The Landlady

Constance Rauch

POPULAR LIBRARY • NEW YORK

All POPULAR LIBRARY books are carefully selected by the POPULAR LIBRARY Editorial Board and represent titles by the world's greatest authors.

POPULAR LIBRARY EDITION
June, 1976

Published by arrangement with G. P. Putnam's Sons

For
Elsa Hansen

Chapter 1

THAT maligned and febrile network, the Penn Central Railroad, was on this day provoking an unusual response. It was a sparkling Friday afternoon early in October, and the occasion of Samuel Porter's first time out as a commuter. To his surprise he found the ride enchanting, and his heart was filled with joy.

The 5:07 to Irvington—pride of the Hudson Division —was right on schedule as it hurtled its clangorous way beside the wine-dark Hudson River. True, wine had very little to do with the questionable sheen now gracing those majestic waters, but for the moment Sam was willing to ignore the perils of pollution. The day was fine, and the Palisades shimmered with autumn colors on the western shore.

Soon Sam recognized the approaches to Wimbledon-on-Hudson and felt a small pang. Over so soon. It had been just thirty-eight minutes since the train's departure from Grand Central. The Victorian jumble of dusty red brick and battered tarpaper they were passing now was the old CopperCable plant; Wimbledon's single, grudging concession to industry. Indeed, CopperCable had arrived at its shoreline location long before the wave of prosperous commuters who now claimed the village as their own. An apparently playful display of enormous spools and reels was littered about its yard alongside the tracks. No doubt gigantic bridges, now slumbering on some visionary's drafting table, would one day be made from them.

Samuel reached the little platform at the rear of the car just as the train drew into the station. "Wimbledon-on-Hudson" appeared in neat white letters on a signboard of cobalt enamel. Fresh blue-green paint preserved iron stairs and railings. A large wall of granite blocks, bearing the legend "1904" retained the press of parked cars.

Wimbledon, a hill town, not unlike the little villages dotting the Mediterranean coast, spread to the river. In Wimbledon, however, the flavor appeared to be determinedly Anglo-Saxon.

From his vantage on the rickety platform, Sam Porter saw a decorous procession of fresh-painted stucco houses. Further up the hill sat quaint half-timbered cottages and gabled New England-style homes of weathered cedar shakes. And at the top of Maynard Street, amid a gaudy display of autumn foliage, there survived a modest handful of small estates.

The train came to a full stop with a resounding jerk. Sam moved quickly, his fellow passengers thronging around him. Had Sam been expecting pleasantly modulated murmurs of "After you, my good man" and "Hello, there, Withers, how's the family?" to go with the genteel atmosphere of the place? Alas, all of a sudden it was as though he were once again on the old IRT Lexington Avenue Line attempting an ignominious retreat at Fifty-ninth Street.

The commotion in the parking area, the speed with which the cars went roaring up the hill, lent an incongruous hysteria to the general good feeling of a sunny weekend in the offing. In less than three minutes traffic cleared; peace returned. And Samuel Porter, looking deceptively like the young scion of a fashionable Eastern family, prepared to begin a new chapter in his life.

Reaching for a prized cigar he'd been saving for this first climb home up Maynard Street, Sam discovered it was all but severed by the precise perforation of tiny toothprints. Damn. Patience had gotten to it first.

How to get up this blasted hill without the solace of those expensive puffs of fragrant blue smoke? He wanted his arrival at 33 Granite Terrace to be an auspicious one. A little spiritual support was definitely in order.

New job. New place to live. But still no money. These circumstances were familiar enough by now . . . yet there was something tantalizing in the air, something he'd always aspired to, about Wimbledon itself. It was so much like the vision of the prosperous, ordered life he had longed for as a small boy.

Yes, he would definitely need a good cigar. Ah, there was a likely place, at the corner of Maynard and Main: The Pleasant Hour Lounge. Perhaps a beer . . . some discreet inquiries into the hows and why of Wimbledon-on-Hudson. An informative, amusing story to take home to Jessie.

No further arguments necessary, Sam Porter made his way through maroon double doors that shone warmly in the sun.

Jessica Porter had watched the 5:07 arrive—looking like an intricate miniature toy, depositing tiny passengers. Standing on this fantastic porch—larger than their former living room had been—bordered by graceful screened-in Palladian arches, she felt both giddy and elegant.

Could one ever become accustomed to such a view? *At this precise moment in time,* she thought, *I am completely happy.* Their new home was situated high above the Hudson, perched precipitously over a full-blown garden on the verge of going wild. Mossy terraces gave a medieval, cloistered look to things. The filigreed leaves of an enormous Japanese maple tree filtered the light directly below her and there was a sharp scent of something very old, yet organic and pure . . . ozone, decay, perhaps a rare berry bush imported by an enterprising merchant at the turn of the century. As the angle of the sun became more pronounced, the river shone and danced with a reflected brilliance that became too sharp to focus on directly. Beyond, Jessie could make out every red and orange leaf, and every dun-colored ridge in the Palisades.

The clumsy, dusty business of moving in awaited her inside . . . and well she knew it. Glad that for the moment Patience, the baby, seemed to be living up to her name, Jessica stepped gingerly around the mass of corrugated boxes the movers had deposited helter-skelter in the living room. She had managed to unpack a few, but as soon as one was emptied, Patience would appropriate it for her building project, a warren of interconnected cardboard caves.

"Whoo! Whoo! I see you! You see me?"

"I hear you, but I can't see you!"

"Here I am!"

"Where's here? Here?" Jessica peered into the box nearest to her. No Patience.

"Here!" Patience, delighted to have intrigued her mother into a game, giggled. Jessica looked into the box on her right. She saw an old extension cord, an oversized sphaghetti pot, and an electric vaporizer.

"Wrong! Where's Patience, Mommy? Mommy lose Patience?" More giggles. Jessica stood on tiptoe and surveyed the room carefully. For an instant she caught sight of a streak of red corduroy and dark blond hair. *There*. But it was gone before she could pinpoint which box it had streaked into.

"Peek a boo!"

"Okay, my love. You win. I give up. Come out, come

8

out, wherever you are." Two small round arms grabbed Jessica's knees from behind.

"Why, you clever little rascal. How'd you get from one end of the room to the other without my seeing you?" Patience sat down in front of Jess and laughed her melodious laugh. If there was a more pleasant noise to be heard in the world, Jessica had yet to hear it. She swooped down to kiss her daughter.

"So. How do you like it all so far, kid?"

"Great. Tweetie likes it, too. Tweetie and I are making a playhouse. See?" Patience withdrew the doll that was her constant companion from the large pocket in her corduroy overalls. "Tweetie's helping me."

"Terrific. Look, when you're all through, the two of you can have me over for tea, okay? Now, I want to get ready for Daddy." Jessica was anxious to change her clothes before Sam's arrival. As she headed toward the bedroom, she looked over her shoulder to where Patience had been just seconds before. Once again the corrugated cardboard tunnel had swallowed her up.

Patience was obviously going to get a lot more mileage out of those boxes before she tired of her game. Good, Jessie decided, because, at the moment, she had more urgent business.

A mental picture egged her on. She saw herself in an expensive "at home" outfit serving Sam a perfectly mixed martini. The martini was very dry, icy cold; and Sam, looking confident and chipper, lifted his glass to her. This was the right way to begin a new life. Toward this end she began a hurried search for the glossy Bonwit's box that contained the required costume.

One of the benefits of moving as often as she and Sam had during the four years of their union (two in formal wedlock, out of respect for the advent of Patience) was Jessie's proficiency as a packer. All their clothing was properly packed and labeled and in its proper bedroom;

just as every carton having to do with either cooking or eating was jammed into the small, high-ceilinged kitchen.

Jessie found the box, withdrew the plum-colored velvet dress, and hung the hanger over the shower-curtain rod; a shiny, nickel-plated circle suspended above the midsection of a voluminous, claw-footed bathtub. It reminded her of a Mary Petty cartoon. She knew full well that it was this incredible Victorian bathroom, with its antique tub, baronial pedestal sink, and stained-glass windows—rather than the view of the Hudson they only partially obscured—that had sold Sam on leasing the place.

Her own enthusiasm hadn't hurt, of course, and they'd decided to take on the doughty dowager who owned the place, a senescent crone named Mrs. Falconer. Jessie hoped that she and Sam, between them, could deal successfully with the old woman. Especially since she lived—in what Jessie mentally calculated to be at least fourteen rooms—directly above them.

The steep hillside location made the upper floor significantly larger than their own ground-floor apartment, which had yet another level below it housing a furnace and storerooms. Mrs. Falconer's address was on Maynard Street, with a separate entrance and garage. The Porter's entrance was half a block around the corner, on Granite Terrace. And, of course, as tenants they bore the brunt of the steps. Hundreds of them. Leading to that magnificent Palladian arched porch. Jessica, who had been a literature major at Wellesley when she met Sam, felt the porch and its steps to be right out of Ezra Pound's Portofino, and was determined to love them all. And, though she sensed musty, cobwebby emanations from the old woman's apartment above, their own place was spotless and had been freshly painted for their arrival.

The trouble was, Jessie thought as she did a quick washing up, there was no tellling whether they were up against Margaret Rutherford or Ma Barker. Either way, the Porter family was bound to find its history altered by Mrs. Falconer's very obvious eccentricity. Jessie smiled, remembering Mrs. Falconer's quavering, gravelly voice, declaring: "Oh, you and your hubby won't even know I'm here. I keep to meself. Mind me own business, don't you know." This after inquiring bluntly, during the first three minutes of their initial interview, about Sam's profession, his ancestry—"not the *Baltimore* Porters?"—place of birth, astrological sign, stock portfolio, and whether (with a covert glance at Jessica) another little Porter was scheduled soon.

"Oh, my, yes. My dears, the architect who built this house built most of the Maynard Hill—but *this* is the house he built for *himself*. And your little residence was designed for his own dear parents. You'll never know I'm here. The walls are stoutly built. Why, I was saying to Dr. Swope on the telephone just yesterday (he's a brilliant internist over at Hopkins, by the way), and he agreed with me. Dear old Dr. Swope agreed with me one hundred percent. They don't build good stout walls anymore. They simply do not have the skills nowadays to build real walls out of mortar and stone." Mrs. Falconer had apparently enjoyed a halcyon period as a nurse, at some time in the very dim past, and loved to punctuate her nonstop verbal stream with medical references of one kind and another.

"You young people today don't even know what privacy is. . . . Why, I expect you may have trouble finding me just to give me the rent check!" Jessie remembered how horribly Mrs. Falconer had tittered at this riotous remark, and how the thought that the old woman might actually be balmy had come to her. But then, after her moment of mirth, she had become quite matter-of-fact. Jessica then decided that perhaps laughter in the very old might always seem a bit mad and decided to walk in

11

the opulent garden, thus giving her husband—an avowed lover of eccentrics—the task of formalizing the rental.

It didn't take long for Jessica to dress; a quick look in the oval, full-length mirror on the bathroom door satisfied her. Not beautiful, still she was prettier than she knew. At twenty-four, there was something childlike and unformed about Jessica Porter. Though patently past girlhood, she was not wholly in command as a woman, and perhaps never would be. She liked to think of herself as a late bloomer whose "time" was yet to come. She smiled briefly at the innocuous little reflection in the old mirror, because she knew Sam would be pleased with the way she looked and would tell her so. That was really all that mattered. She'd hurry Patience to bed, and get those martinis made.

It was six twenty-five. The sun had turned to an orange disk in the still-brilliant sky. With Patience settled happily into her crib, Jessica hurried to the refrigerator to remove the ice-cube tray she'd filled first thing that morning, after the movers had gone. Everything in the kitchen seemed so dim. She knew the sun was setting, but it was a minute or two before she realized that the light in the fridge had gone out. Absently she felt for a light switch, until she bumped head-on into the chain with the luminous bumble bee at its tip. Occasionally old-fashioned wasn't all that charming. The light did not turn on. Oh, lord, now what. Had that silly old woman fouled them up with Con Ed? No, the gas worked. A fuse, then. Sam would have to tend to it. The sun had set for good, and it was harder to see in the tiny kitchen. Though already somewhat deflated, she mixed the martinis as best she could, glad at least of the ice. Jessie knew everything would be all right as soon as Sam walked in. Which, considering that it was only a fifteen-minute walk from the station, should have been nearly twenty minutes ago. Jessica felt her anger and disappointment grow, and somehow lacked the enterprise to suppress it.

Surely Sam wouldn't stop off at some bar on their first night in this wonderful new home? Please, Sam, come home soon. Then, determined to keep a level outlook and not to get soppy about what to Sam, after all, was a god-given right, Jessica rounded up dinner candles and lit them with a certain panache. She tried a few sips of her martini . . . the ice had melted to the right degree; Jessica was not much good at drinking. "Can't afford two drinkers in the family!" Sam often remarked. And things began to look up again.

She could count no fewer than fourteen candles of various sizes reflected in the generous expanse of window glass and mirror in their new living room. A faint lavender-green glimmer was all that was left of the sun. She was feeling festive again—certain that Sam's arrival was imminent. Just then, she became aware of a strange clumping sound, not like anything she'd heard before. The *clump, clump, clump* wasn't mechanical . . . it sounded . . . *painful*. Then she realized what she was hearing.

"The walls may be nice and stout, all right, Mrs. Falconer," she said, her voice loud and clear in the empty apartment, "but you clean forgot to mention your flimsy floors!" The *clump, clump, clump* was obviously Mrs. Falconer's walking stick; so she might as well get used to it. But what a grim, unpleasant sound in the large house! If only she and Sam owned a transistor radio or something. Music might have helped. Jessica was determined to keep her chin up and greet Sam in a cheerful, positive way. It was nearly seven.

The sun, shining so brilliantly just moments before, had begun its descent in earnest when Sam stepped out of The Pleasant Hour Lounge. He glimpsed it now, melting deftly into a secret slot behind the Palisades. Sam had, indeed, spent a Pleasant Hour. With a pang of guilt, he pictured Jessie—and the state she would undoubtedly be in. He'd told her that morning to expect him promptly at six. It would be past seven—and dark— by the time he got home. It would not be the kind of homecoming he'd imagined.

Wimbledon itself looked strange to him. The steep slope of the Maynard Hill seemed threatening. He was confused by the many small cross streets with unexpected names. Rock Ledge . . . Cliffside . . . Firehouse Lane . . . had there been that many? Had he missed a turn? There were few streetlamps once he left the village. He wondered whether he'd failed to recognize the white stucco mansion with the grotesque Spanish tile roof that stood on the corner of Granite Terrace and was to be his "you can't miss it" landmark. He was also irritated to find himself out of breath after such a short climb. He'd have to work out more—get himself back in shape.

The exertion of the climb, the darkness, the gathering suspicion that he might be lost, all conspired to make him feel the drinks he'd had. Jessie would of course notice in a flash. He took a deep breath of the country air, squared his shoulders, and made a new effort to judge his position—noting how far down the river seemed now, glistening and gray under the clear night sky. And then he saw the white stucco house on the corner. Here was Granite Terrace after all. Sam looked up to see whether Jessie had found some kind of porch light to help him up all those steps—but what he saw sent him headlong into a state of clammy terror.

It seemed as though the entire porch . . . the porch Jessica had fallen in love with on sight the day they first saw the place . . . was already consumed by fire. He

14

ran, stumbling on the crumbling concrete steps. The cast-iron pipe that served as a railing was too loose and wobbly; his hands could not guide his feet. When at last he'd reached the porch door, he felt certain he was too late. His heart was hammering with an acrid foretaste of grief. Tears formed in his eyes. As the door opened—a surprise, since he was still trying to find the right knob (there were apparently several locks in use)—Sam fell, landing squarely on a musty-smelling rolled-up carpet.

"Sam! Welcome home! Isn't it beautiful? Here, let me help you. An' I have a lovely, lovely martini all ready and waiting for you."

"Thought you were on fire," Sam mumbled. "Thought the whole place going up in flames. I saw flames." Sam's disjointed speech contained equal parts of alcohol and terror. Jessie appeared not to notice.

"Oh, Sam, *darling*, I lit all the candles I could find. The *lights* don't work. Doesn't it look cozy and romantic? Give me your coat . . . I'll get your drink. Sit down. Everything's going to be just fine."

Chapter 2

THE phosphorescent face on the alarm clock glowed just enough for Jessica to make out the hands at five thirty. She was surprised it was so near morning. The unfamiliar bedroom, the almost palpable darkness surrounding her, and the soundness of her sleep made her feel very "middle of the night." Why was she awake, then? *Clump. Clump. Clump.* So Mrs. Falconer was an early riser. Well, she'd get used to that. The predawn air was intoxicatingly sweet and pure after their months in the city. Sam was asleep, his face absorbed in a dream, and completely vulnerable. He looked about eighteen. He was in fact thirty-three. Jessie tucked the blankets around his shoulders, found her slippers, her glasses, and the flashlight, and walked to Patience's room. Patience slept—and smiled—exactly like the handsome father she resembled so strongly. "I'll give her some milk . . . maybe we'll get to sleep later that way."

The clumping seemed to follow her to the kitchen. "I wonder if *your* lights work, Mrs. F—or are you clumping about up there with a flickering taper?" Jessica filled the plastic cup and tiptoed into the baby's room. She held the cup for Patience while she drank, then covered her gently.

"Thanks, Mommy!" Patience said in her serious, alto voice. "Tweetie loves my new room . . . kiss her good night?"

16

"Shh—you'll wake Daddy. I'll kiss you . . . both." Jessica gave Patience and the drab little terrycloth doll loud, juicy kisses and crept out, closing the door quietly behind her. Now, if the birds didn't start to sing for a while, she and Sam were assured another three hours of blissful sleep. And sleeping with Sam was bliss. Never mind about the sex, which she enjoyed enormously—though she sometimes wondered if it were as important to her as the books she read told her it ought to be. Cuddling up to Sam and feeling completely safe and familiar . . . they fit together so well. His ample, six-foot frame was so deliciously accommodating. Before Patience was born, it had been almost impossible for them to get up in the morning. Every time Sam made a determined lunge at becoming vertical, Jessie's small body would insinuate itself against his—effortlessly and without guile—in such a manner as to render him hopelessly horizontal again—for another twenty minutes at least.

Wound about one another and breathing peacefully, Sam and Jessie were hardly aware of the clumping and the thumping directly above their heads. If Sam heard it, he gave no sign, and to Jessie the noise was merely the lead-in to a brilliantly complicated morning dream that featured the Orient Express pulling in to a mosquelike railway station made of iron fretwork and miles of glistening glass. Through the black billows of smoke and fat puffs of steam Jessie received the knowledge that she was en route to the Bosporus on a vital mission.

Sunlight played about on Sam's face until it was impossible for him to ignore it. First time in months he'd felt this good in the morning. *Ah, all you good gray people back in the city . . . you don't know what you're missing,* he thought. "Jessie," he said, his hand resting gently on her warm, bare shoulder, "just smell that air! Feel that sun! What a place! Let's take a look around. I was so busy trying to charm old Mrs. Falconer into letting us rent this place I don't really remember how the rooms go. C'mon, sweetie, show me our new home?" He kissed her, ritually, on both cheeks, and was rewarded by her soft myopic eyes opening trustingly at him. And by a loving smile.

"Wow. Look at all that sunlight . . . we'll have to do something about curtains . . . all those windows! Oh, Sam, wait till you see. You're just going to love it . . . there are so many funny little nooks and crannies, crazy unexpected touches." She got up, forgetting her robe, which lay crumpled at the foot of the bed. Jessica, naked, was completely unself-conscious—slim and soundly built, her movements were no more voluptuous than those of a schoolgirl on her way to the dormitory shower. This charmed Sam, making him feel lucky, as well as protective. Jessie found her wire-rimmed glasses, put them on, and turned just in time to catch his appraising eye, whereupon she made a conscious effort to undulate her childish hips and execute her idea of a burlesque bump and grind. Sam leaped out of bed and threw his pajama top around her.

"All right, little lady, you can tell me all about it at the station house, now, march!"

"Sam, if you'll make the coffee while I'm in the shower, I'll fix breakfast while you're taking yours, okay?" She didn't wait for his reply and was soon taking her first shower in the Mary Petty bath.

While Sam was putting the coffee on he was joined by Patience. He swooped his daughter up in his arms, sat her on the high, wide windowsill, and gave her a resounding kiss.

"Daddy," Patience began, "have you heard how that funny lady upstairs makes funny bumpy noises? Tweetie told me she's a witch. There are good witches and bad witches. Do we know which kind of, ah, witch she is?" Though her command of language was precocious for a

18

two-year-old, the word "witch" appearing twice in one sentence, yet meaning two different things, was a puzzle that stopped her momentarily.

"She is a good old witch for sure, Patience, me love. Trust Daddy to know which kind of witch is which!"

"Does she do magic tricks?"

"You'd better believe it, Patience, baby. Why, after Mommy put you to bed last night all the lights went out. What do you think of that?"

"Oh, Daddy, I think we have to call the 'lectric company." Patience laughed.

"The bathroom's all yours, Sam!" Jessie called, and appeared almost immediately in the kitchen in a pair of faded denim bell bottoms and a decrepit sweat shirt. "I'll have breakfast on the table in ten minutes, okay?" Sam took his turn, happily proprietary—admiring the stained-glass window, the marble fixtures, the lavishness of the proportions of the room itself, which, owing to some quirk of the architect's priorities, was twice the size of the kitchen he had just left. When he stepped out of the bathroom, he noticed a closet door ajar. Assuming it to be his closet, he opened the door.

It was dark and murky . . . and cold. And it was definitely not a closet. "Jessie!" he shouted. "What the hell is this door doing back here?"

"What?"

"Why the hell is this door open? And where does it go?" In the dim light he could make out steps going to the floor above. They seemed to turn a corner midway, where an old blackish-green piece of drapery hung arras-like at the top. "Jesus Christ! Don't tell me there are connecting stairs between our place and hers. Why didn't we see this before? For all we know Falconer's just a delightful old geezer . . . on the other hand, until we really know, for Pete's sake make sure this door is *always* locked." Sam was outraged.

"I was so busy with the movers and Patience all day . . . and then as soon as Patience was asleep, all the lights went out. I never saw that door. Honest!"

" 'I keep to meself, I do.' " Sam mimicked the landlady's quavering voice. " 'You'll never know I'm about.' I bet she's down here all the time. Damn. Jessie, promise me you'll keep this thing locked at all times, please. Remember how she showed us the front porch door, and the little back door? Why the hell didn't she show us this *side* door if she didn't feel it was something to hide?"

"Sam, calm down . . . it'll be all right. I'll always check it to make sure it's locked. I promise. Now, come have some breakfast, that'll cheer you up."

But the edge had been taken off the morning by Sam's discovery of the connecting stairs. He sensed this was a tip-off to the old woman's deviousness. A deviousness he'd recognized from the beginning but discounted in his delight at finding such a fantastic apartment so close to New York. "Well, let's decide what to do first this morning. I have to get the electricity straightened out and finish unpacking, and we'll have to shop. What else?" Jessie hated to mention it, but there was something else that needed attending to.

"Sam. The keys she gave us don't seem to fit any of the locks. We'd better straighten that out, too."

"Did you try them all?"

"Yes. I wanted to put a couple of cartons out in back, and I took the keys she gave us, but they didn't open any of the locks. There are at least three, and a couple of hook-and-eye deals on the inside. If the front porch door hadn't been open, I would have been locked out."

"Christ, Jess . . . what have we gotten into! Oh, well. I'll take care of it. I guess I'd better call the old lady and present her with our little list. Maybe I'd better call the electric company first. You know it's not Con Ed up here. They have a separate little electric company. Do you have a phone book?"

"Uh, Sam, do you think they'll be open on a Saturday?"

"Damn it, Jessie, how will I know if I don't try? Where's the book?"

"Oh, never *mind*, Sam," Jessie answered testily. "I'll look it up *for* you. Have another cup of coffee."

Jessie found the phone book, asked Sam what the name of the electric company was, and fortunately found the number right away. Wonder of wonders, there was a separate listing for weekends and holidays. She wrote it down and handed it to Sam, who was distractedly looking for something. "Well, what is it *now?*"

"Where are my pipes, Jessie? Where did you pack them? At the bottom of the pots and pans, no doubt."

"Now, look here, Sam. You're not being fair. I packed everything without any help from you. For the *fifth* time in less than three years. Mind you, I'm not complaining . . . but it isn't very kind of you to cast aspersions on my ability as a packer, when thanks to your highly exercised proclivities for changing jobs and pulling up stakes, you are directly responsible for my being highly proficient at it! And, furthermore . . . if you *must* know . . . I laid out all your pipes—and all your blooming tobacco tins—on the sideboard. And, since you apparently don't remember, you were delighted to find them there last night and even smoked a couple of pipefuls in the romantic candlelight." Jessie was ashen pale. Anger did not suit her looks.

Sam said nothing as he walked to the dining room. There were the pipes. He had forgotten, and it made him angry. Maybe he'd forgotten about the side door? Jessie's father, a retired schoolteacher, had pointed out Sam's forgetfulness on numerous occasions, and (because it was true) it rankled him all the more.

"All right, Jessie, where's that goddamn number?"

"In your goddamn shirt pocket . . . where you put it less than three minutes ago." The fat was in the fire. Another Saturday morning quarrel—no stopping it now.

"I knew it!" Sam growled. "We can't get through a lousy Saturday morning together anymore! It is ten o'clock in the morning and the whole goddamn weekend is already spoiled."

"Please. Sam. I'm sorry. Really. If you think these last few weeks have been easy on me—I mean, I've been under a strain, too, you know!"

"Don't tell me. I get it from all your friends. From your crazy family. . . . 'Moving again? Isn't that asking a lot of little Jessica?' Nobody ever asks whether maybe it isn't a little hard on *me*. Do you for one moment think I change jobs on a whim? Don't you realize I'm trying to make a better life for us every minute? Now I've finally gotten a real opportunity, and all you can think of is what a strain it's all been on *you!*"

Jessica knew—from hard experience—that whatever she said now would determine the atmosphere between them for as long as the next two weeks. Sam's temper was under rigid control most of the time, but unleashed, it invariably took him weeks to get back to his apparently easygoing self. She took a deep breath, called to mind how sweet their first night in this new apartment had been, tried to remember how lovable and vulnerable he'd looked sleeping shortly before, when suddenly Patience was heard to say brightly, "Hello! Did you come for a visit? My mommy and daddy are in there."

And Mrs. Falconer—large as life—stood in their living room.

Chapter 3

"NOW, I hope you two lovebirds won't mind a silly old woman dropping by to make a suggestion. My own dear hubby passed away many long years ago . . . such a dear, considerate . . . *well-spoken* . . . man! How I miss him! But, really, you simply *mustn't* leave those side stairs open. As I told you, I keep to meself . . . value me privacy . . . and I particularly don't want drafts. I hardly ever use those old stairs and must ask that you don't, either. Well . . . I see the little Potter family is getting settled."

"Porter . . ." Jessica murmured, but Mrs. Falconer, in changing verbal gears, took no notice. Her peculiar voice had a way of moving abruptly from genteel falsetto to a husky, gravelly pitch—evidently the tone she used for points that were to be emphasized most strongly. She was once again the elderly clubwoman calling the meeting to order:

"What *charming* furnishings. I always did say that oak is a noble, honest, *forthright* wood. But you see so little of it anymore! When we get to know one another better, I may let you see some of the pieces I have—well, my dears, they're *museum quality*, really. Jacobean pieces Frederick and I chanced upon at a country auction back in the Depression years, when one could still purchase excellent furnishings for very modest sums.

"Of course, *your* things are very sweet. That commode

23

is so like one I had in my bedroom as a girl . . . Fancy these simple country furnishings coming into vogue again!"

Mrs. Falconer paced the carton-littered apartment with all the authority and momentum of a luxury liner pulling out of the New York Narrows.

"Now, I'm sure we shall get on *splendidly*. This has always been a *happy* apartment. Why, the Corbetts lived here for nearly twenty years and never, never any cross words between us. Let me know if there's anything you need, and I'll see you have it."

Sam looked at the woman—her dry, wrinkled face etched harshly in the brilliant sun. Her eyes were deeply sunk into their sockets, but coldly blue and probing; age had most definitely not withered their command of detail. The *grande-dame* performance was something Sam had to admire in spite of himself, especially in light of the eccentric assortment of rags she was wearing. Her head was covered with a moldy crocheted beret, and stray wisps of dead white hair poked out like stuffing from a chair; she had on an oversized old man's cardigan secured by three safety pins, one of which was a diaper pin with pink plastic tips. Underneath were two dresses: one, a red-and-white-checked housedress with a multitude of stains, and the other—peeking through at neck, sleeves, and hemline—appeared to be a rather formal silk print from the era of large geometric flowers and bias cut. A real thrift-shop find it would be on the Upper East Side, he decided. On her feet were cracked and graying white nurses' shoes, with spongy crepe soles, accounting for the stealth of her entrance. Apparently she was not making use of her walking stick.

". . . of course there's nothing like a *real* Turkey carpet to lend harmony and distinction to a room. You know, my dear"—she'd been directing her attention exclusively to Jessica, who stood palely galvanized to the spot where

she'd been standing when the woman first appeared—
"I may have a perfectly gorgeous Kirman rolled up
in the attic that would look divine in your little dining room. Do remind me to look for it one of these days.
I want you to have it. I can plainly see that you have
style, and I know you'd appreciate a fine, *authentic* piece
to set off your own sweet things."

"Mrs. Falconer, you're very kind." Jessica forced her
voice with an effort into an unaccustomed steely pitch.
"But there *are* a few things of a more practical and, uh,
immediate nature that I would like to bring to your attention, since you are here."

"You know, my dear, I can't help but confide a little
secret to you . . . just now, standing there in this lovely
sunlight . . . you reminded me so much of dear Gwen
Corbett. Such a brave, strong woman she was! Fought
for her rights . . . nursed that poor dear hubby of hers
for *years*. Cancer of the colon he finally died of—not
pretty—but she was *steadfast!* Yes, you do remind me of
her. Of course she was a *real* beauty—high coloring,
raven hair; that is, before it went gray, poor thing. . . ."

"Mrs. Falconer . . ." Samuel Porter, standing tall, chest
thrown out, voice carrying to the second balcony, managed to interrupt her. "We need keys. We have no electricity. The keys you gave us don't fit any of the locks.
The electricity went off last night at sundown. Can you
explain this, please?"

Mrs. Falconer inquired fawningly of Patience, whose
astonished eyes merely blinked in disbelief, "Did you *eat*
the keys, sweetheart? Such a beautiful little child. You
are fortunate, indeed, to have been so blessed . . . Keys?
But of course I gave you keys. Things get in such a muddle sometimes. It's not easy to keep track of everything
in such a large house. Here. Let me have them. I'll soon
see what the matter is." Jessica reached for the jangling

assortment they'd been presented on arrival and placed them in the large gnarled hand.

"Before we check the locks, Mrs. Falconer, would you please tell me what the problem is with the electricity? I was preparing to call Mid Hudson Electric when you . . . appeared."

"Don't mess about with *those* people, whatever you do!" The old woman's voice was loud, and shrill. "Those thieving idiots will cause you nothing but grief . . . take my word for it! I'm sorry you were inconvenienced. I have this cut-off switch old Mr. Dalrymple installed for me. It conserves my, er, costs, don't you know. I can't imagine how your lights could have been affected. Mr. Potter . . . *you* look like you understand these things. Come. I'll show you where the apparatus is located. I'm sure we'll have your power reconnected in no time."

Jessica watched them go off to the cellar below, hoping Sam could cope with the mess. It really was remarkable to see old Mrs. F in action. Given a practical problem, she seemed to become more alert than ever. Jessie felt a grudging respect for the irritating old woman. After all, she must be close to eighty, if not more, and she *was* running this big old house entirely on her own. Who could tell—maybe Sam and she might one day even grow fond of her. Jessie wondered whether Sam's specialized professional knowledge of building maintenance might not prove useful in cementing the tenuous tenant/landlady relationship. Sam was an absolute wizard with machinery, despite his poet's soul.

She walked back to the kitchen to stack the remains of their unhappy breakfast, once again pondering the curious twist that had caused the handsome, starving actor she'd met the summer of her junior year to become a maintenance manager who specialized in massive boiler installations. It was fun doing the dishes in a new kitchen, fun looking through this still unfamiliar little window above the sink and gazing at the wild garden below. The gentle play of warm sudsy water and the brisk, business-like strokes of her scrubbing brush provided a soothing accompaniment to the sort of reverie she most enjoyed.

Sam-the-actor into Sam-the-boilerman had been a surprisingly smooth and simple transition, though requiring flexibility and a willingness to change address on both their parts. Jessica felt they'd done pretty well . . . all things considered. Patience was two and a half years old; and in that time Sam had had three jobs and they'd lived in four different apartments; this was the fifth.

Sam had been a good actor, and Jessica was now careful not to allude to his former profession, lest the memory of his default give him pain. There were just too many good actors in New York, and Sam was one of the many who yearly fell by the wayside for lack of parts and funds. Despite his handsome, appealing presence, Sam did not photograph well; his televised image was that of a man some ten pounds heavier and twenty years older. This was a primary handicap that had kept him from getting bread-and-butter commercial assignments. Finally, during the winter that Jessica was pregnant with Patience, he accepted a friend's offer to assist in the management of an off-Broadway theater building that had been purchased cooperatively by his troupe. In a matter of months the transition from trodding boards to prodding boilers was a *fait accompli*.

There followed several associations with New York building management concerns, mostly unsavory and disappointing. Yet with each new connection Sam's salary had become more respectable; and finally he'd accepted an offer from yet another old friend—this time an aging, émigré playboy with whom he'd shared many happy, drunken hours since they'd first appeared together on a TV talk show. Pierre Villard and Sam Porter were old buddies; now they hoped to become partners.

Jessica had some reservations, but she preferred not to examine them too closely this early in the game. Pierre was rich. He'd somehow come to the U.S. during the occupation of France under circumstances that were never fully explained. At any rate, he was not free to return; and Jessie suspected the entire affair had been some kind of tax dodge. Sam liked Pierre and Pierre nonchalantly picked up bar checks that would have paid the Porter grocery bill for months. And, on the rare occasions when he visited the Porter ménage, he never failed to bring some extravagantly amusing toy from F.A.O. Schwarz for Patience. As far as Jessie could tell, he seemed a decent sort.

But Sam and Pierre hardly knew one another sober. And Pierre—who looked like a Gallic Lyndon Johnson —was extremely sober about his business. He called it his "leetle beeznezz" in a deprecating way, but it was obvious it meant a lot to him. Manhattan Office Maintenance Corporation was not all that "leetle," and if things worked out, Sam stood to inherit the presidency when Pierre was ready to retire to full-time fun and games at some semitropical playground.

All the dishes were now gleaming in the drainer. Jessie wiped her hands on a paper towel and was carefully applying hand lotion when Sam and Mrs. Falconer returned.

"Try the lights now, honey," Sam said. "I think we've found the right switch." The lights worked, and the refrigerator began to hum.

"Well—it looks like we're in business! What a relief. What about the keys . . . did you figure them all out?" Jessie looked first at Sam and then at Mrs. Falconer.

"They seem to be a little more complicated, honey. But I've found two that match two of the locks . . . and that should be enough."

"You know, my dear, I'm a foolish old woman . . . I've

28

changed the locks on these doors so often. It's frightening to live alone. That's why I'm so relieved I've finally decided to have tenants again. I really feel more at ease up here on Maynard Hill when I know there are some strong young folks in the house with me." She peered at Jessica with spaniellike trust and gratitude. "Just use the two locks we were able to match. That'll be plenty. This is a fine old neighborhood, and very quiet. Well, you two lovebirds have tired me out with your little problems. I really must get to my place now for some rest. Oh . . . one more thing. Please don't nail any pictures to the wall. It costs me very dearly to have this place plastered and painted when tenants leave it damaged. Use molding hooks if you want to hang anything. I'm sure you've both been well brought up, but one never knows nowadays. . . . You will be careful, won't you?" With that she began to shuffle toward the back door. She shook hands formally with Sam, who was surprised by the strength of her grip and managed after her departure to sputter:

"That woman—she's too much! . . . You can't imagine . . ." Jessie tried to figure out whether Sam was shocked, impressed, or horrified, when gradually the percussive gasps took on the more recognizable form of explosive laughter.

"Sam. What's she done now? What does it mean?"

"That 'apparatus' Mr. Dalrymple installed for our lady . . . I just blew the whistle on it! The poor old thing . . . you know, for a minute there, I think she would have gleefully murdered your fine husband. The jig was up and there wasn't a goddamned thing she could do about it." Sam paused to wipe his eyes, laughing silently, and shaking his head.

"Sam. Tell me what's so funny!"

"I wish you could have seen her. It probably won't seem as funny to you. The old geezer's been tying into her tenants' electricity—evidently for years. Only there haven't been any tenants this year . . . so old Mrs. F's been doing without. She's got the electric company bamboozled in some way. Maybe they have it down as a one-family house . . . I don't know. Anyway, I can see why she doesn't want them snooping around. She tried to hook things up the way they'd been and didn't get it right, and of course I just put it back the way it ought to have been right along. We'll be paying for Porter kilowatts only. And Mrs. Falconer's going to have to come by her electricity honestly, if at all. If looks could kill . . ."

Since Sam had decided it was funny, Jessie found herself laughing, too. Although part of her felt it wasn't all that funny.

Jessica recognized that her own personal yearning for nest-building and permanency might be dimming her judgment. She wouldn't say anything, yet. The phone rang.

"Hey! Our first phone call."

Sam walked over and intercepted the second ring.

"Porter residence . . . Samuel Porter speaking." Then immediately his expression darkened. "*Pierre.* I thought we'd straightened this out yesterday. We moved, you know. In fact, you have the honor of being our first caller at our new address. . . . Oh. Well, sure. Just a minute, I'll check the trains." He reached for his billfold, pulled out the Penn Central Hudson Division schedule, gave Jessie a hopeless look, and continued:

"There's a twelve fifteen I can catch, I'd be in by one. Yes, I understand. No. It's no trouble. Right. Check. I'll call you from the building just as soon as I get there." He hung up.

"I'm supposed to check the crew at 423 Park," he explained to Jessie. "They may run off with all of his equipment or something. Hell. I told him yesterday at lunch that I'd be glad to check work crews out from time to

30

time . . . but not today. He seemed to understand. You should have heard him just now on the phone. I felt like I'd been caught in the hall at school without a pass. Damn. Look, Jess, there's nothing I can do but go in. I'll get back as soon as I can. Don't try to do too much while I'm gone . . . we'll get everything settled together." And in ten hectic minutes Sam changed to his city clothes, kissed both Patience and Jessie a regretful good-bye, and departed hurriedly down beautiful Maynard Hill.

Chapter 4

BY the time Sam had boarded the desultory, two-car Saturday train, Jessica and Patience were taking their first stroll through Wimbledon's tranquil byways. With some effort Jessica pushed thirty-five-pound Patience in her battered, Plaid Stamp stroller over the cracked and bumpy residential pavement. Nonetheless, she was pleased to have left the apartment's turmoil behind. The river was a constant guide so she had no fear of getting lost. Until they picked up the used VW they were buying from her brother at the end of the month, she'd have to market on foot; and now was as good a time as any to give it a try.

To Patience's delight Jessica's unschooled steps led them directly to a charming park—with a sandbox, slides, swings, picnic tables, benches, playing fields, and an impressive tennis court. There was a cheerful Saturday swarm of children—with many mothers and some fathers in attendance. It was too nice a day to hurry to the market. Patience scrambled out of the stroller with an ecstatic grin and jogged directly to the sandbox. Jessica claimed an empty bench.

The crisp October sun was summoning the heat of midday. It was as warm as August but more invigorating. Pungent yellow leaves littered the ground, and brand-new corduroy clothing covered most of the children. Jessica sat—content to lapse into the mindless, brooding-hen state of a park mother's not entirely un-pleasant lot.

With the sun on her face, she peacefully surveyed the Breughel-like scene through partially closed lids. Here was everything that Wimbledon had to offer—cleanliness, order, and charm, artlessly joined to produce the unmistakable air of untroubled vitality that must surely be the real meaning of the jargon term "advantaged." Even the sounds these children made seemed different; less shrill than in the city—less aggressive. Worth it to put up with eccentricity and uncertainty. Worth it to gamble on a crazy old lady. When would they ever be able to afford to buy a house in a place like this? Probably never. But *renting* a spacious, appealing apartment in the midst of all this beauty and opulence seemed to Jessie the most fortunate of all compromises.

Patience was engrossed in a one-sided conversation with a pudgy three-year-old wielding a Creative Playthings sand toy. Wheat-blond hair falling in gentle waves to the shoulder, it was either an astonishingly pretty boy, or a very sturdy girl.

"Your little girl is quite an extrovert, isn't she? Tommy doesn't share toys with his peers as a rule."

Startled, Jessica found herself staring directly into intense brown eyes that seemed to will her to conversation.

"He's a handsome boy—you must be very proud of him." Jessica loathed park-bench confidences, but decided to brave this one—she was new in town, and anything this avid mother had to offer in the way of information could only help. Her friendly remark was greeted with a short, boisterous laugh.

"*Ha!* That's the *irony* of it! Tommy's my *fifth*. Boy. And he *is* beautiful, isn't he? I mean, let's face it, wouldn't he have made a *fantastic* girl? The other four are homely, healthy brutes. Jonathan's a senior at Wimbledon High; Stephen is fourteen, Walter is twelve, Matthew's ten—so you can imagine, when I found I was pregnant again, after seven years!—I mean, I'd even forgotten how to pin a diaper! Well, naturally, we all thought *this* time it would bloody well just *have* to be a girl. I know what you're probably thinking. Look. I've read all that crap."

Jessica had been thinking absolutely nothing. That this woman was not going to be one of her favorite new neighbors had been the closest thing to an actual thought.

"Don't worry—there's no chance old Tommy will grow up *queer*—I know better. But frankly, now . . . isn't it a shame he wasn't born a girl? Wouldn't that have been one gorgeous girl child?"

Jessica responded with a tepid smile. "Patience likes him—they're getting along very well."

"Patience. What an unusual name. She's lovely . . . how old is she?"

"Uh, she's big for her age, she'll be thirty months on the fourteenth."

"Really? She talks so well. Well, I guess girls *do* mature earlier! Oh. Let me introduce myself. Nancy Dietz. We live on Maynard, off Firehouse, the old Underhill place . . . do you know it?"

"Well, no, actually, we've just moved in." Now maybe she'd get the new-resident treatment and learn something useful.

"Oh, I *know* what you must be going through—they say every three moves is equal to a fire—I mean, what it does to your furnishings and all. Well, I believe it. Where did you buy? I usually know the *minute* a house goes on the market around here, and I wasn't aware that anyone had sold. . . ."

Jessica detected a newly craven desire within herself not to admit that the Porters were merely renting. Rapidly she rationalized that someone like Nancy Dietz wouldn't matter in her life anyway and that the way to establish herself for the present was to say little about their actual circumstances. No doubt the area was as snobbish as it was "advantaged," and although Jessie was *sure* she wasn't a snob herself . . . perhaps she'd be wiser just to play it cool.

"My name is Jessica Porter," she began, but just then her companion darted up, reached for an aluminum-framed tennis racket and with a graceless, loping gait ran full speed toward the tennis courts.

"Here's my tennis partner. Nice to have met! Keep an eye on Tommy? Must run!" And she was gone.

Jessie closed her eyes, smiling. What a relief. She decided never again to let herself be dragged down to the kind of evasion she'd seriously intended just a minute ago. There was something so grasping about the Dietz woman's attitude that Jessie caught it almost without realizing. She'd avoid people like that. A place as charming as Wimbledon-on-Hudson was bound to offer up people of charm as well. Now she found herself in charge of two children. Park mothers! One had to be on guard every minute.

"Hi. I see you've got Tommy this morning. How'd she manage it this time?"

"I guess it's because we're new around here?" Jessie smiled at the girl with hazel eyes and a pretty face. Despite salt-and-pepper hair, she could be no more than twenty-five.

"Does she do that all the time?"

"Well, you do get to expect it. She's one of our real tennis nuts—plays every second she can manage, and of course Tommy's arrival was simply an obstacle to be overcome." The girl was friendly and complacent, no hint of malice in her smile.

"Thanks for the tip. Although since I'm here with Patience anyway, it isn't much trouble. Tommy seems like a nice little boy."

"He's nice enough . . . but he throws tantrums when you least expect it and starts hitting anything he can reach. You see that little dark-haired girl over there in the red jumpsuit? He hit her so hard last summer we had to have stitches."

"Good grief! Is that your little girl?"

"Violet Smith. I'm her mother, Mary."

"Jessie Porter. Violet is a pretty name—how'd you choose it?"

"My husband's mother's. And it is a lot better than Mary, right? Of course I went through half my life as Mary Wurtenburger, so the Smith seemed sexy for a while! You're new, huh? Moved in yet? Know your way around? Anything I can tell you?"

"Well, you've already told me about Tommy Dietz, and I'm grateful. I was actually on my way to shop and hit this park unexpectedly. Patience needed an outing as much as I did . . . we only moved in yesterday and everything's still very chaotic."

"I'm going to the A&P just as soon as Violet lets me, so why don't you hitch a ride with us? I'll be glad to drop you off after. Let's move to this next bench, and maybe Patience will be lured over to play with Violet." Jessie followed Mary to the next bench, and Patience toddled after.

"What about poor Tommy? Shouldn't someone be with him?"

"Don't worry about Tommy. He *never* leaves that sandbox, and now there won't be anyone within hitting distance." Mary laughed, unconcerned, so Jessica decided her own responsibility for the handsome child was at an end. She glanced over at the tennis courts, a scene of extraordinary movement. None of it expert.

"For tennis buffs, they don't seem to play all that well." She turned to Mary for confirmation.

"We all laugh about it. The ones who play the most—well, actually, what they do is *hog* the courts—seem to play the worst. They take it so darn seriously. All the 'nice shot' and 'six-love' and 'well done!' that gets tossed about—you'd think they were real contenders! All it seems to do is keep them in fighting trim. Funny thing, the best player in Wimbledon—when she can get a free court—is a plump little woman from Australia, who weighs one hundred and sixty pounds and has two grandchildren."

"I believe you." Jessie was delighted with her new friend. "I'll bet she uses the same racket she bought in Australia dozens of years ago and doesn't own a single pair of terry tennis socks with cute little pom-poms at the heels."

"Now that you mention it . . . I think she wears her husband's sweat socks."

"Look, it's terribly nice of you to offer to drive Patience and me to the A&P—are you sure it won't be any bother? I'm only too happy to accept—pushing that stroller over these old sidewalks is bad enough; and I was kind of worried about pushing it uphill going home."

"No trouble at all. Glad of the company. My husband's taken to working Saturdays—and I've gotten so I hate Saturdays!" Mary smiled, and Jessie decided the offer had been sincere.

"Matter of fact, my husband's working today, too—and I was pretty upset about it."

"High cost of living in Wimbledon?" Mary asked.

"No. At least, not yet. It's a new job, and he just felt he'd better, that's all."

"On your first day in a new place? That must have been a blow. Well, look, Vi's about had her fill—she'll be mean and hungry soon. Let me introduce you to the

37

joys of the Wimbledon A&P, and then we can stop for a sandwich and a Coke at Murphy's—that's the real heart of this village—and I think you'll like it."

In Mary Smith's enormous station wagon Jessie asked, "Do you have other children? This is the biggest station wagon I've ever seen!"

"No. Just Violet. We do a lot of skiing in the winter and camping in the summer; and in between we antique all over—it's a lot of fun, and it's a good cheap way to fill in the gaps in our White Elephant barn of a house. I guess that's why I'm so down on George's working Saturdays; we haven't done any of those things for ages.

"Well. Enough whining. Here's the A&P—I'll meet you here in the parking lot in exactly fifteen minutes—okay?"

"Great." Jessie was delighted not to have to push her cart alongside the Smiths'. She invariably made all kinds of errors when forced to shop with anyone. Patience was already trained to keep a respectful silence as Jessie engaged in the ever more frustrating pursuit of good buys.

"All set for Murphy's? I'm starved, and so is cranky old Violet."

"Kanky ol' Biolit," Violet agreed.

Walking down Wimbledon's Main Street for the first time, Jessie felt a wave of nostalgia for only half-remembered images from her earliest childhood in Springfield, Ohio. Clean. Proud. Orderly. Shop after shop displaying tastefully selected goods, which, in their entirety, were wide-ranging enough to make Wimbledon self-sufficient. If forced to, one could start from scratch and become completely outfitted through the merchants of Main Street.

"This is fun. I've not walked this peacefully down a sidewalk in a long, long time."

"We're very proud of Main Street—we actually have a Wimbledon Beautification Committee, and all the merchants are held to a fairly strict code for their signs and storefront paint and everything. But here is my personal favorite, Murphy's Stationery and Soda Parlor. I love Mr. and Mrs. Murphy—they've lived here all their lives and are probably the nicest family in Wimbledon."

But the second they walked into the charming, old-fashioned store, with an authentic and aromatic soda parlor on one side and a tempting display of paperback books, imported toys, and office supplies on the other, something in the atmosphere seemed wrong.

Jessica knew the woman sitting on a high stool next to the cash register, red-eyed and ashen-cheeked, would be Mrs. Murphy. Hovering over her, equally bereft and stunned-looking, was a young police officer. The officer's facial features and coloring were so like those of the woman he was comforting that Jessica guessed him to be a son or nephew. They both wore "the map of Ireland" on their faces—even in abject sorrow.

"My God. Something terrible must have happened," Mary whispered. She walked quietly behind the counter, poured two Cokes for the children, and calmly placed them at a far corner table. "Stay here, you two," she ordered, "and drink slowly." Mary returned to where Jessica stood, and they began to eavesdrop shamelessly.

"Why, William? Why? I keep asking myself . . . who could possibly have had anything against poor dear Nora? Oh, I can't stay. I'm going to break down altogether." A wracking sob escaped despite her effort to control it.

"Mother. Please. It's a terrible, sad thing, and some terrible mad person must have done it. I'm sure it had nothing to do with poor old Nora. An accident of fate. A terrible accident of fate." Officer William Murphy looked ready to break down himself.

"*Stabbed!*" Mrs. Murphy almost shrieked, the image in her mind suddenly too graphic, too shattering, to be contained. "Stabbed at her desk—the desk she's had for forty-two years—blood all over her record books! William. I can't stay here. Please take me home."

Officer Murphy, noticing the two women for the first time, addressed them respectfully. "A terrible thing has happened, Mrs. Smith. I'm taking my mother home. Would you mind the store—don't let anyone in, we're closed—I'll be back soon to close up." With that, he put his mother's coat around her shoulders and slowly they walked out the shop's back door.

Neither Mary nor Jessica could find her voice. Mary walked over to the store's front door and turned the OPEN sign around to read SORRY! WE ARE CLOSED, then walked back to where the children were sipping their Cokes. Jessie decided to pour Cokes for herself and Mary. And, each lost in her own fog of pity or confusion, the four of them sat in silence at the small marble-topped table in the back of the store.

It seemed only moments later when Officer Murphy returned.

"Ah. There you are. Thank you for staying. I'll close the shop now. It's my old Aunt Nora, you see. I don't know what to make of it. She was stabbed to death. At her desk. We only discovered it just now. We had a little committee rounded up—she was retiring on the fifteenth —we were planning a farewell dinner at Max's—my dad was the one to find her." Officer Murphy's tears ran freely down his cheeks. "So, you'll excuse me. I'm obliged to you for minding the store—I've got to get back to the station."

Not until they were all seated again in the station wagon was Jessica aware of actually exchanging any words with her new friend. First of all, she had to direct her, and in the state she was now in, she found it difficult. The ordinary routine of giving somebody directions, however, broke through their shock and they both found themselves talking at once, neither listening to the other.

"*Stabbed!* In Wimbledon! It's too awful. I can't figure it out. There's never been any violence here. Never. Why, the worst problem we've got is some pot smoking at the high school—there aren't any hard drugs, even. I feel so awful. I didn't know old Miss Kelly very well—but I knew her to say hello to, and she was a sweet old thing. You know. Lace-curtain Irish—very refined, easily shocked, on the library committee. I guess she worked at CopperCable—many of the old-time villagers do. . . ."

"To think we moved up here because New York was so scary. Well, I guess moving to a strange place, and all —I just feel terrible. I've never seen such raw, heart-rending grief. I'm all shaky. Oh. I think you make a left turn here at Firehouse, and then you catch Granite Terrace on the next corner."

"Granite Terrace? I know that little block very well. Whose house did you buy . . . the Robinsons' . . . I remember they were thinking of moving to Florida. . . ."

"No. Here's our driveway now. We're at the top of all those steps."

"Oh, *no!* The Falconer place. I should have guessed." Mary sounded as though she'd just received the final blow to her already fragile composure.

"Doesn't she always snare the gentle, hopeful types like you? It should have dawned on me. You poor things! Well, then, of course you won't be staying, after all."

Chapter 5

JESSICA sensed that if they had not been so loaded down with grocery bags, Mary would simply have opened the car door, let them both out at the foot of the steps, and driven off.

But Mary was a good soul. She helped Jessie unload the wagon, mount the steps, and then, though not without some furtive glances toward the ceiling, from which Jessie could detect the faint and now-familiar *clump, clump, clump,* Mary agreed to stay for a snack.

As Jessica put coffee on and distributed four plates, Mary unpacked her groceries for her.

"This isn't going to do at all, you know." Jessie tried the words with a touch of nonchalant humor, but her voice betrayed her.

"I mean," she continued, "you can't just drop a verbal bombshell like that and then clam up. Now. I mean to feed you and Violet a nourishing meal, and then . . . I haff vays off makink pipple talk!"

Mary laughed.

"Okay, so I'll talk. That is, I'll tell you what I know. But, I'm warning you—none of it is good."

Jessie brought out a platter of cold cuts, and the four of them sat around the Porters' large oak table and wolfed down a zesty pickup meal of sliced ham, fresh black bread, sliced tomatoes, chive cream cheese, and German potato salad. Violet spilled her chocolate milk.

Mary wiped it up. Patience dropped her dish. Jessie picked it up. Finally, when they could eat no more, Patience and Violet went to play, and Jessica refilled the coffee mugs.

"You didn't even want to come in just now!" Jessica accused.

"That's right. I'm not ashamed to admit it. I don't ever want to see that Falconer woman again, if I can help it. She's mad, Jessie. I don't know whether she's ever done anything really violent, of course. I almost wish she would, so that she could be put away. As it is, I know that she's done a great deal of harm. Yet when anyone remotely official deals with her, she becomes propriety itself—all lah-dee-dah and to the manor born. But let her decide to harass a tenant or a bill collector; then watch out! She has a bag of tricks that will turn the most kindly, rational, gentle people into blathering paranoids."

"You mean she plays psychological games?" Jessica asked.

"Psychological *warfare* is more like it. You'll never know when to expect her, for a start. Weeks will go by in perfect harmony; you won't see or hear her. Then suddenly she'll be meddling into every tiny corner of your lives. I can't possibly describe it. But I will tell you that the last three tenants all left in such a hurry they didn't bother to take half of their belongings. There's a seedy secondhand shop on Van Cortlandt Street that Mrs. Falconer takes all the leavings to. And, Jessie, I don't want to sound like a crepe hanger, but all three of these couples are now divorced—and I don't know about the earlier ones. They're way before my time in Wimbledon." Mary stopped to sip her coffee.

"Did you know any of these people, or is this all hearsay?"

"I knew the Teels; they were the last tenants. They moved to Wimbledon about three years ago, just when

43

George and I did. George met Norman at the hardware store one day; they'd known each other at school. Norman didn't make much money; he was a social worker in the city. So, naturally, when they found this place . . ." Mary's eyes, her negative feelings about the place notwithstanding, glanced with warm appreciation at the graceful room.

"Well, naturally, they were overjoyed. They invited us over, and, Jessie, the place was enchanting. George and I were almost envious. Our house still needed so much work then, and here the Teels had lucked into this perfect place, so tidy and clean and all in working order; and they were renting it for a song. We had such a good time that night. I remember thinking that Norman and Marjorie were probably the first couple we'd met in Wimbledon who seemed really to be in love. I just knew we were going to be firm friends for a long time. Why, Marjorie and I were even expecting babies the same month. But that was the only pleasant evening the four of us ever shared here. After that, Mrs. Falconer got her hooks into the Teel family, and things became very complicated. Norman moved out to the Coast, and Marjorie and her little boys are living with her folks in White Plains. I blame the whole thing on that creep upstairs." The Falconer cane and footsteps could now be heard clumping directly overhead.

"Jessica, thank you for a delicious lunch. I know you'll think I'm a hysterical fool, but we must go. I promise I'll call you. And let's meet at the park—on Monday around eleven o'clock. We're in the phone book if you need anything—George Smith, Riverview Road, okay? I'm just not prepared for a confrontation with the old lady. And by the sound of those footsteps I'll just bet she's spotted our wagon in your driveway and is on her way to see you this very minute. Violet! Come on, we're going home."

Sure enough, while Jessica stood by the window

watching Mary's station wagon roll down the steep drive into Granite Terrace, there was a knock at the door.

Jessica considered not hearing the knock. But as she hesitated, Patience walked helpfully to the back door and with some effort, used her pudgy fingers to undo the two locks.

"Hello. Do you want my mommy?" And she led Mrs. Falconer by the hand, ushering her proudly into the living room.

"There you are, my dear. I feared perhaps you'd gone out. Wasn't there a car in your drive just now? Your baby is such a good hostess. It's one of my great sorrows never to have borne a child . . . though, my dear, many a soul is walking this earth today thanks to my skilled assistance many long years ago. Oh, the stories I could tell you! Ah well, that's not what I came down to talk about. I *certainly* don't wish to disturb you. I can see you have much unpacking still to do—and dishes to clear, and good wholesome food to put away. You're a busy young woman, and I won't take much of your time. It's just that . . ."

Jessica found herself holding her breath. Mary's suspicions were contagious. Yet even as she stood watching the odd old woman, Jessica couldn't, in all honesty, discern anything remotely menacing about her. She was a bit pathetic, and her talkativeness was irritating; but that was all.

"Yes, Mrs. Falconer? Is there something I can do for you?"

"Yes, Mrs., er, uh, Painter, I came to look for a box that was stored here when I had some wallpapering done upstairs. I have these exquisite old quilts that have been in the family for many generations. My family. The Cavendishes. Though Frederick was a sweet man, his people were *common*, my dear. Common as dirt. No pedigree at all. Wimbledon working class. But these quilts; I be-

45

lieve I put them in your linen closet—though I can't imagine why, goodness knows, they should have gone to the attic. Would you mind awfully if I just take a look, dear? It won't take a second?" Her compelling blue eyes wore their trusting look; hard, indeed, to refuse her.

"No, of course not. Go right ahead, Mrs. Falconer. Though I must say the linen closet seemed perfectly bare this morning."

Mrs. Falconer was already on her way to the hall. Jessie followed, turned on the light, and waited as the woman craned her neck, peering at the top shelves.

"Well. How do you like that? It isn't here. Are you *sure* you didn't see it? It was quite a *large* box, you see, covered with cedar paper. Oh, it bothers me so much to let strange people in here. Things do begin to disappear, no matter how careful one is. I *want* those quilts. A lovely grandniece of mine is getting married next month in Denver. I wanted so much to send her a lovely heirloom as a wedding gift. Maybe I put it in one of the bedrooms. . . ."

This time Mrs. Falconer didn't bother to ask permission. She continued through the apartment in a mounting frenzy, opening closets, peering inside, closing them, and moving on.

When she began to open dresser drawers, Jessie finally spoke up.

"Mrs. Falconer. Those dressers belong to us. They weren't *here* when you had the paperhangers. You won't find your box in them, surely!"

"Oh. Yes. I *am* sorry. Of *course* you wouldn't have *my* box in one of *your* dressers, now, would you? Well, my dear, all I can say is, if the box turns up when you've *finally* cleared all these messy cartons away, you will see that I get it, won't you?"

"If it does, I'll rush it right up to you. I'm sorry you couldn't find it. Perhaps it's in your attic after all. Now,

I really must get back to work. Do have a pleasant evening, Mrs. Falconer." Jessica walked steadily toward the back door as she spoke, and opened it, pointedly, when she concluded.

"Oh. Well, of course I'll leave; you don't have to worry about me interrupting your important affairs. But do remember the box, won't you? I'm sure that handsome hubby of yours wouldn't dream of taking it." She closed the door behind her with something that fell just short of being a slam. Jessie stared at the back door in amazement until, a minute or two later, she heard the woman's receding footsteps, lumbering up the outside stairway.

It had been far too eventful a day already, what with the shock of poor Miss Kelly's stabbing and Mary's dire warnings about Mrs. Falconer. Yet Jessie continued to build her own dream of being settled; putting her own stamp on the quaint apartment high above the Hudson. She was far from ready to give it up, and during the next hour she and Patience finished unpacking all the baby things. Everything fell neatly into place. The result was satisfying to them both. Though it was still too early for her bedtime, Patience consented to a short lie-down with some of her freshly unpacked toys.

Filled with new enthusiasm, Jessica cleared away their earlier meal, and completed unpacking the kitchen things. Small as it was, the kitchen was efficient. All sorts of loving touches—little shelves, a large pegboard with hooks in all the right places, a useful little counter top, testified to the enthusiasm of earlier tenants. And that breathtaking Hudson view above the sink would be a continual source of pleasure. Once again Jessie observed the sun begin its colorful descent behind the Palisades and realized she hadn't heard from Sam.

What would it be tonight? she wondered. Would he appear, bright and cheerful, in a few minutes, so they could all eat a family supper together? Or would she hear nothing at all until after nine o'clock, when the phone would ring to tell her he'd run into some friends and would start for home after just one more round of drinks?

She never knew, with Sam. It had seemed rather glamorous, at first, to be married to such an outgoing, popular young man. Though Sam's cronies treated her well, and the musty, boisterous barroom atmosphere was appealing, she knew a hated, "bluestocking" quality clung to her like some overripe perfume. She came from a bookish, teetotaling family.

To Jessie, at nineteen, Sam's easy gregariousness was like a magic buffer. He opened doors to a formless, vaguely cynical society that accepted her and found her witty. But after Patience was born Jessie went out with Sam less often, and soon hardly at all. It never dawned on Sam to question his right to come and go as he pleased. And Jessie, despite her resolve to be brave and understanding, had become increasingly ambivalent toward him. In Sam's case the style was so very much the man that Jessie was loath to tamper with it. But Jessie's style, she often pointed out, was being tampered with. So they quarreled about other things. Bitter quarrels that led nowhere, settled nothing. She had no idea what to do about it.

For a time she'd read marriage manuals and self-help psychology books, thinking somewhere to find the clue that would permit their two disparate life-styles to blend congenially. Though Sam never appeared to notice, there was a phase when Jessica's approach to him would alter week by week depending on which eminent counselor's book rested on their bedside table. Sam never read a single one.

She knew why she was thinking about all this now. Of all the facts Mary Smith had had to impart about Mrs. Falconer's former tenants, the remark that Jessie found hardest to ignore was the one about divorce. Whatever

48

Mrs. Falconer did to people, it seemed to have produced a one hundred percent record of failed marriages.

Sam and Jessica Porter, who still loved one another, had agreed on the move to Granite Terrace because both hoped it might help to save their marriage.

Chapter 6

PATIENCE and Jessica ate supper quietly by candle-light. Daddy had not been heard from. Their little meal was over so quickly that to stave off the lonely wait for Sam Jessie decided to keep Patience up past her normal bedtime. Trying to think up a diversion, she remembered how delighted the child had been to see her finger paints when they were unpacked. What's more, Jessie'd get into it, too—great therapy for a lonely suburban housewife!

The dining table was covered with newspaper, and two large sheets of finger-paint paper were laid down . . . an irresistible invitation to creativity. Jessie's all turned out turbulent and gloomy-looking. Though she chose cheerful colors to begin with, by the time she'd slapped them onto the paper they took shape as a roiling North Atlantic sea storm or a Baskervillian lake of fog— on this one, she deliberately placed "the footprint of a gigantic hound"—with four quick strokes. Patience, on the other hand, was enjoying more success. Her results, on several sheets of paper, appeared to be a chronicle of her good friend, Tweetie. On fields of glowing pink, green, and lavender, the little doll, primitively drawn, but recognizable, was seen to dance and fly.

"Why, Patience, I think you're quite an artist. That one looks just like Tweetie. What's she doing?"

"That one is me. Patience. The green one is Tweetie. Here we are in the park. You are pushing me on the swing. This yellow stuff is the leaves. We going back there again?" Patience seemed almost wistful, remembering the park. Could it be she hadn't understood about the move? Did she think they'd be going back to the city again?

"But of course we'll go there again, sweetie. We can go there every day from now on. We live here. That's our park, now. So you like the swings, huh?"

"Yeah! And I like the trees. And Violet. This is nice. We're not going back to the 'partment?" Jessica brushed a wisp of Patience's fine dark blond hair from her face. It felt a little damp and was curled into a delicate spring that bounced back the second she released it.

"This is our home now, dear."

"That lady . . . upstairs? . . ."

"Yes?"

"It's *her* house."

"We rent this place from her."

"She doesn't . . ."

"What?"

"She doesn't want us to be here." Patience was tired. But she held onto the thought and continued. "She's scared all the time. . . ."

"Scared of *us*, you mean? Nobody could possibly be scared of us. Why, we're about as harmless as they come!"

Patience grinned at her mother. "No! Mommy, don't be silly! Not of us. She's just scared. All the time. She's a sad old lady. We going to the park tomorrow? And see Violet?" Jessica nodded. Patience yawned.

"Tweetie and I want to go to sleep now."

When Jessica returned to their work table after putting Patience to bed, the paintings had dried and were curling at the edges. Suddenly they were precious to her. Flooded by some unnamed apprehension, she felt an urge to protect them from harm. There was no doubt

51

in her mind that the paintings Patience had done indicated a real gift. So much promise! It seemed almost a burden. The feeling passed quickly. Jessica hung the paintings on the kitchen wall with masking tape. "Patience," she murmured to herself, "whatever did Sam and I do to deserve you?" She couldn't wait to show the wall to Sam. But Sam never called.

Shortly after midnight, just as Jessica was drifting into a shallow, troubled sleep, she heard keys rattling in the porch door. Startled, she sat up with a sudden lurch, her heart beating rapidly. She realized that she'd been asleep long enough to dream and that her dream had been a frightening one about Mrs. Falconer. The door opened, however, to reveal Sam, and he was full of lively talk. He carried a crisp, autumnal night smell into the room, and his city clothes gave him an air of command.

Swallowing any hint of her own prolonged loneliness, Jessica pulled on her robe, found her slippers, and set a teakettle on to boil.

". . . so Pierre and Dorcas took me to the station in a cab—I just caught the last train to Irvington. I can't figure him out, Jessie, he was so difficult on the phone this morning, forcing me to come in today. You know, there wasn't any need for me to be there at all. Oh, well. I guess maybe I scored a few brownie points. Anyway, around five o'clock he called me on the nightline at 423 Park and told me to meet him at P.J. Clarke's for drinks. I've been with him and this crazy new girlfriend of his, Dorcas Dillingham, ever since. The upshot of it is, by the end of the evening we were all so chummy that I told them we were having a housewarming party next Saturday and that I hoped they would both come. I'm sorry to do that to you, Jess, but maybe it'll turn out to be fun.

"Dorcas said it would be her first chance to see the

'American suburbs' she's heard so much about. She's veddy, veddy British, but I kept catching a kind of Cockney inflection underneath. Pierre must be losing his touch. Every time she went to the ladies' room, he'd sort of apologize for her—which I hate to see a man do—and say how they'd started living together because he needed 'companionship' since Nicole ran off with that dancer. 'Companionship!' Wait till you see Dorcas. Though she's a bit long in the tooth, at that."

Sam gratefully took a sip of tea from the mug Jessie'd placed before him. She was grateful in turn that he was apparently sober despite a night on the town.

". . . And then, Jessie, the most extraordinary thing happened. One of those weird coincidences. We were just talking about Wimbledon, when finally I could see the location clicking in Pierre's mind—you know how vague he can be. And just as Pierre was saying, 'Ah, yes, but of course, Wimbledon-on-*Hudson;* that's where my leetle CopperCable is—I'm a pretty beeg stockholder, you know . . . a newspaper boy came in with *this.*" Sam pulled out a slightly battered copy of that night's early edition of the New York Sunday *News* and threw it on the table, face up, by Jessie's mug of tea.

ELDERLY CLERK FOUND
FATALLY STABBED AT DESK

Underneath was a horrifying picture showing poor Nora Kelly's body crumpled up at her desk in the CopperCable offices. Jessica hated the picture, hated the *News* for printing such a demeaning, sensational thing.

"Oh, Sam. Please. I already know about this . . ."

"Imagine, Jess—right here in Wimbledon. No sooner do we arrive at a place than wham! it's spread all over the front page! See, read the caption:

Quiet Wimbledon-on-Hudson the scene of puzzling murder. Special phone installed by Westchester Police to receive any leads in brutal slaying of Nora Kelly, accounting clerk for 42 years at CopperCable Wimbledon facility.

Story on Page 3

"You already know about it . . . what do you mean?"

Jessica told Sam of her meeting with Mary Smith that afternoon. And when she took the time to describe Mary in detail and explain how helpful she'd been to them, Sam interrupted impatiently.

"Yes, that's fine. I'm glad you made a friend. But what's that got to do with this murder?"

"I was getting to that. We went to Murphy's together. Murphy's is sort of the hub of Wimbledon—a combination soda parlor and stationery, very charming. The Murphys are related to this poor Nora Kelly. When Mary and I walked in, Mrs. Murphy had just gotten the news from her son—who's a policeman. Her husband discovered the body. Oh, Sam, it was just awful. They were so shocked and heartbroken. See, Miss Kelly was going to retire on the fifteenth, and they'd been planning a dinner in her honor. They were having a planning meeting at CopperCable this morning and Mr. Murphy was in charge of the committee . . ." Her voice trailed off; she found she was more upset now than she'd been that afternoon.

"My god, here I think I'm bringing you some spicy news from the outside world, and you were in on it practically from the ground floor. I'm sorry you were upset; the Murphys must be very nice people for you to care so much. Calm down, honey. After all your years in the wicked city you must know that it's a mad world." Sam walked over to Jessie and put his arms around her.

To her surprise and confusion, Jessica found herself sobbing uncontrollably, and the comfort his arms offered only seemed to make the tears flow faster.

"Jess—what's the matter? Did something else happen to upset you? Did you have another meeting with old lady F? What's wrong? Come on, now." He helped her out of the chair and led her gently to the overstuffed wing chair.

"Here, sit on my lap and cry all you want. I'll wait. I've got all the time in the world, and tomorrow's Sunday and we'll sleep late and have a nice breakfast, okay?" He patted her back and predictably the sobbing eased. Jessie groped in the pocket of her robe for a tissue.

"Sam. I'm sorry to behave like this. The day was upsetting; but I thought I'd been handling everything so well. I didn't think any of it was really getting to me. It wasn't just the murder—although you can imagine it wasn't the best of all possible welcomes to Wimbledon. And I'd been so pleased by everything until then. It all looked pretty and, well, *safe*. And I was so glad to have met Mary . . . but, then, when she drove us home . . . well, when she saw where we lived—oh, hell, I'm going to start crying again. . . ."

"What about where we live? Did Mary know this place? Well, all the better. We can use all the information we can get about this crazy place. You've found us an ally, probably."

"Ally? Do you think we need one? I mean, for Pete's sake, Sam, why all this mystery about a dotty old landlady? Just because she's a little senile, why turn her into some kind of sinister threat? That's what *Mary* was doing."

"How, exactly, Jess? What did Mary have to say?"

Jessie repeated the bulk of Mary's remarks to Sam. Without fully meaning to keep anything from him, however, she did not in fact quote Mary accurately. She did not mention the Teels' divorce, nor did she mention the broken marriages of the two previous tenants. Yet that was what had disturbed her the most.

"Psychological warfare, eh? I wonder why? I mean, what motivates *her*? Oh, well, Jess, don't worry too much. Forewarned is forearmed, right?" Sam leaned back and gave a massive yawn. Then he turned Jessie's face to his by placing his hand under her chin; his other hand still absentmindedly patting her on the back.

"Besides," he went on, "you don't know this Mary Smith that well. Her name sounds like an alias! Maybe she's a gossip . . . likes to exaggerate things."

At this point Jessie pulled herself away from the tender, though absentminded, ministrations of Sam's hands.

"Now, wait a minute, Sam; I do know Mary well. And as for her name, she's married to George Smith, and her maiden name was Wurtenburger—how's that for an alias? When she left this afternoon, I felt like I'd known her for years. She doesn't seem like a gossip at all. She's candid and helpful. And, Sam, she literally did not want to come up those steps. She was afraid of Mrs. Falconer."

Sam laughed a little.

"Come on, Jess, let's sleep on it. We've both had busy days. And, you know, I'm going to look on this whole thing as a challenge. I don't know what makes old Mrs. Falconer tick, and if I didn't have designs on this apartment, I couldn't care less. We ought to be able to work out some kind of *modus operandi* that lets us get along with her well enough to stay on here until we can afford something less eccentric. I really don't see that we have too much to worry about." As was his habit, Sam began to undress before he reached the bedroom. His tie was tossed over the wing chair, his shirt unbuttoned, and his shoes and socks lay abandoned strategically on the rug. "And what the hell, Jessie," he went on rather sleepily, "if it doesn't work out, we'll just move again, that's all.

Now that we're in this area, it shouldn't be too hard to find something else. Personally I don't think that old woman is any match for us. We're younger, stronger, and know a helluva lot more about psychology than she does. By the way, did you see her again today?"

Jessie filled Sam in on the brief visit and her odd search.

"She's just losing her memory, I guess. Look. Let's go on being as polite to her as we can without forfeiting our own privacy." Sam mimicked Mrs. Falconer's affectedly cultured voice. Jessie laughed. They went to their bedroom. A coppery harvest moon shone above the black Hudson; and Wimbledon slept snugly beside it.

"I'll just look in on Patience before we go to sleep. Won't be a minute." Jessica walked sleepily to the baby's room next door. Here, too, the moonlight poured in through the enormous, still-uncurtained windows. Patience was sleeping so peacefully she seemed almost not to breathe. Jessica bent over the crib and kissed the lovely cheeks. As always, Patience slept with one round arm encircling the ubiquitous Tweetie. Tonight Tweetie apparently had a friend. Jessica picked up the extra doll, absently wondering which one Patience had selected for this signal honor. The doll felt strangely clammy. Jessie walked to the window to look at it more closely. Then, with an involuntary shudder, she let the thing fall from her hands to the floor.

"Sam! Sam. Come look at this awful thing!"

"Shhh . . . you'll wake her up! What is it now?"

"That *thing* I just dropped; it was in Patience's *crib.* I've never seen it before!"

Without a word Sam picked it up, and they tiptoed out of the baby's room. When they got to their own bedroom, Jessica switched on their bedside lamp, and both examined the doll, whose mere touch had caused Jessie to drop it in disgust.

"Ugh. How in the world did we come by this?" Sam's revulsion was as instinctive as Jessica's. The doll was made of aging, half-sticky, half-dry and corroded latex stretched over a spongy composition frame, its "skin" luridly jaundiced. It was, admittedly, a slightly naughty toy. Perhaps a novelty item sold by mail through the pages of a bygone stag magazine some thirty or forty years earlier. Its head was disproportionately larger than its body. Though it may at one time have had some kind of "human hair" wig, all that remained on the scalp were a multitude of pinholes, thus making its encephalitic head look like the work of some mad acupuncturist. The facial features, those of a coy, Kewpie doll, wore the plucked eyebrows and ruby-red cupid's-bow lips of the late twenties and early thirties.

The body was as obscene as the head was grotesque. Its naked breasts—grossly exaggerated—showed the passage of time in the corrosion of the pointed nipples. One nipple was worn off altogether, revealing crumbly, spongy stuffing. The other, though faded, showed what the original erotic conception had been—erect, immense, crimson. A fake "jewel" was inserted in the navel, and the pubic area, though sculptured in rare detail, was partially obscured by a few ragged wisps of black silk net.

With horrified fascination, Sam turned the doll over. Its rear view was every bit as tawdry. In small letters on the base of its neck was the imprint: "Whoopee Novelties. Made in U.S.A." With a speechless shrug, Sam threw the thing angrily into the wastebasket, then threw the Sunday *News* on top of it for good measure.

"I don't know about you, Sam," Jessica said, "but I've had it. This is just more than I can take right now. It's so ugly . . . so weird. Maybe there's a perfectly ordinary explanation. But I've got to get some sleep. In fact, I feel as though I already am asleep. This may all be a bad

58

dream." Jessie crawled between the sheets, and as she reached to turn off the lamp, her eyes were accosted by an image that continued to register long after darkness came. The newsprint photo of poor dead Nora Kelly, bathed in cold, black blood, covered everything but the awful yellow doll face, with its dreadful needled scalp. The image repeated and expanded in her mind's eye, until, exhausted, the blank solace of sleep finally came to her.

Sam left the bedroom, sleep unthinkable. He was desperately, passionately angry. The idea of that leering, nasty— He tiptoed back into the darkened bedroom and retrieved the grubby doll . . . even being in the same room with Patience! In her crib! Vile. Some decrepit old man's slimy fetish—that's what it looked like—it fairly oozed evil. He held it defiantly in his hand, gesturing to the ceiling, waving his arms, pacing the apartment trying to accommodate a rage that he could find no real focus for. How had the thing got to Patience? Mrs. Falconer? A previous tenant? One of the moving men? He began opening closets, closing them, peering into cupboards.

Eventually his peregrinations led to their liquor supply, which was fortunately modest. The doll was dropped on a low kitchen shelf by the stove, and he once again began his pacing. It was as though he sensed the answer he was looking for was there taunting him. If he could only discover the right question to ask. Drink in hand, darkness around him, he sat down on the big wing chair and tried to be rational about the lurid doll. Actually Patience could have picked that thing up anywhere . . . playing with the boxes as Jessica unpacked, crawling into little nooks no grown-up could get to. That doll could have been wedged into some crevice for twenty, thirty years, until Patience's coolly observant little eyes spotted it and her nimble little fingers pried it free. It was a perfectly satisfactory explanation; but he didn't believe it. A heavy, prurient atmosphere lingered in the darkened room, and with it, a nameless fear. Try as he might, Sam could not shake an apprehension that the doll had been placed in the crib deliberately.

By dawn Sam had gone through half of one bottle of house-brand scotch and a third of an inferior bourbon. Somewhere along the line he'd grasped a glimmer of an idea that haunted him with its remembered clarity and perception. Something to do with Mrs. Falconer. It had to be. Exasperated, he skulked off to the bedroom; it was nearly five in the morning. He would be hung over at breakfast. Whatever theory he'd been formulating had left him. He was completely in the dark.

He tripped over an unopened packing box, stubbing his toe painfully. His oath, as loud as it was colorful, seemed to shatter the quiet night air. And a split second later the sound of Mrs. Falconer's cane responded directly above his head. Her day, apparently, had already begun. He listened to the clumping of her stick, the more muffled scuffle of her rubber-soled nurses' shoes, and pointed an angry finger straight at the sound.

"Old woman!" he said. "If you had anything at all to do with that doll in the crib, I promise you'll regret it." An empty, mindless threat.

Jessica stirred in her sleep as he crept into bed, but did not wake up. Now that his anger had dissipated, and with his mind oddly comforted by some half-forgotten drunken insight, Sam fell soundly asleep beside her.

Chapter 7

"OUR first rainy day in Wimbledon. Thought I'd let you sleep." Torrents of noisy rain streamed vertically down each window. Jessica, dressed and looking crisp and competent, had brought in a little tray with toast and coffee.

"What time is it?" Sam accepted the precious, life-giving coffee with extraordinary gratitude.

"It's just after one. Patience and I have been up since eight . . . we've had a good morning. I've even got the *Times* for you. It didn't begin to rain like this until around ten. Now it looks as though it'll last all day. Drink your coffee, take a shower; I'll fix some eggs, all right?" The hangover Sam had expected wasn't all that bad. He found himself in a cozy, muddled state that welcomed rain, savored the thought of the fat Sunday *Times*, delighted in domestic joys . . . indeed . . . desired this comely, capable creature who was his wife.

"Where's Patience now?" he said.

"She's lying down. I think she's fallen asleep."

"Does this door lock?"

"Why, Sam! You're feeling pretty good, after all, aren't you?" Jessie smiled. And, accommodatingly, the door did lock.

So it was after two o'clock before Sam—showered, shaved, and breakfasted—heard the latest on the village murder. Jessica purposely led their talk around to the subject, thinking it would distract Sam from the incredible scene they'd tried to contend with the night before. Before Patience had awakened that morning, the very first thing Jessie had done was to take the wastepaper basket and invert its contents gingerly into a partially filled plastic garbage bag. Then, holding it as far away from herself as possible, she'd marched straight out to the back steps to their trash can and without hesitation dropped the bag and sealed it noisily with the dented lid. That, she decided, had best be the end of that. And if there were any way they could get through the day without the doll's being mentioned— she would find it. The murder, on the other hand, seemed safely impersonal.

"Let me tell you about my morning, Sam," she began.

At nine that morning Jessica had walked with Patience in her stroller down Maynard Hill. She found a shortcut that made the matter of pushing the stroller down to the village easier. Murphy's was closed. The only other newsstand in town—in a characterless chain store—was doing extra-heavy business. Jessie caught the drift of conversation coming from a cluster of Sunday-paper buyers standing by the door.

"They've ruled out robbery," one man said.

"Well, the poor old thing—she wouldn't have had money or jewelry on her, now, would she?" an older man pointed out.

"You know, Nora was about to retire . . . she was sixty if she was a day. . . . Still, she was kind of a pretty old thing. Even now. She never did marry, did she?" interjected a plain-looking woman around fifty wearing a faded raincoat over her housedress.

The first man answered, "Oh, she was a real little doll years ago . . . many of us'd like to have had a try at her—remember, Ed?"

"Remember? Why, I went with her! Let's see, that'd

be the summer of 1930. Plant was shut down. Bad times. Ah, we were all so damn young, we didn't know what good times was, did we? C'mon, Rita, it's starting to rain, we'd better get moving." Ed and Rita and the others broke up their gossip. Once they were out on the street Jessica overheard one further remark.

"I'll just bet whoever killed her thought she was somebody else."

Jessica found herself wanting to know even more about Nora. The Sunday *News* was all but sold out. But the *Times* was available in generous quantities. Jessie made her purchase, bought a red lollipop for Patience's ride home, and walked squarely into Mary Smith.

Mary was buying the *Times,* and she was alone.

"I only have a second . . . I left the coffee on. The wagon's parked outside with the motor running. . . . Hop in, why don't you?" Jessica, aware of the rain beginning to gather force, was amenable. As soon as they drove off, Mary began speaking with an easy intimacy. Jessica found herself marveling that they'd only met for the first time less than twenty-four hours before. Already Mary felt like a comfortable old friend, and Jessica was pleased. Despite the warnings Mary had given her about the Falconer place, Jessica found that just being with Mary made their life in Wimbledon seem assured of a comfortable and predictable continuity.

"Guess what, Jessie," Mary went on, and Jessie realized that her earlier chatter had passed right over her.

"What?" she asked brightly, to hide her previous inattention.

"Mrs. Murphy called me last night to thank us for being so helpful and understanding yesterday afternoon. Imagine, with all she had on her mind, to think of us. She even asked who you were . . . said you were a new face."

"Do the police have any ideas about it yet? I just overheard some people talking, saying they thought it must have been a case of mistaken identity," Jessica reported.

"Well, all Mrs. Muphy said was that they'd ruled out robbery as a motive. They seem to think poor Miss Kelly's job may have had something to do with it. Nora'd spent the last months helping programmers convert the accounting system to a computer. She wasn't going to be replaced when she retired. They're only guessing, though. They don't seem to have very much to go on yet." Mary was making the turn off Maynard onto Firehouse, and it was beginning to pour.

"Mrs. Murphy said she knows that nobody who ever knew Nora would want to kill her."

Jessie, thinking out loud, said, "Still, a brutal knifing like that, it makes you think it's some kind of 'crime of passion,' don't you think?"

"Crime of passion, huh? I guess you read the Sunday *News*. I personally think it was some mad person passionately interested in covering something up. Something crooked in poor old Nora's books."

"Poor Nora Kelly," Jessie said. "Well, have a good Sunday, Mary. Just drop us off here. I'll leave the stroller in our driveway and dash up those steps with Patience. Oh, by the way, it seems Sam has decreed we're having a housewarming party next Saturday night—would you and George like to come?"

Mary smiled.

"You sure don't scare easily, do you? Well, I'll ask George. Maybe you two will succeed where others have failed. Mind you, George isn't so wild about your Mrs. Falconer, either. I'll be in touch." Patience and Violet were sitting with their arms around each other in the back seat, laughing.

"C'mon, you two. You can play together again tomorrow."

"Take care, now!" Mary called, and drove off.

The account of her day completed, Jessie asked Sam seriously, "Well, what do you think? Do you think Nora Kelly's murder was a 'crime of passion' or a coldly calculated scheme?"

"I don't think it's any of our business, thank God. Still . . . a bizarre crime like that usually involves strong feelings of one kind or another. Of course, it could be that the person who did it had some kind of grudge against CopperCable; and it was Miss Kelly's bad luck to be on the spot when he decided to act out his grudge." Sam seemed less interested in the murder than he'd been the night before. And of course, he was right. It wasn't any business of theirs.

"You could ask Pierre what he knows about Copper-Cable," Jessie suggested, not quite willing to let go of the conversation. "I mean, if he's such an important stockholder and all, maybe he's heard something about a grudge or feud or something."

"Why don't you ask him, Jessie, at the party? He'd be flattered. And it'd be right down his alley—even if he doesn't know a thing. There's nothing old Pierre likes better than a sweet young thing looking at him with big eyes and asking his opinion about some earth-shattering subject he knows next-to-nothing about. No disrespect intended, Jess!"

"I'll do it, Sam, but are you asking me to play up to your boss? That isn't like you. There's a first time for everything. You know, it's going to be hard having Pierre here as your boss. I've always felt so casual about him. Now I'm going to have to think about everything I say and do. Ugh." Yet secretly Jessie relished the idea of playing the role of helpful wife to the rising young executive. The whole idea was patently absurd. That's what she liked about it. Then a new concern entered her thoughts.

"My God, how much money do we have left until you get paid?" This was serious. Sam's face reflected her alarm.

"This party you've invited him to—it's going to cost us. I'll have to spend quite a bit on things like curtains and other odds and ends. And I don't think there's much liquor left." Sam's face clouded even more. "And party food. I'm warning you, it's going to cost much more than we can afford." Already Jessie was absorbed in listing items they'd need on her yellow-lined legal pad. Sam, who wasn't certain when he'd receive his first paycheck, was very certain about their bank balance. The move from the city had just about cleaned them out. Jessie would have to conjure up some kind of miracle to have a party ready by Saturday. The remorse he felt for his impulsive invitation was written all over his face.

"As bad as that, is it?" Jessie looked pale.

"There's probably about fifty dollars left in the bank, Jessie—and I have to spend thirty-five dollars for a commutation ticket tomorrow. I've got maybe twenty dollars in my wallet. What do you have?" He looked miserable.

"I tipped the moving men fifteen dollars; and I bought some groceries. Let me get my purse. . . ." She walked to the kitchen, came back, opened her purse, took out her wallet . . . and produced a five, a ten, two singles, and a fistful of change.

"Well. This will feed us for the rest of next week, at least, because we have all the staples we need; but it won't pay for a party."

"Maybe I can get an advance," Sam suggested.

"Not if I have anything to say about it. That's a bad

way to start a new job." Jessie was dismayed at Sam's even considering such a thing.

"Oh, I don't know, Jessie. Pierre knows we don't have much money. And, let's face it, he's loaded. What difference would it make if I hit him for an advance?" Sam was ready to seize this way out, perfectly willing to consider their awkward problem solved. Not Jessica.

"Don't you see," she argued, "Pierre doesn't know the first thing about not having any money. He knows we're not rich. But he's never been broke in his life. If you hit him for an advance, he'll just assume you're a bungler . . . can't manage your finances. It would never occur to him that our income was too small to cover something like moving expenses. Don't do it. We'll figure something out. Besides, Friday is the fifteenth; you'll probably get paid by then." Jessica attempted to be as logical and rational as she knew how, because she felt Sam's biggest danger in his relationship with Pierre would be this very nonchalance that ignored the essential difference between them.

"Fitzgerald was right, you know," she went on, "the rich are very different."

"That was Hemingway, wasn't it?" Sam put in mildly. And Jessie smiled, relieved. She'd made her point. And they hadn't fought. Now all that remained was to set the stage for a successful party in a new apartment, with less than twenty dollars to spare. She asked, "How are we going to set the stage for a good party in six days, with only twenty dollars to spare?"

"God, Jessie, remember those great set-striking parties we used to have? B.Y.O.B. and send out for pizza?"

Jessie remembered. "Or for blintzes from those little dairy restaurants on Second Avenue! That already seems very long ago. . . ." The memory of those brave theater days provoked an idea, a perfect idea that could just be the solution they'd been groping for.

"I think I've got it! Stage. Striking set. Sam! What about all that stuff we stored when the theater went under? It's all still there at Victor's loft, isn't it? God, when I think of all those yards of gauze we only used once for the scrim in *Death of a Salesman* and how furious we were when nobody'd buy it back from us. And I bet Victor'd be delighted to get rid of it all. There were some marvelous props, too, remember? Lamps and carpets and pillows and mirrors and candlesticks—I can just *see* it all here. We'll store it— and use it while we're storing it. Then, if Victor ever gets some new backers, we'll let him have the stuff back. And we can ask him and Sarah to the party, they'd be fun to have. Sarah can play her guitar. . . . Well, say something. What do you think?" Jessica beamed.

"By George, I think you've got it!" Sam was already considering the proper approach to Victor, and couldn't foresee any problem in selling him on the idea. Lord knew, Sam had pulled Victor out of similar scrapes hundreds of times. Victor owed him a favor. To think that's where he'd first come face to face with boilers and number six oil! He'd had something very different in mind at one time. Still, no regrets. It sounded like an amusing plan.

"Bless you, me girl. Victor and Sarah will make the party. Just what we needed. I'm sure I can talk him into letting us store all that stuff for a while. You're a genius, you know that?"

"It's going to be fun. Do you think you could get down to Victor's on your lunch hour tomorrow? Can you figure a way to get the stuff up here? It'll take a lot of stitching to turn that gauze into curtains by Saturday —the sooner I get it the better. Oh, it's going to look beautiful! They'll filter the light and make everything look terribly *fin de siècle*. Just you wait, Samuel Porter:

By next Saturday, this room will look like a page from Boris Aronson's sketchpad!"

From that Sunday afternoon until the following Saturday, the Porter ménage was mobilized into the single-minded pursuit of a memorable housewarming. The plan, embarked on so casually by Sam, almost as a slip of the tongue, turned out to color the remainder of their moving-in week with good cheer. Their busy schedule dimmed their initial preoccupation with Mrs. Falconer. Sam's arrival, late Monday evening in a borrowed company station wagon, was a triumphant thing. Breathing heavily but grinning from ear to ear, he unloaded his theatrical loot in several mad dashes up and down the steps.

During the days that followed, Jessica put in countless hours at her sewing machine; and every evening Sam would hang her latest efforts at each successive window. The living room took on a lush, luxurious look, as the floor-to-ceiling folds of gauze were attached to traverse rods Jessie'd bought with their last bit of folding money.

Every day proceeded without incident—save one. One mild Indian summer day, just slightly tarnished by air pollution, Jessica called Mary early in the morning to enlist her help. Mary arrived with Violet and her portable Singer in tow. The children played in the little side yard protected on all sides by a towering privet hedge. Mary and Jessica could hear their placid babble even though they couldn't actually see them. Between them the curtains were completed at last. Mary was impressed.

"Who would have thought it could look so . . . so—" she reached for the right word—"so opulent!" The plain white curtains were embellished with only one extra decorative touch—provided by the discovery of several reels of Victorian ball fringe among the props. As Mary and Jessica were stitching the last of the fringe, they suddenly heard a new voice above the cheerful chatter in the side yard. It belonged to Mrs. Falconer. Mary, her face guarded, leaned her head closer to the window, where she could catch a glimpse of what was going on and monitor the conversation. She saw Patience pull her doll Tweetie out of her overall pocket, to show to Mrs. Falconer.

"This is Tweetie."

"How nice," Mrs. Falconer replied. "Do you love your doll?"

"Uh-huh," Patience said.

"Yes, little girls, love your dollies. Dollies come alive when they are loved. Your mommies and daddies don't know this, of course, but your dolls are alive. They hear what you say to them, and once in a great while they will say something to you. Did you know that? Do you know the story of the two dollies who loved each other?"

No answer. Apparently Mrs. Falconer felt the girls wanted to hear it, because her peculiar voice once again changed gears, deepening and becoming more gravelly, as the story progressed.

"She seems to be telling them a story," Mary whispered. "Listen!"

Jessica put down her scissors and pins and tiptoed to the open window.

"Once upon a time there were two beautiful dolls, a boy doll and a girl doll. They lived together in a little hilltop love nest that was filled with happiness and comfort."

"Did they belong to a little girl?" Patience wanted to know.

"Shh. Listen while I tell the story. It doesn't matter who owned them. They were all alone up there in that

70

dark and cozy world. Just two little dollies who loved one another."

"Then what?" Violet demanded.

"Then came their trouble. A wicked witch grew jealous of their happiness and beauty. She cast an evil spell. The girl dollie was sent away. The boy dollie was taken prisoner by the wicked witch. Oh, but these two little dollies missed one another something fierce, they did! There the girl dollie sat on a strange shelf, in a strange new room, forgotten by the world. Except for her lover boy who was taken prisoner. He was brave. He tried to escape and rescue her. Over and over again he tried. They would meet, secretly, at night. They would plan their revenge against the witch. Until, sure enough, one fine day they managed to trap her! And they killed the wicked witch! But it was too late. Because just as she died, the wicked witch cast her last evil spell over the girl doll.

"There, before the boy doll's eyes, the beautiful little dollie began to change! Her sweet pink skin turned old and wrinkled. Her graceful legs became stiff and creaky. Her tender smile became a nasty frown. In a few seconds all the life went out of her! She is probably sitting on some nursery shelf to this day—cold and lifeless and forgotten."

"What about the boy doll?" Patience asked.

"He's free, now. Alive and about. Still looking to find again the love he once had. So every night he scurries from house to house looking into nursery windows, hoping one day he'll find a new, beautiful little girl dollie to live happily ever after with, in a cozy love nest for two."

The two children stood in the yard, shuffling their feet uneasily. It was plain to see they had not enjoyed the story.

At the window Jessie looked at Mary. She felt they

ought to break things up but didn't want to force Mrs. Falconer on Mary.

"You go, Jessie," Mary suggested. "I'll stay out of sight."

Jessie stepped into the side yard, and both Patience and Violet came running to her—glad to have the story-telling spell broken. Mrs. Falconer rose with some difficulty from the wrought-iron garden bench.

"Ah, I felt sure you wouldn't leave these two angels unattended. Still, one never knows, does one? Mothers are so different today. You must ask me to baby-sit for you—any time. I love children. And, I fancy that they love me, too. I seem to have a way with little girls, especially." She tittered modestly.

"There's soda and cookies in the kitchen, kids, hop to it!" Jessie said, and the toddlers made their way into the house. She stood in the hallway, wondering whether Mrs. Falconer expected to be invited in. As she turned toward their apartment door, Mrs. Falconer moved toward her.

"A cookie or two would be delicious, I think. And some of your soda would rinse my throat. My voice does tire more easily these days." The old woman's steps followed closely on Jessica's until both were in the small Porter kitchen. Jessie's only thought was how to get her out again as fast as she decently could. Mrs. Falconer's amazing collection of facial wrinkles assembled themselves into a sociable smile.

"Why, you've made real progress, haven't you, my dear? It's charming." She walked expectantly into the kitchen. Jessie busied herself with getting out the soda. As she reached for the ice-cube tray, she heard a curious sputter.

"Take these damn things down immediately!" Mrs. Falconer sputtered, her blue eyes gray with rage. With an obvious effort at control she took a deep breath.

72

"I told you never to hang anything on my walls without molding hooks. How could you put these awful modern paintings on my new kitchen wall? I went to great expense to refurbish this flat. I will not have my tenants willfully destroy my property. *Take those awful things down at once, do you hear?*"

"I hear you Mrs. Falconer. You can be heard up and down the block, I'm sure. Those finger paintings were attached with masking tape. It's harmless to walls. Painters use it to protect walls. It doesn't leave a mark. You're letting yourself get upset over nothing."

"Nothing, eh? I'll be the judge of that!" Mrs. Falconer reached up, tore down the innocent display. Jessie watched open-mouthed as the paintings she'd come to treasure were ripped from the wall. This was the limit.

"I hope you're satisfied, Mrs. Falconer!" she shouted. "As you see, your precious wall doesn't have a mark on it. But you've just destroyed my little girl's paintings, and I'm going to ask you to leave before any more angry words pass between us. You owe both me and my daughter an apology. Now, I'll thank you to leave."

Suddenly deflated, Mrs. Falconer saw that the wall was indeed free of damage. She mumbled a brief apology and shuffled miserably out the back door.

Mary emerged from her hiding place in the bathroom. "What did I tell you, Jessie? She's a freak. Look what she just did to those paintings. It hurts. But it's not serious enough to report. Believe me, there'll be other incidents—just as painful, and just as hard to pin down. It reminds me of the time she accused the Teels' little boy—he couldn't have been more than three or four—of stealing her false teeth. It sounds absurd, but she scared the child half to death. She chased him all over the yard with her garden rake, ordering him to give the teeth back! Poor kid had nightmares about it for months afterward. One good thing, though, I bet she leaves you alone for a while." Mary stopped to pick up the paintings, trying to smooth them out, seeing whether perhaps some of them might be hung again. "She seems to slink away into solitary after a scene like this. I'll bet your party's a roaring success and the old creep leaves you in peace no matter how noisy it gets."

"Thanks, Mary. That's a help." She was not accustomed to shouting at old ladies, and the scene had unnerved her. Though she had never mentioned the grotesque Kewpie doll to Mary, and wasn't going to mention it now, she was suddenly certain beyond any doubt that the nightmarish toy could only have been connected somehow to Mrs. Falconer. The juxtaposition of Patience's tattered pink and lavender innocence with the clearly remembered evil of that leering yellow doll was untenable. She gave an involuntary shrug.

"Let's piece these together with Scotch tape and hang them up again. I'm ready to forget the whole thing. How many people do you know that break their necks getting ready for a housewarming, when they already know they can't possibly stay in the house much longer?"

"Don't talk that way! Why, after the way you handled the old bag just now, I found myself thinking, 'By golly, the Porters are going to make it.'"

Chapter 8

"DO you remember *Stairway to Heaven,* with David Niven and Kim Hunter? . . . No, of course you wouldn't, way before your time. That may explain why you two have the stamina to climb those monstrous steps. Whoosh! Ah, thank you. You remembered." Victor Tarpinian accepted his favorite brandy and soda, took a sip, and then glanced around the festive Porter living room.

"Enchanting. Very atmospheric. Wonderful mysterious vibrations all over the place. Sarah, maybe it's time we left the city. This is a bit of all right, don't you think?"

Victor and Sarah, recovering nicely from their climb, smiled approvingly at their young friends. The first guests to arrive, they were clearly enjoying the sense of intimacy a pre-party interlude gave them.

"Jessica, I must see Patience . . . do you realize it's been *months* since I've seen that incredible child? She's probably learned to read by now!" Sarah, in her forties and childless, had taken a touchingly personal interest in Patience from the beginning.

Jessie blushed. "Now, Sarah, I'll be the first to agree that she is advanced for her age, but . . ."

"Don't be too sure, my love, you should have seen the way her eyes followed the page when I read her bedtime story to her, just now." Sam saw no reason to be modest where Patience was concerned.

"Oh, is she asleep, then? Won't I get to talk to her?" Sarah looked crestfallen.

"She's probably still awake, why don't we go see her . . . and let these two catch up on their theater talk." Jessica was feeling strangely suspended now that the week's feverish preparation was behind her. She was glad to leave the room where party trappings implored her to fuss, to fidget, to fret—though everything that could be done had been done—hours before. Their money problems had been solved Friday night, when Sam came home jubilantly waving his first paycheck, and they'd gone straight to the A&P and loaded up on a generous supply of gourmet party treats.

When Jessica and Sarah had gone, Victor turned to Sam.

"So, how is the 'young man of promise'?"

"Getting older—and less promising—every day, I'm afraid, Victor. This new job with Pierre Villard has me worried. I've known him for years, ever since we were on that crazy Alan McFadden TV show together. We've seen each other maybe six or seven times a year since then . . . you know, go out and get gloriously drunk somewhere, him picking up the tab every time. I never took him seriously, but we always had good times. Well, to be perfectly honest, he liked having me along for the ladies. He's always been something of a playboy, and now that he's over sixty, I guess he feels he needs a bit of an assist in that department."

"Wasn't he married to a beautiful actress when you first met him?"

"Nicole. Yes. Half-French, half-Swedish—one hundred percent gorgeous. Yes. She was really something, but it all deteriorated a couple of years ago . . . rather rapidly, at that. First she had a breakdown. He sent her to a very good private clinic. Nevertheless, she managed to get hooked on pills. She left the clinic, left

76

Pierre, and moved in with a male ballet dancer. Then, last I heard, she'd turned lesbian, was becoming something of a fixture at Gay Activist type things. Still beautiful, from all reports."

"All that must have been hard on old Pierre," Victor was nodding with sympathy, it was the kind of story he'd heard before . . . and would hear again.

"Well, I guess that was my other function when we went out. He'd tell me all his troubles as the evening wore on. Frankly, Victor, Pierre gets rather boring after a while. But he's a good egg. And, if I was the only one he had left to talk to at his age, well, it made me feel a bit sorry for him. He just doesn't seem to have many friends left. He belonged to a flimsy sort of 'café society' set that just disappeared as the years passed.

"Then, after he'd tell me all his troubles with Nicole —she even had a daughter from another marriage that Pierre helped educate; I mean, all in all, he always seemed to do the decent thing—well, after that phase he'd invariably get on to the subject of his 'leetle beeznezz' and how he had no one to take over from him when he retired. When he'd get on that subject, I knew he was getting ready to call it a night. . . . He'd look at me with those devious brown eyes of his, lids half-closed, and say what a good *ami* I was to him, and how nice it would be if I could join his little company."

"Well, that's just what you did, so what's troubling you?"

"Victor, it's not something I'm too proud of, believe me. And please, don't ever tell Jess, because I don't plan to. The last time we went out together, I was really in a tight spot. That other job I had with the Miller Brothers wasn't panning out. Ben Miller hated my guts . . . oh, hell, it's a long, dull story, and doesn't amount to a damn thing, now that it's all ended.

The point is I was out on the town with old Pierre, and I knew I was about to be fired. I could feel it in my bones. So, there I was with Pierre, and I couldn't help thinking, why not? Why not just say yes to him this time? I knew the subject would come up. It always did."

Victor's eyes gleamed with recognition. He understood his friend. Fond as Victor was of Sam, he couldn't help recognizing the pattern. He'd seen it happen before . . . first Sam would be euphoric over a marvelous new job and would paint glowing pictures of a bright new future; and then, weeks later, he'd be all played out, bitter over some superior's jealousy, and would darkly predict his imminent dismissal. It seemed that some kind of basic weakness doomed this clear-eyed, ingenuous-looking young man to failure. Victor feared for Sam and Jessica, because he sensed Sam's repeated failures would eventually cause them to break up. He tried to brush this from his mind and said, amiably enough, "Wouldn't surprise me if you didn't help Pierre get to the subject that night. Right, Sam?"

Sam winced at the recollection.

"Victor, you can't make me feel any worse than I already do. Tell you the truth, man, I don't believe Pierre ever meant a single word of any of those some-one-to-leave-the-business-to monologues. What's more, it was something we both—drunk as we were—respected and understood. It was just tired, late-night boozy talk. Taking him up on it was a rotten thing to do."

"You must have been pretty desperate."

"But that last night—I will say this—he sounded more like he meant it than he ever had before. I mean, it was the first time he went so far as to talk in dollars-and-cents terms. And, boy, did it sound good! Princely, even. I was that hungry. He looked me right in the eyes, and said: 'Sam, *mon ami,* I am seexty t'ree years

78

old. I shall retire when I become seexty fife. If you join the beeznezz now, you will be able to take over completely when I go.' I accepted. We shook hands on it. All very man-to-man. I started in two weeks ago. We moved up here on the strength of my fine new prospects. But Victor, my friend, it's been sheer hell ever since! It's perfectly obvious to me that Pierre would love to back down on the deal—but he's too much of a gentleman of the old school to do it."

"And too ineffectual to figure out a decent way out of it, I'll bet."

"Right. As for me, well, though I feel like a heel, and deservedly, I can't help but feel Pierre could really use me. I could help him out, if he'd only let me! I'm quite the hot-shot salesman, you know. I could get him all kinds of new business—and he could stand some expansion. But instead he seems to take great delight in starting me at the bottom . . . letting me get my hands dirty . . . all that."

"Sam, Sam. You'd better put up with it for a while. God knows, you need the bread. And, you know, you just may be reading too much between the lines. Old Pierre may actually do just as he said, and hand over that nice, profitable little business to you in a couple of years. Don't overlook that possibility—stranger things have happened. Give it a little more time. You've got a chance here, old buddy, to knuckle down and make something of your life. You've got so much going for you now—Jessica, Patience, this great new pad. I'm pulling for you. But you're the one that has to make the effort. Nobody's gonna do it for you. Say, when is this problematical Frenchman due to arrive, anyway?"

Sam looked at his watch. It was seven forty-five. "The rest of them should be here by eight. It'll be you and Sarah, Pierre and Dorcas—wait till you see her!—oh, and Len and Sue are coming, too. You remember them,

79

don't you? Sue was Jess' old roommate at Wellesley. Bought a big fancy co-op down your way."

"Yes, I remember. They also bought shares in the playhouse. I fear we lost them a packet. Len's been very good about it. Tax loss."

"Yeah, well, Len can afford it. We're also having some locals in. Mary and George Smith. I haven't met them. Jessie's made friends with the wife, we've neither of us met the husband. He's a lawyer, I think. And that's the cast of characters for tonight. That is, if our resident shrew upstairs doesn't put in an appearance." Sam shot an eloquent glance at the ceiling.

"She's really batty, huh?" Victor's mobile Armenian face showed curiosity. "I wish she *would* put in an appearance, sounds like a real find."

"Don't wish her on us tonight, Victor." Jessica had come in at the last exchange. "She may be amusing to us someday, but right now, if I may borrow Queen Victoria's immortal words, *'We are not amused!'* I, for one, am crossing my fingers she leaves us alone."

Sarah, who loved a good story, asked, "But you *will* tell us about her, won't you? Sam's dropped a few hints, and, frankly, she sounds too eccentric for words."

"Well, maybe later, after we've all had more to drink. I guess it all depends on how you look at her. She seems pretty funny to me at times. But Jessica's rather down on her at the moment."

"And the Smiths don't like her, either. They had a run-in with her a few years ago. So, let's cool it on old lady Falconer for the moment, all right?" Jessie wanted the evening to be an amiable, relaxing one. Lord knew, she'd worked for it. Victor was about to say something tactful to clear the air when the air was in fact shattered by an extraordinary rattling, buzzing clatter. It was repeated, twice.

"What on earth?!"

"Hey, that's some doorbell! I haven't seen one like it since my aunt sold the old Remsen Street town house." It was Len Roth, with Sue. When they saw how surprised everyone was at their noisy entrance, Len laughed.

"You never noticed your doorbell." He nodded a cheerful hello to each of them and motioned them out to the porch door. "Here, I'll show you . . ."

"I'm sorry!" Sue said to the other women. "I told him not to, I mean, the door was open, it's a *party;* but I guess he got a nostalgic kick out of seeing a bell like that and just had to try it. Some racket, huh?" She was resplendently Pucci'd and Gucci'd and bussed Sarah and Jessie on their cheeks. "Let the men play with the bell. I want a drink. Jessie, as long as you live here, you're sure to keep your dear little size-seven shape. Those steps! Yes, a vodka martini, thanks."

Jessie almost spilled Sue's vodka on the rug as the raucous buzzer sounded again. And again.

"I sure hope Sam disconnects that right away! Where on earth is it? . . . I never saw a bell out there."

Sam, Len, and Victor came back in, all grinning delightedly. "It's like a wind-up toy, Jess. A big old key you turn. Must be sixty, seventy years old. It's over a foot from the door, never saw it. Some fun, eh?"

"Yeah. Could have woken the baby. Some fun."

Just then, the bizarre buzzer sounded again—in a triumphant dot-dot-dot-dash, Beethoven's Fifth rhythm. The noise was shattering and very funny.

"Allo, we are here. Are you there?" It was Pierre Villard at last.

"Ah, but this is *charming*. I have not seen such a fine old doorbell since I left the house of my father on the Avenue Foch. Nineteen thirty-seven that was. Hello to you all. Allow me to present my dear friend, the beautiful Miss Dorcas Dillingham, of London, England."

"Oooh, didn't we make a racket! I'm pleased to meet you, I'm sure." Whereupon Dorcas shrugged out of her floor-length bunny-fur coat, to reveal a dress of lush purple velour fastened by rhinestone-studded straps. Victor leaped into action at the bar table.

"Name your pleasure, Miss Dillingham!" he cried with nothing short of alacrity. Len escorted her to the bar. Jessica faced Pierre and presented her cheeks for his bilateral kiss.

"Ah, Jessica, *ma petite*, such a stylish flat. Such ambience . . . and, you, you look *ravissante!* I wonder, now, do you think Sam is good enough for you?"

"Of course not, Pierre." Jessica laughed. "But, no matter. *You're* here now. Let me introduce our friends."

When they'd all gotten something to drink and found comfortable perches, there was a brief pause. Dorcas sat on the arm of the wing chair, leaning over Pierre in a proprietary and—to the men, at least—provocative manner. She sipped her Dubonnet-on-the-rocks-with-a-twist and sighed.

"Sam. This is so nice of you. Your house is not at all what I expected. I always thought American suburbs were all sort of chrome and glass—you know, picture windows looking out at other picture windows, and hot and cold running appliances everywhere. This might just as well be England. Of course your hills are a bit steeper; and the Hudson . . . that's rather special, that!" She dimpled daintily at Sam.

Pierre took her free hand in his. "But, Dorcas, you must remember, neither Sam nor Jessica are what you would call typical Americans. Those suburbs you talk about do exist, I'm sure—though I've never seen them myself. Samuel and Jessica Porter are much too cosmopolitan to live that way."

And too poor, thought Jessica to herself. What was so bad about hot and cold running appliances everywhere? she wondered. It beat the weekly trip to a laundromat—and twenty-odd hours a week of standing at the sink doing the dishes. Oh, well. What would Pierre know about such things.

"Too cosmopolitan and too artistic, don't you think? I must say, the décor here is stimulating. Rather theatrical. Yet one gets a very cozy feeling, overall. Samuel, Pierre told me the other night, after you'd gone, that you'd once been connected with the theater. Is this true? Why did you ever leave? Such a handsome face— why, I shouldn't wonder you'd be the toast of the West End if you came to London. Have you ever considered trying again?"

"The theater is a very demanding mistress, Miss Dillingham," Victor interjected. "I happen to know that Samuel has a real gift. But—here in the States, anyway —that is never enough. And with a little family to feed and care for, Samuel decided to put his college training in business administration to use, after all. I'm sure he's made a wise choice. Now, tell me, you delectable creature, were *you* ever connected with the theater?"

"Me? That's a laugh! The only time I ever tried it was in grammar school. My poor mum had to make this awful costume for me out of crepe paper—black, with yellow stripes, it was. I was the queen bee, you see. All the other girls were flowers. They got to wear pretty shades of pink and blue and primrose. I got all perspired, and the black paper bled all over the yellow. It was a complete disaster. You know, my mum and dad have called me Queenie ever since!"

"Was that in London?" Sarah asked.

"No. Tunbridge Wells, actually. I came up to London when I finished school."

Jessica was setting dishes of food about, buffet style. She wondered what was keeping the Smiths. It wasn't that late yet—maybe they'd run into a baby-sitter problem. Their oddly assorted guests seemed to be warming to each other. Dorcas had gone over to chat more intimately with Victor and Sarah. (Jessica caught Victor addressing her as Queenie, for which he was rewarded by a delicately cascading giggle—clever rogue.) And the Roths were talking animatedly with Pierre. There was a good hum in the room. Pierre gave Sam a pleased, kindly smile in response to a fresh drink and a tray of canapés. Jessica went to the kitchen to put some rolls in the oven, and Sue soon joined her. Sue's news was that she was expecting a baby in April.

"Oh, but that's great, Sue! You must come up and see me some day during the week, and I can give you the whole truth about motherhood. I don't half mind it, you know."

"I'll call you. We'll do it soon. All the same, I'm glad they give you nine months to get used to the idea. Say, you were expecting another couple, weren't you? I think I just heard some new voices."

"Good. The Smiths! Come, I'll introduce you. You'll like Mary. I haven't met George yet myself."

Sam was doing his best, introducing Mary and George. Yet there was an apparent edge of constraint as they stood in the middle of the room, with all the other guests already some two drinks ahead of them. The constraint seemed something they'd brought with them, though. George, a narrow-faced, horn-rimmed, tallish man, reminded Jessica, unkindly, of the sort of man who does cold-remedy commercials. She could see him lying in a very tidy bed, propped up with pillows, while Mary tended capably to his aches, pains, and drips, as he lay there with a diffident smile on his face. Although, to look at Mary, it was hard to hold onto that first domestic image. She looked lovely. Gone was the unassuming little housewife in blue jeans—in her place stood a delicate, elegant woman. The brown and silver hair gleemed with a diamanté clip, and she was wearing a beautifully cut dress of orange jersey. It was the first time Jessica noticed that Mary had a stunning figure.

The tension passed. George, divested of his black bankerish coat, became instantly more human. He surprised Jessie by sitting easily on the floor, long legs folded lotuslike, and requesting a Heineken. Sam had bought the beer in a last-minute surge of payday largesse; how nice there was a call for it. Jessica went over to him.

"It's so nice of you to come, George. I can't tell you how lucky it was for me to meet Mary in the park . . . she's made us feel so at home!"

"Our pleasure, Jessica. Mary was glad to meet you, too, you know. Wimbledon's kind of a funny place. Mary keeps looking for what she calls 'real people.' She considered you quite a find."

"Did you have any trouble getting a sitter?"

"No. We had trouble. But it wasn't that. We had a small difference of opinion. I'm afraid it was my fault. You see, the last time we came to this house . . . well, we witnessed a very unpleasant scene. It ended with the breakup of a marriage between two of our favorite people. . . ."

"Yes—the Teels—Mary told me about them. You mean you didn't want to revisit the scene of the crime?"

"Something like that. I guess I'm superstitious or neurotic or both. I really hated having to come here tonight. I wanted to meet you and Sam, of course. It's just this damn place. Now that I'm here I feel pretty dumb. You've fixed it up so that I barely recognize it. It looks like you and your husband now. I wish I hadn't given Mary such a rough time."

"She seems completely recovered, George. You know, this is the first time I've seen her out of blue jeans." When Jessie saw the look on George's face as he glanced across the room at Mary, she realized that whatever their quarrel had been, it was over now. George was very much in love with his wife.

Pierre, seated once again in the big wing chair, smiled expansively. "Jessica, Sam, your little parties are so *intime*, so . . . European. In Paris you would have a *salon* and hold weekly *soirées*. Everyone would fight for your invitations!"

Jessica flushed with pleasure. Sam, delighted, said, "Well, thank *you*, Pierre! Now wait till you hear Sarah play—I'll bet she even knows some old French favorites of yours." Sarah played both classical and folk guitar and was highly accomplished. Best of all, she enjoyed playing. No coaxing was necessary. She sang some of the songs, in a light, clear voice. After a while she began to play corny old favorites that seemed suddenly fresh and pure again . . . *I Know Where I'm Going . . . Sometimes I feel Like a Motherless Child* . . . even *Greensleeves*. The most satisfying surprise came when George Smith and then Dorcas joined her, their voices tentative at first, then emerging with confident ease.

Tears came to Jessie's eyes. The room was filled with a spontaneous happiness. She slipped away to the kitchen to see about coffee. Ever since her earliest childhood Jessica's response to moments of joy was so intense that she had to be alone with it. As she walked to the kitchen, she gave the walls of the hallway a gentle pat and thought, *Tonight we are all casting a spell. Those nice people are making this a happy place. Please, please, let it be a happy place from now on!*

She put the coffee on and whipped heavy cream for the *mousse au chocolat*. She closed the kitchen door so that the noise of the beating wouldn't interfere with the music. When the coffee was ready, she cleared a place on the little counter for the tray of dessert pots and applied a dollop of cream to each. Done, she tossed her big oven mitts out of the way on the shelf below and carried the tray into the living room.

The entrance was perfectly timed. Everybody stood up, stretching, smiling, and applauding the music-makers.

"Ah! Dessert!" George said. "Now that we've sung for it, I guess we can really dig in, right, Dorcas?"

"Sam, could you help get the coffee from the kitchen?" Jessie asked.

"No, no, let me!" Dorcas urged. "I want to see the place where you prepared this feast with my own eyes. Maybe you have a special secret!"

"My little Dorcas sings far better than she cooks, Jessie ... *mais c'est la vie, n'est-ce pas?*"

Jessie laughed. Dorcas was already in the kitchen. Jessie wanted to say something nice about Dorcas to Pierre but merely gave a blithe wave in his direction on her way from the room. The kitchen was so tiny and cluttered she felt she really ought to be out there giving Dorcas a hand.

But Jessica was still in the hallway when Dorcas screamed.

She rushed to the kitchen to find Dorcas, her arm stretched out in horror and disgust. One of the oven mitts was on her outstretched hand, and attached to it, dangling in a menacing, tenacious way—was the doll.

Chapter 9

"IT jumped at me! Get it off! It's *stuck*."

"Oh, Dorcas. I'm so sorry. *Sam!*"

"What in the world—" Sam, Victor, Pierre, with the women as close behind as the little hallway would permit, were peering in the direction of the tiny kitchen. Sam squeezed in behind Jessica to take in the cause of the commotion in a flash.

"That damn doll!" In a sudden, sinking moment of clarity, he recalled his drunken pacing through the apartment a week before. "My God, Jess—I tossed it down on that shelf there, last Saturday night. I'd forgotten all about it. This is going to take a little explaining. Here, Dorcas, let's have a look. . . ."

Dorcas, still standing with her arm extended, held up her oven-mitted hand for Sam to examine. The doll, now surrounded by rational, well-dressed people in the bright party atmosphere, had never seemed more evil. It was firmly attached to Dorcas's wrist. Sam pulled it off.

"I get it!" he said, shaking his head.

"Magnets."

"Magnets?" Jessica asked, bewildered. "Oh! Of course. The oven mitt has a magnet . . . see?" Jessica took the mitt and slapped it against the side of the stove, where it stuck.

"You mean the doll has one, too?"

88

"Curiouser and curiouser . . . the doll has a magnet in it. Why, I'm sure I haven't a clue."

Victor edged his way into the room,

"What's this all about? Dorcas, do you mean to say this tawdry toy *attacked* you?"

Dorcas gave a weak laugh.

"Victor, darling, you must think me an awful fool. I didn't know it was a doll. It seemed alive. And on first glance it was so fierce looking! I don't know when I've been so startled. Surely, that's the most awful doll you've ever seen!"

"Why that terrible thing looks as though it knows me, Victor!" Sarah had put her finger on it. It wasn't that they'd any of them seen the doll before, so much as an unspoken but unanimous feeling that *the doll knew them.*

"It's positively evil," Sue murmured.

Victor, relying on his keen antennae as a theatrical director, decided the uncanny atmosphere had better be broken up—and quickly.

"It's a Kewpie doll, Sarah. You remember Kewpie dolls. Remember how my skill with a bucket of tennis balls won you something like this at Palisades Amusement Park?" He picked it up and handed it to Sarah in the hall. Sarah, exactly as Jessica and Sam a week before, gave an involuntary "ugh!", almost dropping it.

"Oh, no, Victor. It wasn't like this at all. My God, just look at it . . . this is really crude. And old. Look how it's all yellowing and crumbling. This must have been some porno outfit's idea of a Kewpie doll."

"And yet. There's something, I don't know, something so *familiar* about it . . ." Sarah continued. "I don't mean the fact that it's a Kewpie doll, either. This is the first time any of us has seen it. . . ." Several murmured yeses and serious, nodding heads agreed.

"Yet, doesn't it seem, oh, I dunno, sort of inevitable? . . .

I mean, if ever I wanted to describe my idea of that thing in the dark we're all afraid of . . . the thing we fear will crawl out at us from under a rock someday . . . well, it would look very much like this doll. Wouldn't it now?"

Before anybody else could say anything, Victor went on. "Ah, Sarah, you're going to scare us half to death with that fevered imagination of yours. Not that I don't catch your drift. May be something in what you say. But that's not what old Whoopee Novelties had in mind. This was meant strictly as an aid to the tired libido. It's the aging process has given it this surreal quality—that's all." Victor spoke with conviction, but Sam could tell he was ill at ease.

"Look. Let's all go back to the living room, where coffee and brandy will be served. Everybody out. Samuel Porter is now in charge." Sam gestured them all—a very nervous Jessica included—out of the room. Then he got the coffee things together by himself and officiated most expertly at the serving ceremony.

"Now, let's enjoy this delicious dessert. Dorcas, we both apologize for your little fright. I'm afraid I dropped that doll on the kitchen shelf last week. Jessica'd thrown it away . . . and I picked it up again. It startled us in much the same manner, under slightly different circumstances. I couldn't for the life of me figure out how such a god-awful thing found its way into our house."

"To think it was there all during the week . . . and I never saw it!" Jessica exclaimed.

"Well, no matter. After all, we've just moved in, and there are any number of ways a strange object might have gotten mixed up with our things. Who wants brandy?" Sam wanted the doll episode closed. As he looked around the room, he saw that two people were not going to forget the incident. George and Mary Smith looked distinctly unhappy. Neither had spoken during Dorcas' scene in the kitchen.

"I'll have some of that lovely brandy!" Dorcas declared, apparently recovered from her fright. In fact, she was rather enjoying the intensified celebrity she'd acquired.

The mousse was superb. Gradually the atmosphere in the room once again expanded with shared pleasure.

Pierre finished his mousse with *éclat* and smiled at his hostess. "Ah, Jessica; that was very, very good. Now I, too, will have some of your fine Napoleon brandy. Tell me, Samuel, what about your Wimbledon-on-Hudson murder? Have you heard anything more about it?"

A lively discussion of the murder story began. Even George and Mary grew more relaxed, as all that was known about Nora Kelly's sad demise was sorted out. The Roths and the Tarpinians, who had not heard the story before, demanded all the facts.

"Why, it's a real puzzle, isn't it? No motive!" Sue commented.

"Of course there's a motive. We just don't know what it is yet. For that matter the police may know by now and just aren't saying," George replied.

"That reminds me, Pierre. Sam told me you're a stockholder at CopperCable. Do you know anything about the company that might have a bearing on this case?"

And just as Sam had predicted, Jessica's flattering, naïve gaze was all that Pierre required. He squared his shoulders, put on a very thoughtful, businesslike face, cleared his throat, and gave the assembled guests the benefit of his knowledge.

"Ah, of course, Jessica; that's why I am so interested. If this murder were to affect the stability of my investment—which is in fact quite a leetle amount—I would like to know about it *tout de suite!* CopperCable has always been a most conservatively run organization. I'm sure you realize this Wimbledon plant is just one of

hundred CopperCable operations all over the
. It was built originally to supply electrical wiring
for the Otis Elevator works down in Yonkers."

"You mean it's electrical wire they make, then? What
a disillusioning thought. Here I'd been passing their
yard on the train these last few days imagining the
wonderful suspension bridges those cables would support
one day!" Sam's fancies died hard.

"Well, it has become a far more diversified operation,
of course, Sam. But I very much doubt they produce
that kind of cable. Certainly not in Wimbledon. What I
do know, though, Jessica, is that the members of the
Board agreed, two years ago, to automate much of the
operation here. Contrary to what most people think, this
automation does not mean the letting go of any workers.
Automation has been . . . uh . . . phased in . . . gradually.
It's actually created some new jobs. *Naturellement*, certain jobs have been eliminated by attrition. It did occur
to me at first that some employee, angered by the new
automation, might have sought vengeance . . . but there
are simply no facts to bear this out."

"Well, Pierre, I do know that Nora Kelly wasn't going
to be replaced. She was their head bookkeeper. She'd
worked there forty years. And her last job was helping
the computer programmers convert all the records to
tape." Mary Smith continued earnestly, "According to
her cousin, Mrs. Murphy, the very last thing she did was
convert all the profit-sharing and retirement records.
As you know, she was to have retired. A dinner in her
honor was to have been held tonight, poor thing."

"Mary and I were talking about that last night, Pierre.
We think there may be a motive there. Somebody could
be adversely affected by those records being computer-
ized. Matter of fact, I called the police about it. Even
though my law practice is in the city, I do know the local police pretty well. They listened politely; I couldn't

judge, though, just how seriously they took what I said. For all I know, they're already working along the same lines, and didn't need my suggestion at all. A couple of detectives from Yonkers have been attached to it." George occasionally indulged in Walter Mitty dreams of a practice in criminal law. His actual field was tax law, and in his heart of hearts he was beginning to loathe his work.

"Say, I just thought"—it was Len Roth's turn to contribute—"if everything's on tape now—it could take several weeks before they uncover anything that isn't strictly kosher in the records. I've run into that myself. Computers are very efficient. But you can't ask them a question the way you ask people. You've got to run program after program from start to finish. Then you go over the printouts with a fine-tooth comb. God! I've been there. It can take months! Remember last year, Sue? When the entire Midwest region stock-control file was bollixed up . . . just because Winnetka, Illinois, had been entered incorrectly?" Len's family business, which manufactured children's sportswear, was one of the best-known and most up-to-date in the industry.

"What's more, you can't just plug computers in when you want to. I'll bet a small local installation like Wimbledon shares computer time with other CopperCable plants and has to wait its turn. Over and above the standard day-to-day demands that have to be met. It can be quite a hassle.

"So you see, Pierre, it looks like CopperCable and the police investigators are going to have to play a waiting game. That is, if they really do think the motive is hidden somewhere in the records! Imagine—trying to solve a murder and having politely to wait their turn for computer file maintenance!"

"You know, Len, I'll bet that's exactly what the police are doing. That explains why they were so, well, defensive, when I spoke to them last night. How about that—deduction by computer!" George Smith was convinced they were right.

Pierre laughed.

"Ah, but that is too bad! I was awaiting the entrance into the case by a Monsieur Maigret. Instead, the case is in the hands of a beeg box with blinking lights! It is perhaps just as well. *Eh, bien,* my friends, I would like to invite everybody to join Dorcas and myself for a nightcap before we catch the last train into the city. It will be *trés amusant* to see what the night life is like in this leetle place. Sam? Jessica? will you agree to join us? This has been so nice. But, you know me; I am what the English call a pub crawler."

It was only eleven fifteen. Jessica was surprised by Pierre's sudden suggestion, hesitating for a moment, considering what a Wimbledon pub crawl might be like. Then she remembered Patience. Of course, she'd have to stay behind. Sam took to the idea right away—as did Victor, George, Sue and Len. Sarah demurred.

"Why don't the rest of you go?" Sarah suggested. "I really don't feel like it . . . I've got my shoes off and am much too cozy right here. Besides, you don't have to worry about any last train to New York. You can all ride back with Victor and me—we came up in the old playhouse station wagon. Jessie and I will clear up the dishes and have a nice time talking."

"I'm going to stay, too," Mary decided.

The party divided itself into two groups. The live wires, injected with a fresh spurt of enthusiasm, quickly got their coats, and, bestowing indiscriminate kisses, lavish praise, and thanks for the evening's festivities, fled noisily and clumsily down the steps, amid a flurry of giggles and boozy catcalls.

George Smith's gleaming station wagon was parked in the Porter driveway, awaiting the short downhill journey to the village. Behind it was the Tarpinians' car. Surprisingly both were Ford Country Squires. The Tarpinians', however, wore a distressed patina of dents, scratches, rust, and grime that bespoke a valiantly fought eight-year campaign of alternate-side-of-the-street parking in lower Manhattan.

Their first stop was Sam's Pleasant Hour. George had never been inside the place before. He confided to Sam that he did his unwinding at the Commodore bar before catching the train home for Wimbledon. Sam told him that what The Pleasant Hour might lack in sophistication, it more than made up for by the size and economy of its drinks. They made plans to meet during the week ahead.

Dorcas walked directly to the garishly lit jukebox in the rear of the bar. It had been silent when they entered. Dorcas gleefully poured in two dollars' worth of Pierre's coins, whereupon it emitted a savage rock beat, and she began to dance. Victor, though rather portly and definitely a sedentary type, joined her with uncharacteristic abandon.

The handful of old regulars who'd been cloistered at the end of the bar, giving their lugubrious attention to a 1932 James Cagney relic on television, ordered more drinks, and fastened their gaze on the party—for all the world as though somebody had merely switched channels for them. Evidently Dorcas in the flesh was worth two James Cagneys on the small screen.

Len and Sue joined the dancing. Sam decided to cut in. Len decided to pretend to an intense jealousy.

"My dear fellow," he intoned solemnly, stretching his slim frame to its full five feet and seven inches, "though you are a dashing type and no doubt accustomed to using your charm to gain your every nefarious craving, this little lady came to this here affair with me. I'd ap-

95

preciate it very much if you'd kindly take that Paul Newman charisma of yours . . . and stuff it!"

Whereupon Sam, with a perfectly straight face and not missing a beat, managed to signal Sue to step aside and, throwing his big arms and massive chest around the startled Len, engaged him in an impassioned tango. Dorcas and Victor broke up laughing and vigorously cheered the new couple on.

"Hey, Sam!" Victor asked, "Do you think that swell dish of yours can do the Big Apple?"

Pierre then signaled to the bemused Irish face behind the bar:

"Another round, bartender. My funny friends will need sustenance—and soon."

On cue Sam and Len executed a very professional 1940's dip, thus ending the spontaneous *pas des deux.* All hands applauded and then grasped fresh drinks gratefully. Victor proposed a toast:

"To you, Sam. To Jessica. And to Patience. And, most especially, to your fine new home."

They moved over to one of the booths. Before Sam could join them, Pierre motioned to him to stay behind.

"One moment, please, Sam. Let them go. I want to have a leetle talk."

"Sure thing, Pierre. What's on your mind?"

"Sam. Please let us be serious for a moment. You worry me. You must show me more of an interest in the business. *Naturellement,* Dorcas and I have very much enjoyed your charming hospitality. You are such an amusing friend! But, my dear Sam, business is business. I have watched you since you joined my firm. You are never in the office. You are never supervising the men and the equipment in the field. . . ."

"But, Pierre . . . for Christ's sakes. I'm your new sales representative, remember? That's what it says on the fancy engraved cards you gave me. You and I agreed that the most important contribution I could make to Manhattan Office Maintenance would be to acquire lots of new business. And that's just what I've been doing! I have Mr. Bennet of Realty Associates just about ready to sign. Koch of 451 Madison wants us all to get together for lunch on Tuesday—"

"Sam. How can you miss my point? I want you to learn this business from the bottom up. That means learning how Miss Teagarden keeps our accounts, supervising Mrs. Kern in purchasing, and most important of all, being there, on the job, Saturdays and Sundays when the work is done! Fernandez and Jackson should know that wherever they may be, you could come in at any moment to see that they are running the crews efficiently. My good fellow, you must apply yourself! Learn the business. All this partying and being the charming young man at lunch is not what I'm playing you for. Do me a favor—for your own good!—and show by your actions in the next month that you are really taking an interest. Otherwise . . ."

Here, Pierre broke off.

In hsi astonishment Sam could only reply in a dazed, hurt way. "What about these new accounts? You have four memos on your desk right now. These men are ready to come over to us. Four good accounts in less than four weeks, Pierre! Don't you want to follow through on them? It could mean two hundred thousand dollars' worth of new business in the next year."

"When you show me that you know how my business is run, I'll be glad to meet with any new clients you think you can produce."

The subject was closed. Sam excused himself. He was pale. Victor had been observing this little confrontation and feared he understood its general direction. Pierre had his drink refreshed and calmly walked to the booth where the others were sitting. He gave them all his best

Gallic smile. "Drink up, *mes amis!* Soon we must proceed to the next Wimbledon watering hole!" Victor was still watching Sam. Before joining the group Sam downed his drink and ordered a double. Victor patted Sam on the shoulder.

"Bad as all that?"

"Victor . . ." Sam's pale, serious face already told Victor it was bad, indeed. His voice was a strangulated whisper. "Old Pierre's just kicked me right in the gut. All I know is that I'm afraid I'm going to get very, very drunk before I can return to Jessica . . . to Patience . . . and to our fine new house."

Chapter 10

SAM set out to accomplish his declared goal in a matter
of two or three hazy hours—never more than a half
mile from his new home. He became separated from his
guests, and Victor made excuses for him. The party
continued energetically enough until it found itself in a
little Italian place in Dobbs Ferry. Here, they conceded
the lateness of the hour and made their noisy way back
to the sloping driveway at 33 Granite Terrace. Sarah
trundled down the steps to meet them, competently
putting on a pair of driving gloves for the long haul back
to the city. All the coffee she'd recently consumed in the
Porter kitchen made her conspicuous in her clarity and
rather smug in her sobriety. Mary, too, was horribly
bright-eyed and clear of speech. Their stagey tolerance
of the returning group's cotton-mouthed muzziness was
not appreciated. Sarah backed the big wagon briskly
down the drive, expertly escorting the rumpled remnant
of what had so recently been the live wires. George
nuzzled up to Mary in the front seat of their wagon, as it
moved around the Tarpinians' and left for home just
blocks away. His tall angular shape had gone soft and
rubbery. He rolled the window down and his narrow
head popped into view like a benevolent sea turtle.
George's memorable, carrying baritone could be heard
all the way to Firehouse Lane:

99

Ha, ha, ha, you and me
Little brown jug, how I love thee!

Just before the Tarpinians' wagon left the driveway, Jessica's poignant voice was heard calling down from the porch:

"But where is Sam? Isn't he with you?"

She sounded so forlorn. Victor, though drunk, was touched. He turned to Sarah.

"Just a moment, my dear, I don't want to leave our little hostess with a worry. Pierre, Len, be patient for a second or two—I'll be back down right away." He stumbled gallantly up the steps, perspiration glowing on his large genial face. He was all out of breath when he reached Jessie, standing defenselessly by her door.

"Jessica. Sam will be home later. I don't want you to worry about him. But I think he will be quite drunk when he does come home. Pierre said something that upset him. So don't be too hard on him. I think of you two as the best-matched pair I know. But nobody's perfect, remember! Sam and Pierre are having a little problem adjusting to each other as business partners . . . it isn't going to be easy. Ah, Jessie, Jessie, don't look so scared. You're a brave, smart girl. By now you must know Sam almost as well as I do. And I know you love him more than I do—so be generous to him in your thoughts. He'll come home. Let him be. Wait until tomorrow to find out what went wrong. He's lucky he has you and Patience behind him."

"Victor . . . you give me too much credit. Someday I just may come down and cry on your shoulder. I'm tired of being brave and smart. I want us to be happy—that's all. Why is it always so damn hard?"

"Take my advice, sweet Jess. Just go to sleep now. Tomorrow everything will seem much better. And . . . if it's any consolation, you sure throw one hell of a good party." He kissed her avuncularly on the forehead, gave her a fond hug, and made a careful descent of the steps.

Jessica kept the porch light on until she heard the city-bound car chug around the corner, then turned off the light. She'd been so looking forward to his return. They'd done the dishes, put all the party things away, the place really looked like home. It would have been so nice to sit around the big oak table with a final drop of brandy and compare notes. But it wasn't going to be like that. She was about to crawl into bed, when a sudden feeling of love and compassion for Sam made her get up again. No point in being petty. She walked to the porch door and turned the light back on. Sam was sure to need all the help he could get just to make it to his own front door.

Sam had drunk himself into a thoroughly anonymous muddle. His mouth tasted rancid. His charismatic blue eyes were dimmed and foolish. The process of locomotion required every bit of his concentration. This was his first real misery drunk since Lorraine Schmitt had turned him down. Voluptuous Lorraine Schmitt . . . wonder whatever became of her. Those were two of the softest, roundest—oh, what the hell. They'd never have been happy together. But, then, who was? Were he and Jess happy? Now that Pierre was obviously going to be just another in a whole dreary string of mistakes. How many "fresh starts" could he ask Jess to endure? Why couldn't that sweet little thing have married a nice accountant! Anyone could tell just looking at her that was what nature had intended her to do. He should never have given up acting! That was his second mistake. Marrying Jessie, he implied bitterly to himself, had been the first. Acting was the one thing he was really *good* at. Everything else, well, that was just pretending to be good—not the same thing at all; though it fooled some

. the people some of the time. Even him. Even Samuel Porter had been fooled, some of the time. As recently as this evening, when an orderly, prosperous life was finally seeming to unfold for the rapidly aging "bright young man of promise." What a laugh! He laughed. A passerby frowned at him. He skulked sheepishly into the next brightly lit door. It was a bar.

Rita and Ed and four or five of their old-time Copper-Cable buddies were ending the evening that was to have been the occasion of poor Nora Kelly's farewell dinner. They were not as drunk as Sam, but only because they were not as miserable. A thick paste of nostalgia bound them to their seats, holding them in maudlin thrall. Poor Nora was dead—and they were alive. As with all survivors, there was a secret undercurrent of triumph to their genuine dismay.

"Did you know why she never married that guy Frank Whatsis?"

"Naw, it wasn't Frank, it was *Fred*, remember he worked over in Quality Control back in those days, before he started wearing those white shirts and calling himself Frederick."

"Yeah. Fred. Well, weren't they engaged or something?"

"Or something, more likely. She never married, period. I never could figure that. She was one fine-looking woman."

"I dunno. Old Fred married that hoity-toity Cavendish dame on the hill. No accounting for tastes, huh? But then he never was one of my favorite people. Always thought Nora was lucky to be rid of him. Though, come to think of it, they was always friendly—even after she and Freddie broke up. Sure enough, he married that terrible old bag—she never gave him a moment's peace, turned him into a regular Casper Milquetoast! But many's the time I seen him sitting with Nora at the cafeteria. They always seemed real friendly."

"He's dead, now, too, right?"

"Oh, my, yes. Been dead for years."

"Remember what a tightwad he was? Everyone used to kid the daylights out of him." Here Ed, visited by a long-forgotten recollection, began to chuckle.

"Remember how we always got a new guy to go to him when there was a collection to be taken? Or raffle tickets? Funniest thing. Old Red Krasnowski; we got him to go to Fred practically his first week on the job. Somehow he was able to do what nobody'd ever succeeded in doing before or since. Sold him one goddamn raffle for the Elks Club. Just one, mind you. Two bits. Remember? Damned if old Frederick didn't win the goddamn Pontiac! We were all madder'n hell! I see that loony old widow of his driving it around sometimes to this day. Course it looks kind of old-fashioned now, but it still runs, and she keeps it clean as a whistle. Though it's a crime to let a crazy old bag like that on the road. She'll kill somebody some day."

Sam, a solitary figure hunched at the bar, had his back to the group that was sitting around a large booth in the rear. He heard them the way a sunbather half dozing on the beach almost hears the portable radio on the blanket next to his. He recognized the topic as being familiar the same way he would register the theme of a popular tune. If he gave poor old Nora Kelly any further thought, it was only a fleeting moment of envy for her. She, at least, had left this troubled world for keeps.

This would be his last stop. He was just as miserable as he'd been when he started out, but he no longer remembered why. He slapped a crumpled bill on the bar and rose to go.

Climbing up the steps to their porch finally proved an

exercise in futility. He just couldn't make it. It would be easier to turn the corner and go up to Maynard to approach their place the back way. The additional walk required another ten or twelve minutes—but not a single flight of steps. Samuel congratulated himself on his resourcefulness.

Flushed with genuine pleasure—his first in three or four hours—he approached their unassuming little back door. Dear Jessie had left a light burning for him. Finding the right key took a while, but finally one of the many keys on the ring made contact. The back door led to a rear entry the Porters shared with Mrs. Falconer. A service area for storage and garbage cans. The Porter door was immediately to the left, Mrs. Falconer's basement door straight ahead. And, just as Sam closed the outside door behind him, the Falconer door opened in front of him.

For a fraction of a moment of time they stared at one another across a great chasm: tenant and landlady . . . youth and old age . . . David and Goliath? Sam felt suspended; his actions had long ceased to be governable by any conscious force of will and he did not trust his speech.

"Heh, heh. Stepped out to have a few, did you?" Mrs. Falconer, as he might have known, were he sober, took immediate command of the situation. She poked him playfully in the arm, almost upsetting his balance.

"That'll show that goodie-goodie who's boss, eh? Treat 'em rough. You're too good-looking to be tied down to such a namby-pamby. Take my word for it; you'll get fed up. I know that type . . . she doesn't want you to have any fun. Never trust little girls with long noses who wear glasses. They're mean-spirited."

"Long nose? Jessie? Are you talking 'bout my li'l Jess? She's got a button nose. So's Patience. They're both cute as buttons. What're you trying to do? Make me mad

104

at my sweet little wife? I beg to differ with you, madam."

Sam squared his shoulders and hoped his recent excesses did not tell on his breath, as Mrs. Falconer was moving in ever closer until she was peering at him eye to eye.

"You take a good look at your wife, young fellow-me-lad. You'll see a mean-spirited spoilsport. She'll squeeze all the life out of you, if you let her. Just take a word from the wise, from somebody older and wiser. I like the looks of you, young man. But that wife of yours . . . I wouldn't give you a plug nickel for. She's holding you back. You'll see. Don't say I didn't warn you!" With each word her tone became more venomous, the hatred exuding from her glittering blue eyes more compelling, until, by the time she finished, there was actual foam forming at the corners of her mouth.

Since the outburst was entirely unprovoked, Sam assumed the old woman was reliving some weird incident in her own lifetime, and decided to become a disinterested observer. What a crazy night. He was not so far gone as to foolhardily enter into an imbroglio with the senile old bitch.

"Madam, I bid you good-night. I most assuredly do not agree with anything you've just said—but respect for the burden of your years forbids my taking issue." He gave a stiff little bow and lurched into his back door. It was an awkward exit, but he did succeed in closing the door on her retort, which was vituperative. Yet the closed door took all menace out of the tirade for Sam. He didn't even try to make out what she was saying. Nor did it occur to him to wonder why Mrs. Falconer was on her way out at two in the morning . . . or whether she was in fact going out at all. The sound of her voice was still unpleasantly discernible as he turned on the shower and drowned it out.

All was quiet when he stepped out of the steaming

shower several minutes later. He grabbed an old terry cloth robe from the hook. Painstakingly he pulled the robe around his shoulders and recognized his transition into the ghastly, chastening state midway between drunk and hung over. Still quite wet, barefoot, and shivering with cold, he stepped into the chilly hall. It was growing windy outside. He could hear the trees being churned up, leaves being blown off in gusts, hitting the windows like a soft sleet. The howling and sighing reminded him of the sea—what an atmospheric place this was! How rich in evocative settings. Despite his incredible evening, he felt buoyant for an instant, as a glimmer of the good life goading him and Jessica on reappeared. Then he noticed a new quality to the rushing, turbulent sounds buffeting his fevered sensibilities. Dimly at first, then with a fearful flash of recognition, he heard it.

A piercing, plaintive wail coming from the baby's room.

He ran to the sound. Patience was standing in her crib—pointing to her door.

"Tweedie. Twee-dee!" she wailed. "Tweedie! Twee-die."

He picked up the red-faced child and hugged her. He patted her on the back and was astonished at the depth of the terror being transmitted through every tight little muscle in her sob-wracked frame. It was as though the colicky days-old infant he could remember Jessica ministering to in those early, fragile days had suddenly returned, grown grotesquely to toddler-size.

"Where is Tweetie, sweetheart? Let's see if she didn't just fall on the floor or something. *Shhh. Shhh.* Calm down, love. Everything's all right. Daddy's here."

"Twee—*gone!*" More sobs. Her chubby clenched fist kept gesturing toward the door. He began to fear convulsions—something mothers were always mentioning

106

to one another in relation to high fevers. He'd never seen one, but now found he could imagine very clearly what one would be. He was afraid Patience was just about at the breaking point.

He reached into the crib, just to make sure the tattered doll on whom this pitiful grief was being lavished might not be shoved into a crevice, but found nothing. He picked up one of the blankets, wrapped it around her, and headed for Mommy. Together, in their own comforting big bed, they would surely manage to calm her.

The hall was even colder than when he'd left it. A terrible draft was shooting up and down its entire old-fashioned length. Their back door was now wide open, and rattling on its hinges in the wind. Still carrying the baby, patting her, and crooning to her that everything would soon be all right, Sam walked to the back door and closed it. And, having closed it, he latched it, and closed the hook and eye. He'd not done that before.

Chapter 11

SAM came into the bedroom carrying the wailing Patience, just as Jessica woke to full alertness. She'd managed to turn on the light and put on her glasses but had not consciously heard the baby until the moment of their entrance. Now, as Sam laid Patience between them on the big bed, she realized that this was the first time in her life that she was truly afraid. This was real. Her child was in trouble. She felt the baby's dry, red forehead. No fever. The cries were dry and raspy . . . no tears were being shed. Jessica felt the contorted muscles, stroked the white-knuckled little fists that were clenched so tightly they were drawing blood from the palms. Patience was not sick. She seemed to be . . . terrified.

"But what's wrong, Sam? Did she say anything . . . I don't think she's enough in control now to talk at all. . . ."

Sam's face, in bleak contrast to his daughter's, was gray.

"She thinks somebody took Tweetie away. I looked for the doll just now and couldn't find it anywhere. She seems to have had a terrible fright. Surely it must be more than the doll. I first heard her screaming when I got out of the shower."

Gasping, hoarse, Patience's usually clear alto was distorted, pleading. Once again her hand gestured plaintively toward the door. Jessica picked up her child, patting her, trying to soothe this monstrous terror out of her. She carried her to the bathroom. The only medication on hand was some Phenobarbital Dr. Norris had prescribed more than a year ago when Patience had once run a fever of 105 degrees. Did the stuff go bad? Lose strength? Well, she'd try it; this child needed sleep. How to get it down? Would Patience accept a glass of milk? Jessica could only try.

The hallway was bitter cold. Huddling the blanket around Patience and crooning softly to her, Jessica walked into the kitchen. The gasping seemed to be quieting down a little. When she'd filled the cup with milk, she added the pediatric Phenobarbital drops, not increasing the dosage prescribed for a much younger baby.

She tried to cradle Patience in her arms, letting her hold the cup, just as she had done when the child was younger. It didn't work; the fists wouldn't unclench to grasp anything. Then she decided to try one of Patience's old bottles, given up months ago, but still on hand. She carried the freshly washed and filled baby bottle and Patience back to their big bed. Sam was now in his pajamas, piling another blanket on the bed. The temperature drop in the last hour was marked—it was probably below thirty outside. And of course, there wouldn't be any heat in the middle of the night. Not even the most generous landlord would squander fuel at that hour. Jessica wrapped a comforter around her shoulders and placed Patience gently on the bed. She began to sip a bit of the milk. Jessica murmured encouragingly to her. "There, there. Drink up. You'll feel so much better. Mommy and Daddy are right here. There's nothing to fear. Sleep, sleep, sleep, my love."

Sam couldn't help noticing how very much younger Patience—lying back drinking out of a bottle again—seemed, despite her size. The poignant desperate cries, gradually becoming less shrill, were those of a much younger child.

"Twee. Dee. Eee. Too. Twee. Dee!" A mere whimper, now. Milk being taken. Wild, anguished eyes beginning to blink. Fists looser. Brief, shuddering spasms were all that remained of the sobbing.

"*Shh.* Sleep." Jessica kissed her forehead. At last Patience was giving in. In a few minutes more she was out like a light. She'd taken hardly any milk. It wasn't the soporific drug that had overcome her—it was simple exhaustion.

Jessica stood up and prepared to take Patience back to her own room. The child, sleeping soundly, seemed twice her usual weight. Sam, seeing Jessica struggling to balance the sleeping child without disturbing her, came over and picked her up in one swift, gentle maneuver. Jessica followed him to the baby's room. They tucked her in, adjusted the curtains, fussed about ineffectually; there really wasn't anything left for them to do. Patience now seemed perfectly normal; Sam and Jessica didn't quite trust their memory of Patience's recent extraordinary behavior. Had it really been terror?

"What was it she said to you Sam, about Tweetie?"

"She kept pointing to the door. I think she was saying that somebody took the doll. It could have been a nightmare, of course. She was as much outraged, I think, as she was terrified. Poor, poor Patience! I really can't believe the way she was, just now." He tiptoed to her crib and peered in. She was perfectly calm. Not a trace of the gasping, wrenching sobs. There was even a slight smile on her face. How would she be in the morning? Would she remember? Of course. She'd look for Tweetie when she woke up.

"Do you think we can find that blasted doll before she wakes up?"

"Sam, I think somebody really did take it. Patience
110

simply does not have nightmares. Why, the only time I hear her making noises in her sleep is when she laughs. You've heard her, love; she even giggles sometimes." Jessica, relieved her daughter was now safely sleeping, suddenly admitted her own anxiety. Sam put his arms around her. She looked into his kindly, familiar face and saw that this time he had no reserves to offer her. He somehow appeared diminished to her eyes. This was Sam . . . the man her world steadfastly revolved around, wasn't it? Why did he look so strange to her? Was this the first time since they'd fallen in love that she was seeing him clearly, seeing him as he really was? He was—at this moment—hung over, nearly out of his wits with concern for Patience, and completely at a loss. With a deep sigh, Jessica shifted position so that her arms encircled him, and it was she who absently patted his back, and said, "There, There. Everything will be all right. You'll see."

Feeble, milky sunlight was doing its wintry best to greet Jessica's awakening at six thirty on Sunday morning. She found herself curiously refreshed and calm, as though she'd successfully survived some dreaded ordeal. Had she just recovered from an illness? Passed a final exam? Given birth to a baby? Baby. Patience! She leaped out of bed. Her bare feet found the wide, old-fashioned floor boards welcoming and warm, and her keen nose recognized the nostalgic, schoolroomy, winter-is-coming smell of steam heat turned on for the first time of the season.

She grabbed her glasses and left the robe and slippers behind. She was still adjusting the eyeglasses frame on the bridge of her nose as she opened the door to Patience's room, so that focus and reassurance occurred simultaneously. Patience was sitting up, babbling gently to herself. She smiled matter-of-factly at her mother.

Jessica leaned happily over the crib railing to give Patience an enthusiastic hug. Patience accepted it calmly enough, giving no indication that she had any recollection at all of last night's fright. Maybe she wouldn't remember! Jessica gave Patience some milk to tide her over until breakfast, and crept back into bed.

At eight thirty Jessica returned to Patience's room. Patience had fallen asleep again. She looked fine, but she had wet her bed. This still happened sometimes. It was nothing to worry about. But, come to think of it, it was the first time she'd been wet like that in the morning since before they moved to Wimbledon. Well. She had taken some of that Phenobarbital . . . it could be that she'd been a little doped up and just didn't realize. She wouldn't wake her now. She changed her pajamas, put a blanket under her, and let her continue sleeping.

She and Sam had a quiet, unhurried breakfast. Jessica was troubled by so many unanswered questions, she decided they would all keep until they'd had something to eat. When Sam's eggs and bacon were gone and he was reaching for a second cup of coffee, Jessica made the mistake of asking him casually, as she was filling his cup, "Will you be going in to work today?"

The bitter look Sam flashed at her seemed entirely out of proportion to the blandness of her inquiry. He threw his napkin on his plate and pushed his chair back from the table. Standing, he jabbed his finger toward her, accusingly.

"I suppose your friend Pierre put you up to that, huh? What else did he have to say to you about me? You may as well tell me now . . . you'll let me know sooner or later in any case . . . how I'm such a washout as a business partner . . . how I merely bring in a couple of hundred thousand dollars worth of new business in two short weeks, when I could be fraternizing with some blue-haired biddy in accounting, admiring the neatness of her double entries. Did he tell you that, too? God-damn it, Jess . . . get off my back! Yesterday was probably the worst day of my life . . . you know that. But, no, the first thing the next morning, you've got to get right down to cases, don't you? Twist the old screws. You know something? I think that old lady upstairs just may have you pegged, after all!"

Everything he said set off a series of small shocks. Jessica sat, her mouth open, and felt the color drain from her cheeks. How could he have become so angry, so fast? What did Pierre do to him last night? Everything seemed on the verge of sliding away from her. In a curious way she was embarrassed. It was as though all of the earnest efforts she had made to live like a responsible member of society had been a mere disguise, and she was about to be caught out.

As Sam saw her face undergo its several changes, with her eyes now blinking back shocked tears behind the familiar glasses, his anger—if not the pain that caused it—dissipated. Poor Jessica'd always been as transparent as a three-year-old. Obviously she'd done nothing to hurt him . . . why be angry with her?

"Pierre didn't say anything to you last night?"

"No. I don't know what you mean . . . Victor came back and said you and Pierre had some kind of falling out . . . not to expect you until late. I worried about that some . . . but I had no idea what was going on. At the party Pierre was just his usual charming self. He didn't say much of anything to me that bears remembering . . . but then, he never does. What was that you said about Mrs. Falconer?"

"Oh, hell. Forget it. So much is going wrong I'm probably losing my grip. Let's just concentrate on Patience today; that's all that really matters. I just felt played out there for a minute; I think I'll have that second cup of coffee now."

"You're sorry?"

"I'm sorry."

"Thank you."

"You're welcome."

"Oh, Sam, we're going to have to be very careful. Things can slip away from us without our even knowing." She got up and put her arms around him. She kissed him on his forehead. She kissed him on his mouth. He returned the kiss, very generously.

Jessica moved her face away from him for a brief breath of air.

"Well! At least that hasn't changed between us yet. A good thing, too." And she turned back to Sam and continued with an enthusiasm that was as mindless as it was satisfying. For a few minutes they were perfectly absorbed in the comforting, comfortable affection it had taken nearly five years of living together to achieve.

"Oh, Sam, when I get to feeling everything slipping out of control, the way it did just a few minutes ago, I see how fragile everything we've tried to build up together really is. Two or three wrong moves could destroy it all. I'm not kidding!"

Sam was about to interrupt. She stopped him.

"I'm not finished. What I want to say is, well, more *profound*, than 'Let's hold on' or 'Let's be nice to each other.' What I'm trying to say is . . . this is going to sound callous to you . . . out of character, maybe. Sam. If it's this hard to keep going . . . if it takes this much effort just to live an ordinary life together, the way we think we'd like to . . . well, let's be smart enough to give up before we give out! It hasn't happened yet. But I can picture it happening. I can see us struggling harder and harder, and having less and less to show for it. I can see us getting so caught up in the day-to-day struggle that we hardly know one another anymore, let alone like each other. It isn't worth that. I don't want *anything* that badly. Not a pretty apartment. Not a lovely river view. Not a prosperous, orderly life without any unseemly rough edges. The fact is anything you have to work too hard for is never worth it in the end. There's a point where you begin to feel foolish and cheated . . . even if you end up getting exactly what you thought you wanted."

Sam listened to her with a kind of dread. Her crisp, articulate, Wellesley-trained little mind was merely putting into words something he himself had apprehended lately—all too vividly.

"Jessie, don't be morbid!"

"You know exactly what I'm talking about. I just want us to be strong enough to call it quits before our merely staying together has begun to damage us. Honest. I mean it."

"Jess! Okay. I agree. Now, let's drop it, shall we? Things haven't 'slipped away' all that much. Yesterday may have turned out to be the downer of the year, but that was yesterday. I'll get over it. I have no intention of going in to work today. I'm going to stay here and enjoy my family. Don't you think Patience has slept long enough? I think I'll just go check."

Patience was still asleep. She had a slight smile on her face and seemed perfectly normal. Except that she never slept in the mornings, and it was nearly ten thirty. Sam bent down and kissed her awake.

"Hey, Sleeping Beauty! . . . No more of this beauty sleep nonsense. You're beautiful enough now. Wake up!"

Her lids wavered, but she was reluctant to open her eyes. Yet her sleep was shallower, and her hand searched the pillow, nervously.

Oh, God, Sam thought. *She's feeling around for Tweetie.* Patience felt around some more, her eyes still closed. She was apparently still asleep, but the searching movements of her hands became more extensive. When they did not find what they sought, she sat up—abruptly.

"Da Da!" she greeted him.

"Good morning, sweetheart! How about some chow? You must be starving."

She stood up, her movements a little clumsy in the crib she would soon outgrow. He hugged her and lifted her out. She toddled loyally after him to the dining room.

Jessica flashed a smile at them that was nothing short of beautific. Patience looked so heartwarmingly normal! Whatever had frightened her so terribly the night before didn't seem to have left a trace this morning.

"Here we are, baby-love, a nice bowl of cereal with bananas, just waiting for you to gobble it up."

Patience let Sam help her to the table and sat down docilely in her high chair. She ate quietly. Sam and Jessica had some more coffee and succeeded, between them, in watching Patience's every mouthful. The child showed no apparent awareness of their intense scrutiny.

"All finished?" Jessica was smiling broadly, indeed, fatuously. Sam found himself waiting for her to adopt the hospital "we" at any moment.

"Do we want down, now?"

"Oh, for God's sake, Jess . . . come off it! Let her be. If we're both so convinced she's all right, why don't we just leave her alone for a while? She knows how to get down off her high chair . . . don't you, sweetheart?

"Dow!" Patience raised her arms and smiled imploringly at the father she'd just made a liar out of. Sam helped her down and watched thoughtfully as she toddled off to the toy box they kept for her in the living room.

Patience looked at her toy box. *Tweetie there?* She could see her trusty friend so clearly. She could *feel* her—that beloved old terry cloth, so comforting to rub her fingers over. One by one, she emptied all her toys

116

out of the box. She looked at each one carefully before tossing it aside. Without a backward glance Patience headed back to her room. She was muttering to herself, but neither Sam nor Jessica could make out any words.

"Jessie . . . where could that damn doll have disappeared to? She's going to keep on looking for it."

"I've béen thinking, Sam. That's a pretty common doll. Funny old Mrs. Farbstein across the hall on East Fifth Street gave it to us when Patience was born. They're safe to chew and washable and the terry cloth makes them seem cozy and lovable. They sell them in practically every baby department. The same dumb face, the same cheap terry cloth. If only it weren't Sunday! I know I could pick up another Tweetie right here in Wimbledon."

"What about that drugstore . . . they have baby toys down there, don't they? You want me to look around? We'll want the *Times*, anyway, right?"

"Okay. You get the *Times*, and see what you can find in the drugstore. But, look, if you do find a doll like Tweetie down there, be sure to let me doctor it to look like the old one before you let Patience see it! I'm going to have to do a very artful job of distressing before she'd even consider a substitute. Even then, I'm not sure we'd get away with it."

"Well, it's something positive to try anyway. You can tell she's upset. I don't like the way she seems to be . . . uh . . . sublimating it, somehow. It's weird the way she hasn't cried or asked for Tweetie even once. She's been much too quiet. It's almost like she's shut us out and is trying to find the doll by herself." Sam looked to Jessica for confirmation.

"I know exactly what you mean . . . and I don't like it at all."

While Sam was away on his errand, Jessica tidied the apartment and got dressed. She missed the cheerful

117

audience she usually had during this morning routine. Patience remained in her room. Jessica strained to hear what the baby was doing. Sometimes, when Jessica was working around the house, she'd catch bits and pieces of Patience's play talk and overhear little advances she was making in her speech. Some months ago Jessica had heard Patience's first actual sentence in this way. She'd been admonishing Tweetie not to spill something.

"Don't spill!" was evidently not expressive enough to suit her game, so she'd tried to embroider the statement.

"Don't you dare spill a drop!"

It had come out so loud and clear and sounded so much like an irate mother that Jessica'd laughed out loud. She couldn't wait for Sam to come home to tell him how verbally advanced their daughter was. And from that day on Patience's speech became daily more fluent until everyone who knew her grew accustomed to conversing easily with her, making few concessions to her age. Yet today Patience was silent. Jessica thought a moment, trying to play back in her mind anything that Patience had said this morning and found she couldn't recall a thing.

Jessica walked into Patience's room.

Patience was sitting motionless in the middle of the floor. When she saw her mother, she gave that docile little smile again and raised her arms as though asking to be picked up.

"Ma Ma," she said sloppily.

Jessica walked over to her, picked her up, and found, once again, that her daughter was soaking wet.

"Well, well," Jessica said grimly to herself. "What we have here appears to have all the earmarks of a classic case of regression."

And once she'd admitted this to herself, she knew she'd been aware of it all morning long. A wild pulse was throbbing above her eyes; her hands were trembling almost out of control, and she could barely see through her tears. Even so, Jessica managed to find a pair of old diapers and pinned them to Patience's passive little bottom with clearly remembered expertise.

Chapter 12

"DEE DEE"

"Yes . . . it's Tweetie . . . we found her for you!"

Tentatively, not quite daring to believe her eyes, Patience reached for the hopefully proffered, artfully aged, counterfeit doll.

Jessica was afraid it simply wouldn't feel right to her. She'd spent nearly an hour trying to make over the spanking-new, hygienically clean infant's toy into a faithful replica of Patience's boon companion. She thought she'd remembered every spot, every little scar that the original had had to show for nearly three years of loving.

Patience accepted the doll. She held it to her chest. There was a slight curve to her mouth that didn't have enough faith in itself to become a true smile. She held the doll away from her, to look at it very carefully one more time. There was a deep sigh, a little shrug, and Patience hugged the new Tweetie with something like conviction.

"Dee. Dee," she said once more and walked off to her room without another word.

"Well, Sam, at least it's a start. I just can't bear to hear that baby talk coming out of her. Even her voice is different—sloppy—not like her, at all." Sam walked over to her and put his arm around her.

"Whatever scared her last night did a proper job of it. We'll have to let Dr. Norris take a look at her, if it

120

doesn't get any better. She can probably recommend a specialist, or something. . . . I can't accept the idea that somebody might actually have been in her room! If that's really what happened . . . well, it could only have been while I was in the shower. When I came out of the shower, I remember I heard Patience crying . . . almost immediately. And, when I left Patience's room, I did notice the back door open—I came in by way of the back door last night—too drunk to manage the porch steps! And too drunk to think very clearly. I remember noticing the back door open, hearing the wind, and just barely entertaining the thought that maybe Mrs. Falconer had come in. But I didn't think about it, really, it was a vague idea, and I was too concerned about the baby to pursue it. See, she was right there when I came in. If I remember correctly, I think it was a very strange scene, indeed. I seem to recall having words with her. She looked very angry . . . crazy, even. But . . . God damn it, I was so drunk, and sick, and exhausted! I don't really know whether it actually happened. I haven't been that drunk in years. I really can't remember anything I did. Oh, God, Jess . . . I think I threw up . . . somewhere along Maynard! Old Pierre really socked it to me. And now, this has happened to Patience, and I can't even fit together the events that might have led up to it. But . . . you've got to admit . . . the idea of some strange person coming into a baby's room and stealing a bedraggled old doll is rather hard to accept! I just can't imagine somebody walking into Patience's room—big as you please—and scaring the daylights out of her like that! What for?"

"What for, indeed?"

"Who in hell would steal a crummy doll out of a kid's crib?"

"Somebody crazy?"

"You think it's Mrs. Falconer? Obviously she'd have

the best opportunity. But what for? And how could she have scared poor Patience like that? Besides, I was right there—in the shower—and if I remember clearly and didn't dream it all, we'd just been *talking*, for Pete's sake! She can't be that crazy!"

"Still and all, Sam, I can't dismiss the possibility. It scares the hell out of me. That woman could be downright dangerous ... violent ... how do we know?"

Just then the telephone rang, and they both jumped.

"Good grief, Sam, it's just the phone. Probably one of our guests paying his respects. I'll get it." She hurried to the kitchen.

"Is that you, Mrs. Potter?"

"Yes," Jessica replied.

"How is that poor baby of yours? Its little cries sounded so heartbreaking! I was concerned. You know, my dear, we have had many little ones living in that flat, but only rarely have I ever been able to hear cries during the night. I almost came down to see if I could be of assistance, but as it was getting very cold, I didn't want to risk catching a chill. But I had to know how the child is this morning. . . ."

"She is much better, Mrs. Falconer," Jessica pronounced distinctly for Sam's benefit.

"I wonder if you'd care to accept some advice from an old woman, my dear. When a child cries that hard, it is possible there has been some injury not apparent to the eye. I would feel much relieved if you'd take it to a doctor. You never know! Why, poor old Mrs. Riddell— she had your little flat back some years ago, when my dear hubby was still alive—her son began to change before her very eyes, but she kept hoping he would improve. Well. I mustn't trouble you with my silly stories. I just hope you'll take my advice. You have such a sweet child, as I recall. So helpful and alert. I forget, now ... is it a little boy or a girl?"

"Thank you for your interest, Mrs. Falconer. Our little girl suffered some kind of fright. We were planning to ask you about it. Did you hear anything strange before you heard my little girl crying? I didn't think her cries were all that loud, Mrs. Falconer. How come you heard them, when I didn't? Just where were you, Mrs. Falconer, when my little girl was making all this noise?" Sam was now gesturing wildly to Jessica to stop this line of inquiry—cutting his throat, putting his hand on his mouth, shaking his head no.

"Just what has your hubby been saying to you? If he has implied anything about me to you, I must simply urge you to make up your own mind, Mrs. Potter. Now, I will admit I saw your husband come in. I was emptying my trash. Old people do keep irregular hours. Sleep is not easy when eternal sleep is just around the corner. Of course you wouldn't understand that. It isn't easy, is it . . . putting up with a man who drinks." She hung up.

"It is her! It's got to be! She's a malicious . . . oily, nasty —ugh! I don't know when I've been so mad! What *is* her game, Sam?"

Then they both heard the familiar sound of her cane. Thump. Thump. Thump. She was coming down to see them. They both steeled themselves. Was there going to be a showdown?

As Jessica and Sam stirred themselves to answer the back door, they were surprised to see Patience approach the door, and, as she had done before, stand on the very tip of her toes to turn the knob and open it. She smiled at Mrs. Falconer with genuine pleasure. She looked almost like her true self. Almost. She didn't say anything, as Mrs. Falconer entered.

"Ah, there you are. I'm here for two reasons. Mrs. Potter—"

"Our name is Porter, Mrs. Falconer. P-o-r-t-e-r."

"Please forgive an old woman . . . it's hard to remember everything. Mrs. *Porter.* I do apologize for being abrupt just now on the telephone. But you see, I remembered something important, after all. There *was* a queer sound, last night. I had just returned to my living room and was about to turn on the radio—they have such interesting men who talk all night! I do enjoy listening to the radio when sleep is difficult—"

"You say you heard a queer sound."

"Yes. I was saying. I don't know what it means, really. Before I heard your little girl cry . . . I think I heard her laugh. I heard a little child laughing."

Sam and Jessica stood dumbfounded. Then, warily, Jessica said, "Well, Mrs. Falconer, it was good of you to come down and tell us. But, as you see, our little girl is just fine this morning. I think it is remarkable that you have such keen hearing, considering your advanced years. But thank you for your concern." Jessica was heading for the door. She didn't trust this strange, two-faced, now malicious, now unctuously concerned, old person. She wanted her out of their home.

Patience had been standing to the side; how much she could understand of the grown-up talk they were unable to judge. She seemed to be listening, though. Sam noticed that, when Mrs. Falconer said she heard a child laughing, a smile flashed across Patience's face. Sam was still studying his daughter when she purposefully walked toward Mrs. Falconer. Without any hesitation she walked right up to the horrid old woman, took one of the gnarled old hands . . . and kissed it.

"Goo whch?" she asked.

"Good-bye, my child. You do seem very fine this morning." Mrs. Falconer was suddenly as dithery as a bride. She turned to the Porters, flashed a brilliant, porcelain grin at them, and repeated, "Good-bye, my child! Stay well!" She let herself out the back door.

"Well, Patience," Sam asked, "is she a good witch or a

bad witch?" So she remembered things. Things other than Tweetie. That was good. Maybe she'd un-regress quickly!

When Mrs. Falconer had gone, and they could hear her cane thumping up the steps, Jessica burst out, "Sam? Do you realize what it means?"

"I saw it . . . I can't quite believe it . . . but I saw it. Evidently our baby's decided that the crazy old broad is a good witch. I don't know why. Patience always did have a strong compassionate streak in her, though."

"But, Sam! If it had been *her* last night—I mean, Patience wouldn't, *couldn't* have behaved that way toward her just now. Surely whoever scared her like that would get a different reaction from her if they ever were face-to-face again?"

"*Pas devant l'enfant,* okay?"

Sam was right. They shouldn't discuss it anymore in front of the baby. Jessica walked back to the kitchen and busied herself with unimportant make-work, knowing Sam would join her as soon as Patience was settled back in her room.

With a studied casualness, Sam walked Patience back to her room. His mind was spinning with the possible implications of Patience's peculiar affection for the unpleasant old woman they'd both decided was at the bottom of the child's terror the night before. Once in her room, he sat down wearily in the old rocking chair Jessica'd used to nurse the baby back in their crowded little bedroom on Fifth Street. Patience hesitated for a moment. The new Tweetie lay on the floor, abandoned when Mrs. Falconer had knocked on the door. Patience went to it and picked up the doll. Sam watched his daughter quietly, trying to assess this new Patience— seeing the differences between her and the one he'd foolishly come to take for granted. Would that bright little companion come back? He felt horribly defeated. Patience came over to him, and he picked her up.

"You sa?"

"Daddy is sad. You're right, my love. And how are you?"

She snuggled closer to him, and they hugged each other. Sam began to rock the chair in a steady rhythm that soothed them both. It was a brief, cozy moment, and he let his mind go blank. His eyes wandered about the room with indulgent approval. Had he ever complimented Jessica on the swift job she'd made of their moving in? He noticed several neat, signature touches scattered about—little things Jessica did so well. A very large Steiff teddy bear, the gift of Pierre Villard, was perched on the big old curtain rod, surveying the scene below with a rakish gleam in his eyes. Patience had never singled out this sumptuous toy for special devotion, so it had been put to decorative use. An antique earthenware crock stood in one corner, filled with dried wheat, wild flowers, and cattails. Now, when had Jessica found the time to arrange that? There was even a wide velvet ribbon—orange to match Patience's quilt—tied in a careful bow around the jug. Jessica should go into the business someday, she really had a flair. As he thought about Jessica's eye for detail and design, his own eyes were disturbed by something that seemed decidedly out of place in this charming old room. He put Patience down beside him in the rocker and got up. He took a couple of steps across the room. Patience, with that poignant new passivity of hers, sat where he left her, Tweetie resting forgotten in her lap. The old Patience would have been right behind him, curious to discover what he was now looking at and picking up. Sam stooped down in the corner, behind the crock of dried flowers, and picked up an object with some distaste. It was the short, fat, chewed-up stub of a cheap cigar!

He looked at Patience as he stood up. She was beginning to babble privately to the doll in her lap. He walked quietly, almost stealthily, out of the room to join Jessica in the kitchen.

"Look what I just found on the floor in the baby's room." There was no expression in his voice. His face, too, was noncommittal.

"Oh, my God, Sam! How could—"

"Somebody was in her room last night, all right. And it doesn't appear to have been our suspect, does it?"

"Don't you think we ought to go to the police with this?" Jessie said it hesitantly, but Sam could tell she'd been thinking about it even before he'd come in with this latest discovery.

"Are you sure it isn't one of yours?" she asked, almost as an afterthought.

"*This?* Jessie, these cost about twelve cents apiece! I only smoke cigars as a special treat, and then only very good ones. This is a stinker. I'd *never* smoke something like this." He carefully put it down on a paper napkin and wrapped it gingerly. Then, to demonstrate his loathing for its inferiority, as well as for its connection with an intruder whose identity they couldn't begin to imagine, he scrubbed his hands vigorously at the sink.

"But, Sam—last night—remember, you told me yourself, you were very drunk. You don't remember everywhere you went or who you talked to. I mean, I can remember other times when you've accepted cigars from old geezers at bars, to be friendly. When you're drunk, you're not always that particular in your tastes."

"I didn't! I didn't smoke a cheap cigar. I don't remember any such thing. I came in. I went straight to the shower. I'm sure I did!"

"Are you, Sam?" Jessica's gaze was level, there was no reproach in it. But nonetheless it had its effect.

"I think I am. I have no recollection of coming into

Patience's room until after I got out of the shower and heard her cry."

"Sam, the reason I want you to be sure is that I've been thinking about whether we should go to the police for some time now. But if we aren't completely sure about this, we could look pretty foolish. You know, it's just the way Mary Smith said Mrs. Falconer always intimidates her tenants. We have real trouble here; God knows, poor Patience is obviously a changed child. But what can we tell somebody about it? Is it enough just to report our suspicions? We can't even say for sure that somebody was here last night. That cigar butt—it could have belonged to an intruder. It could have been something you were smoking and were too drunk to notice. You've done worse things under the influence. . . ."

"You still think the Falconer woman is behind all this, don't you?"

"Sam, as long as we stay here, I'm going to suspect Mrs. Falconer for everything that goes wrong. I sense something terrible in her. But I think I'll go to the police anyway." Jessica had made up her mind.

"Why don't you let Mary help you tomorrow, Jess? Ask her to drive you into the city to see Dr. Norris. It might be a good idea. We're probably getting paranoid about all this. It'll help us sort things out to see what a professional makes of it."

Chapter 13

ON Monday morning all three Porters overslept. With his job already in jeopardy Sam dressed and shaved and bolted out the door with such haste Jessica had no chance to say more than "Have a good day," a lame phrase at best, under the circumstances.

After he'd gone she checked the train schedule they'd tacked up by the phone to make sure there was still another commuter train stopping at Wimbledon that morning. It was eight twenty-five. He should get to the station by eight forty. Thank goodness—there was a train at eight fifty-two. It got into New York at nine thirty. Better late than never, she reflected grimly. Poor Sam ... Pierre was bound to make capital of this.

"Now what?" She sat at the table with an acrid cup of instant coffee in front of her. This was to be the day she was going to the police about their intruder. The odious cigar, still wrapped in its paper napkin, sat like "exhibit A" on the sideboard. Yet at eight thirty on a mild, clear Monday morning, it seemed a futile errand. Police? Jessica Porter, go to the police and babble on about her fears? She doubted she could do it.

Patience appeared at the door and smiled at her. She looked refreshed and walked in with an energetic bounce; but her eyes still had that guarded, dimmed cast to them. There'd been no overnight change apparently.

"Well." Jessica scooped Patience up to sit on her lap. Her bottom was wet, once again, but what the hell.

"First things first, baby. I'm going to call Dr. Norris about you right now." She gave Patience some cereal and went to get her purse. She found her ineffectual old address book with all its scratchings-out and odd slips of paper full of hasty notations that now meant absolutely nothing to her. A brief wave of homesickness for the city came to her. There were as yet no Wimbledon entries. Suddenly "E 73rd," "W 12th," "295 Jane St.," seemed infinitely more desirable than "Firehouse Lane," "Maynard St.," or "Granite Terrace." No matter. She'd get over it. Besides, she'd make a point of putting in the Smiths' name. Ah, "Norris," here it was—under "J"? "J" for Jean, maybe? Dr. Jean Norris was a beautiful woman, capable, tough, and rather glamorous. Jessica was very fond of her. The night Patience was born, Dr. Norris, a full-length mink draped casually over her hospital garb, and Sam, in slept-in clothes and a day's growth of beard, had gone merrily off to a corner bar together to celebrate. Jessica had lain back proudly between the stiff hospital sheets and watched them go. She felt then that somehow some of Dr. Norris' elegance would become a part of her beautiful new baby's legacy. And, until the other night, it had been perfectly true.

She dialed the number that had once been such a familiar part of her routine.

"Dr. Norris' office." Jessica recognized Irma, Dr. Norris' friendly nurse.

"Hello, Irma, it's Jessica Porter, how are you?"

"Jessie! How's that sensational-looking baby of yours? We were just talking about you the other day! Are you still living downtown?"

"We've moved to the suburbs, I'm afraid, Irma . . ."

"Traitor!" It was Dr. Norris; she'd picked up her extension.

"Hello, Doctor. I've got a sad problem here."

"Patience?"

"Yes." Very carefully, without going into all the confusing details about their curious situation, Jessica described Patience's severe crying fit and the apparent regression in her behavior it had provoked.

"There's been no change today?"

"No."

"Does she seem to have lost her memory in any way?"

"No."

"That's good. It's probably not due to any physical trauma, Jess. Look, I can't treat her, but I'd like to see her as soon as possible . . . and then I'll send you to a friend of mine who specializes in child psychiatry. Let's make it for one P.M. Can you be here by then? And, Jessica . . . try not to worry too much. Patience is an unusual child, you know that. It's probably because she's gifted and intelligent that she reacted to whatever happened to her in this way. Her sensitive mind has built a protective wall around something that caused her pain. As soon as my friend Dr. Weller gets to the root of that pain, the chances are very good she'll snap right back. I wouldn't say this to you if I didn't mean it. Be brave. I'll see you at one." Dr. Norris hung up.

Jessica, feeling numb, looked up Mary Smith's number, wrote it down on a scrap of paper toweling, and slipped it in with all the other cryptic scraps in her address book. She found she already knew it by heart, anyway. On the phone Mary agreed without any hesitation to drive them to the city.

"Of course I can . . . it's no bother at all. We'll pick you up at noon."

Jessica went to Patience's room to prepare her for the trip. It was eleven thirty. She'd become accustomed to the daily sounds of the place. At eleven she'd heard the little mail truck go by. At eleven fifteen there was a

131

doughnut man, whose van used a jingling bell. And now, she could hear the clatter of the Monday garbage pick-up. It all seemed so alluringly normal and everyday . . . if only their own life would just settle down to such soothing predictability. When Patience was ready, Jessica gave the room a quick once-over, to make sure she hadn't forgotten anything. The window looked odd. The curtains were pulled back too far, and were all bunched up. She walked over to put them right, and noticed that something had been stuck in one of the panes. A postcard. She picked it up. It was addressed to:

Mr. and Mrs. Samuel Porter
33 Granite Terrace
Wimbledon-on-Hudson, New York

How could it be? The card had a canceled stamp, postmarked New York. She didn't recognize the large, flamboyant handwriting . . . Dorcas! A thank-you note. "Lovely evening. Hope to see you both again. Thanks ever so much for inviting Pierre and me to your new home. Dorcas D." There was an artistic print of pink and red geraniums on the back of the card. But how had it gotten to Patience's window? Who had put it there? Obviously it had to have been a part of that morning's mail. She examined the card closely, as though it might yet impart more information. There was nothing. What about the rest of their mail? As new residents, they were bound to be receiving a number of bills. She ran down to the mailbox on Granite Terrace. Empty. A postcard in the window—and an empty mailbox. *Somebody had tampered with their mail.* There was no way around it. She couldn't believe it. Why, that was a federal offense! She looked up at Mrs. Falconer's apartment . . . could that crazy woman have gone to such lengths? For what earthly reason? And why a postcard

132

in the window? Oh, God, they were going to have to leave this place. And there was nothing she could do about this now. She'd have to try to get to the bottom of it later. Right now she must concentrate on getting Patience to the doctor.

Yet minutes later, when Jessie again trundled down the steps, this time with Patience, to meet Mary's station wagon, she found herself still brooding about what might have been done to the rest of their mail. The idea of somebody actually diverting mail addressed to her and Sam gave her an uncanny feeling. Once more, she determined to brush the episode from her mind. She got into the station wagon and thanked Mary again.

"You're really doing us a terrific favor . . . thanks, so much."

"It's no favor at all, really, Jessie! I've been wanting to go into town for weeks now. You've simply given me the push I needed. You can't imagine how dull you get when you stay put all the time in a place like Wimbledon. I keep putting things off. Bonwit's has sales . . . Lord & Taylor's has sales . . . exhibits open and close at the Met . . . at the Modern Museum . . . and I never stir. While you're at the doctor's, Violet and I are going to cash in on the fall sales. It's going to be fun!"

Jessica threw her friend a grateful look.

"And go gallery-hopping in between, I suppose?"

"Well . . . I don't know. Violet doesn't dig pre-Columbian pottery. Maybe next time—when they do a Picasso retrospective." Then, more quietly, Mary added, "I saw the difference in Patience right away. You must be frantic with worry! But I'm sure they'll find the trouble and she'll be her old self again."

"Thanks." Jessica was close to tears, and she looked out the window over Patience's placid head, to ward them off. The dreary gray expanse of Yonkers sped by.

Several hours later, a rather bedraggled foursome

133

drove up Granite Terrace. It was already dark, but there were no lights in the Porter apartment. Sam would be working late, no doubt, to make up for the morning's tardiness. Wearily Jessica helped Patience out of the car.

"I can't thank you enough, Mary. Don't bother coming in. George is probably home waiting for you."

"Well, okay. That Dr. Weller sounds terrific, Jessica. You did the right thing. Call me tomorrow."

Mary drove off, and Jessica slowly climbed the steps. At first she tried to carry Patience, but the child was too heavy and interfered with Jessie's vision. Patience was able to hold onto the rail, though, and made pretty good progress behind her mother. When they reached the porch door, Jessica poked around in her purse with increasing irritation. The keys! Had she forgotten them? She was sure she hadn't. It was so dark, and there was such a muddle in the big Greek Islands pouch that served as her only pocketbook. She almost despaired of finding them. She was desperately tired. The trip to the city and the two lengthy doctor's appointments—as heartbreaking as they were, finally, hopeful—had exhausted her. To make matters worse, Patience, though not a whiner as a rule, was whining. At last she felt the keys; they'd slipped into an extra sweater she'd tucked in for Patience. She turned the key in the lock, and it clicked open. But the door remained closed. She tugged at it and nothing happened. This was too much! Frantically she felt the edges of the door. It wouldn't give.

There was nothing for it but to climb back down all those steps, and walk up the hill to Maynard. She took a deep breath and spoke to her whimpering child.

"Patience, dear, guess what? We're going to go back down the steps. We'll go in the rear door. Be a good girl a little while longer, and I'll have you tucked cozily in your bed before you know it." It didn't work. Patience began to cry.

Nevertheless, the pair made it back down the steps. *This must be some kind of nadir in my life*, Jessica thought. She felt pathetic and conspicuous. Though she knew none of the neighboring houses could possibly be aware of her ignominious descent, she felt that the cozily illumined windows shining so complacently behind the privet and the hemlocks and the now nearly bare maples were passing hostile judgment.

Slowly they made their halting way up to Maynard. There was no traffic. Patience was still crying as she rounded the corner. Jessica picked her up as they neared their back entrance. Here, too, it was completely dark. Finding her way while shouldering the baby's weight was no mean feat. At last she reached the door. She still held the keys in her hand, and found the right one almost immediately. It, too, clicked competently in the lock. Yet the door remained closed. It wouldn't budge. By now anger was beginning to revive her. She was furious. She gave the door a final kick (which hurt her feet, but made her feel better). It was that damned Falconer woman. She'd fastened all these crazy bolts and hooks and eyes from the inside. On their *own* doors! It was unbelievable. She rang the Falconer bell. Over and over again. No response. The bell probably didn't work. She felt around in the dark to see if there was another bell to ring, but there was nothing. What could they do now?

Jessica stood there with Patience in her arms and almost laughed. It was beginning to rain. From the little stoop she surveyed the opulent homes to the right and to the left. Both dark. To her knowledge, she'd never caught a glimpse of the people who lived in them.

Across Maynard there was another house. Its windows glowed brightly. If she asked to use their phone,

135

surely they couldn't refuse her? She'd telephone Mrs. Falconer. Make her unfasten the bolts. It was worth a try. As she stood there gathering her courage to impose on her unknown neighbors, she heard a telephone ring. It was theirs. And there was nothing she could do about it. Who was it? Sam, telling her he'd be late? (As a matter of fact, he already was.) Maybe it was Dr. Weller with some urgent message about Patience? How would it seem to either of them when there was no answer? Oh, God, she'd better get moving. Patience heard the phone, too, and looked inquiringly at her mother.

"Let's get moving, kid," Jessica said. "We're going to meet our neighbors."

Once again Jessica shifted Patience and walked across Maynard Street to the house whose brightly lit façade shone like a beacon. It had a fairly impressive garden and was surrounded by enormous old trees. The house itself was modest in size, old-fashioned clapboard, lacking any architectural distinction. Once across the street, the Falconer house was barely discernible. She walked up the old wooden porch steps. Now it was apparent that an ambitious renovation project was under way. To the side of the house a huge cantilevered deck announced the direction the rest of the house would soon follow. One living room window had been replaced by a large sliding-glass door. The front door was new, too: a massive, modern thing with an aggressive silver knocker that looked vaguely oriental. Should she use it? It put her off, somehow. She chose the bell. A veritable carillon ensued. Almost immediately the door opened.

"Yes?" It was a small, elderly woman, and she peered sweetly up at Jessica through thick-lensed glasses that made her light brown eyes appear disproportionately large.

"Hello," Jessica said. "I live across the street and have locked myself out. Could I please use your telephone to ask Mrs. Falconer, who lives upstairs, to open the door for us?"

"My goodness, what a predicament! I had no idea that woman still lived there. By all means, use the telephone up in the study." She pointed to a door at the top of a steep flight of steps. "Don't worry about your little girl, I'll watch her for you. The television is on, and we can both watch it together." She flashed a cheerful smile at Jessica and reached for Patience with competent ease. "One more can't possibly bother me." She laughed. "I'm Mrs. Truitt, the Ecklunds' baby-sitter; they both work in the city." Jessica smiled gratefully back at her and dashed up the steps. The room straight ahead was obviously the study Mrs. Truitt had indicated. There were more upstairs bedrooms than she would have guessed from the outside—and most of them were boisterously occupied by an assortment of noisy towheaded children. They ranged in age from a little one of about two, to the middle teens. Could they *all* be boys? Well, it was no concern of hers. She entered the austerely Scandinavian study and picked up the phone. Mrs. Falconer's number was scratched in orange crayon on the flyleaf of her address book, so she found it right away. She waited as the phone rang and rang.

"You're going to have to answer that phone, Mrs. Falconer, because I'm going to stand here and let it ring until you pick it up." After some twenty rings, the old woman finally answered.

"Mrs. Falconer, it's Mrs. Porter, your tenant. I'm calling from the house across the street. Both my doors have apparently been locked from the inside. Would you please undo the latch on the back door to let me in?"

"Well, my dear, you mustn't count on me to always be here to act as your doorman, you know. You absentminded young people always expect others to do your bidding, don't you? Now it just so happens that I was

137

planning to go downstairs anyway, so I'll open the door for you this time. But in the future I refuse to be taken advantage of in this way. If you must go traipsing in and out, you'd better be sure you have your keys with you."

"I *have* our keys—Oh, what's the use? *Thank you, Mrs. Falconer.* My daughter and I will be standing at the back door in just two minutes."

When she got back downstairs, she was pleased to see Patience sitting contentedly on Mrs. Truitt's lap.

"Thanks for letting me use the phone. I reached Mrs. Falconer. She should be letting us in the back door right away."

Mrs. Truitt stood up and walked Patience over to where her mother stood.

"Good. Imagine, old Loretta Falconer. I thought I recognized the house across the street when I took this job in September; though it's been years since I've been up this way. As I recall, most of the house faces the river, right? You can hardly see it from this side of Maynard, though. I've been living in Dobbs Ferry for years now, ever since Jim retired. But I remember Loretta Falconer like it was yesterday. Mighty strange woman. Hope she doesn't give you any trouble. This is a sweet little girl you've got. I bet she's waiting for her supper and a good night's sleep. Right?"

"You must have your hands full, yourself, with all these little blond Eklund children to take care of."

"Well, six is a lot. But the Eklunds are very nice to work for. He teaches at Columbia, and she's a fashion designer. They always come home on the same train together . . . they're very well organized! How long have you been living across the street?"

"Just about two weeks now."

"Well, let me know if ever there's anything I can do to help you. Don't hold back. My goodness, Loretta

Cavendish Falconer, after all these years. Still alive. I remember when poor Frederick died. Let me see now, that'd be . . . oh, 1962, somewhere in there, I guess. The few of us who still knew him were that surprised. It was August, I remember. Plant was shut down for vacation. CopperCable does that—closes down altogether for two weeks, and everybody takes off for the mountains or the shore. I remember we got back from Lake George, and Jim, my husband, says Frederick had died somewhere upstate. Imagine! Frederick had retired by then; but he was still young . . . years younger than her. Never saw her to talk to after that. None of us ever liked her, you know. But old Fred, well, he was kind of pathetic. And he was one of us—a Wimbledon boy. So we had to care about him, in spite of whom he married, you know? You'd've thought she could at least have had him buried here, among his own. But not her. No memorial service. No notice in the paper, even. Nothing. Just came back from vacation on her own. Poor old Fred died in a strange place, all alone.

"Look, you be sure to call on me now if she gives you any trouble." Mrs. Truitt was looking up at Jessica in a candid, meaningful way. "She tries any of her crazy tricks on you, don't let her get away with it, understand? Only time I ever had to grapple with her was during the war. World War II, that is. I was trying to collect money for the Wimbledon War Bond Drive. She all but threw me down all those porch steps you've got on the other side. I didn't get a penny! My, my, that was more than thirty years ago. We all grow older.

"Run along, then, dear . . . I mustn't keep you!"

"Yes, thanks, Mrs. Truitt. You're quite right. She's just crazy enough to lock the door on me all over again, if we're not there just as she opens it." Jessica waved good-bye over her shoulder and practically ran back across the street.

Mrs. Truitt had a way of making Jessica's fears seem less sinister. She'd made Mrs. Falconer seem like somebody to laugh at—a village crank everybody could enjoy hating. She felt a bit better, for having talked to her. As she neared their little back door, she hoped that for tonight at least there would be no more problems. If she could just get into the house and put Patience to bed, she'd flake out right away herself. The back-door light went on as they approached. The door shook as a series of bolts and latches were released. Finally it opened. Jessica meant to rush right in, but Mrs. Falconer, dressed in an ancient Burberry raincoat, with a grimy beret pulled down flat over her old head, and leaning menacingly on her cane, blocked the way.

"Why you should go out in the pouring rain with a child that has not been well is beyond me. You young people take your blessings for granted! My poor hubby and I were not so fortunate. How we would have loved to have a child of our own. But you, Mrs. Potter, think nothing of gallivanting with that poor, tired baby in all kinds of weather—"

"Mrs. Falconer, thank you for opening the door, we'll go in now—"

"I'm not finished with you yet, young woman!" Her cold blue eyes fairly popped out of their crafty bed of wrinkles, and her mouth was curling unpleasantly about the perfect china teeth. . . .

"Now, you listen to me . . ." she went on.

"*Now you listen to me*—" Jessica heard herself interrupt. "You will not harass me this way. We're getting soaked out here, and you rant on about how *I'm* mistreating my child. I don't know why you're so hostile, but my conscience is perfectly clear—your behavior is entirely unprovoked."

Mrs. Falconer sputtered. She raised her hand. *My God,* Jessica thought, *she means to hit me!*

She went on desperately, "You are our landlady. We are your tenants. We pay you rent so that we can live here. The rent is paid. Now let us live here in peace. Otherwise—"

"Go ahead and leave then! You come here and wreck my beautiful things, steal my treasures, ruin my walls, hold noisy parties, dash in and out, call me up at all hours. . . ." She ran down.

"Mrs. Falconer, you are simply not being rational. Please leave us alone." Jessica edged her way past the old woman—close enough to smell her body odor—and was at the Porter entrance. She gave Patience a tug and they both tumbled in the door together. As Jessica pulled the door behind her, it was suddenly—and with surprising force—wrenched from her hand. And with one swift, irrevocable step, Mrs. Falconer gained entrance behind them.

Chapter 14

HAD Jessica not been so angry, she might have noticed that she was more frightened than she'd ever been before. Just moments ago this mad old woman had raised her hand as though to hit her. Now she had forced her way into their apartment. What did she want of them?

"For God's sake, what do you want of us?" she asked, facing Mrs. Falconer, but turning from her almost at once, not expecting an answer. With an irritable, absent-minded gesture, Jessica switched on the light and moved further into the apartment. Most important of all was getting Patience out of the way and safely into bed. She headed toward the kitchen—let the old woman follow, if she must. Still leading Patience by the hand, she turned the kitchen light on, too. Automatically she reached for the teakettle and put some water on to boil. Patience she picked up and perched on the wide windowsill. She faced the door, and there the old woman stood—now brightly lit and doubly disconcerting to behold.

How could somebody so old seem so menacing? Despite her apparent great age, Mrs. Falconer was large, and there was a curious strength about her person. Her head was large, and her large eyes—now protruding wildly—darted avidly from one side of the kitchen to the other. Her arms were quite long, and looked strong, and there was considerable bulk to the body. The more

Jessica looked at Mrs. Falconer, the less confident she became. *This woman could kill us both if she wanted to . . . I wouldn't know what to do to stop her!* Just as these desperate thoughts were beginning to get the better of her, the teakettle began to sing.

Mrs. Falconer's wild eyes underwent an immediate change. Her face, now more composed, seemed smaller, almost refined. She patted the awful dead-white bristles of hair that poked out from beneath the filthy beret on her head, and with a benign little smile, said, "Now, wouldn't a good cup of tea be just the thing!"

Why, she's nutty as a fruitcake! Jessica marveled, almost with relief.

"I'll have it ready in just a second, Mrs. Falconer," she replied, as matter-of-factly as she could manage. Taking her cue from the abrupt change in Mrs. Falconer's behavior, Jessica became, despite her extreme fatigue and irritation, every inch the sociable hostess. She prepared to preside over an impromptu, forcibly imposed tea party.

She selected good cups and good spoons, brought out a hideous but valuable silver server, and seated the malodorous old woman in the living room.

"Now, you just sit tight, Mrs. Falconer, I won't be a minute. I have to put the baby to bed." She'd given Patience a quick peanut-butter-and-jelly sandwich while she set up the tea, and now, with a full bottle to accompany her, the exhausted child was close to sleep.

"Why don't you light some of these lovely candles, my dear?" Mrs. Falconer chirped when Jessica reentered the room. "They make one feel so festive and are so kind to our complexions."

Jessica obliged. *Now that she's calmed down, how am I ever going to get rid of her?* It was after eight o'clock. Mrs. Falconer dipped greedily into Jessica's hastily assembled tray of Oreos and Fig Newtons. She proceeded to devour every last morsel with labored gentility. Had Jessica but known it, she would have savored the relative silence of the old woman's voracious feed. Because once she stopped eating and began to talk, the monologue was to continue unabated for several hours. Jessie prepared successive pots of stronger and stronger tea, in hopes of staying wider awake and more alert than the loquacious adversary on her couch.

"Yes, all of Frederick's people were common, my dear, common as dirt. Where did you learn to brew such excellent tea? I thought the art had all but died away. But we Cavendishes are a proud old New York state name. There are streets named after my father and my grandfather up around Utica and Rome. Still, Frederick set his cap for me, and he did have a way about him! Another branch of the family—the Oliphants, on my mother's side—are prominent from Buffalo to Burlington, from the canal trade to railroads. Yes, I was properly reared. How many people can truly lay claim to a gentle upbringing in this terrible day and age, my dear? My coming-out at Saratoga was a social event of national importance. You can well imagine how appalled my father was when I announced my intention to become a student of nursing! It was an unheard-of ambition for a refined young woman. We had just returned from my grand tour of the European capitals. There we stood amidst the hustle and bustle of New York's busy port— the *Mauretania,* we'd sailed on—and I said, 'Papa, I shall not return to Springvale Farm'—that was the family residence, perhaps you have seen pictures of it in the rotogravure—'I am going to attend the Bellevue Hospital School of Nursing.'"

On and on she droned, barely acknowledging Jessica's presence, yet all the while riveting her with a set stare. Occasionally Jessica tried to stem the flow, but as the night wore on she tried less and less, because she was obviously not going to succeed. Mrs. Falconer repeated herself often; though each time the details varied. If there were any consistent thread to her thrice-told tales, it was, at least, her upstate New York origin and her halcyon days as a student of nursing. Although even the actual school she attended would be hard to pin down.

At one point, when Jessica's eyes were beginning to close in spite of herself, Mrs. Falconer suddenly snapped her fingers with alacrity. Startled, Jessica's heavy eyes opened wide, and she heard Mrs. Falconer say, "Why, I just remembered, I have some lovely photographs taken when I was a student nurse at New York Hospital. If you'll wait here a minute or two, I'll be happy to show them to you!"

"Oh, Mrs. Falconer, I wouldn't dream of asking you to go all the way upstairs at this late hour, only to come back down again. Why don't you show me your photos in the morning, when we've both had a good night's sleep?" A huge yawn escaped unbidden from her mouth.

Once again the dark blue eyes protruded. The flinty stare again became a threat.

"Surely I am not boring you, young lady?"

"Not at all, Mrs. Falconer. It is your own welfare that concerns me. I'd hate to see you climb all those steps—you use a cane, after all, it must be painful . . ."

"Pshaw! This cane . . ." She leaned toward Jessica confidingly, a conspiratorial gleam in her eye. "If I were to tell you my little secret, would you promise not to breathe a word of it to any living soul?"

"Of course."

"My legs are as good as yours, young lady; though I'm many times your age!"

"Then why—"

"Frederick had this cane made specially to order, many years ago." She patted it lovingly and held it aloft for Jessica to admire. "There's more to this cane than hickory burls, my dear. . . ." She nodded knowingly at Jessica, though Jess didn't quite know what was being imparted to her with such import.

"Yes, indeed, more than meets the eye! As long as I have Frederick's trusty cane, I feel perfectly safe in this wicked world." She laughed gleefully and slapped her knee.

Jessica merely nodded and murmured, "How nice."

"So don't worry about the Falconer legs, young lady; they'll make it upstairs and back in jig time." Up she stood, and out she went, with a wicked giggle. At the door she stopped and looked rakishly over her shoulder.

"Now don't go away . . . I'll be right back!"

Where is Sam? Why doesn't he come home and rescue me? I can't keep her out now, she'd go insane with rage if I were to lock the door in her face! Inexorably, just three minutes later, the cane's clumping was heard once again to descend, and Mrs. Falconer came breezing gaily in with her precious photographs clutched importantly to her chest.

The photos were mounted on heavy cardboard, and the photographic studio's name, *"Simmons and Halstead, 127 East 14th Street, New York City—Photographers to the Best Families,"* was stamped ornately in gold leaf at the bottom. Jessica held the photos in her hand, realizing they must be more than sixty years old. A pale young girl, dressed in the nunnish habit nurses wore in those days—starchily aproned and crisply coiffed—faced the photographer with level-eyed determination. When Jessica recovered from her initial amazement at the pre-World War I vintage of the photos, she studied the strange young face in the photo. There was absolutely nothing in it to suggest the assemblage of wrinkled old flesh now before her. Time had apparently been cruel to Mrs. Falconer. As cruel as she herself might be. Was there in fact a correlation? Somebody'd once said to her that the face you have at forty is the face you have earned. Doubly true, it seemed to Jessica, at eighty! She made appropriate gushing noises and admired each photo in turn.

"They're charming, Mrs. Falconer. I'm sure you must be very, very proud of these lovely mementos."

Mrs. Falconer, satisfied with Jessica's sincerity, whisked the photos back. Then she reached into her dress once again and withdrew some papers.

"By the way," she said, "you really ought to go down to the post office and tell them where you live. I have been getting mail that is addressed to you and your hubby. It's such a bother." She smiled at Jessica and handed her a bunch of envelopes.

"But how can this be, Mrs. Falconer? We've received other mail since we've been here. Our mailbox is down on Granite Terrace . . . yours is up on Maynard. It doesn't seem at all likely that the post office would . . ."

Mrs. Falconer drew herself up to her full height and cleared her throat dramatically. It was enough to interrupt Jessica's mild and rather tired attempt at argument.

"Well, you know how things are today, my dear; nothing works the way it should . . . the post office least of all."

Jessica gave up. She took the mail from Mrs. Falconer. A quick glance told her there was nothing much of interest there . . . just bills and advertisements.

She heard a noise on the porch steps. It was Sam!

"Well, Mrs. Falconer, this has certainly been . . . interesting. . . . Now, here's my husband, coming home from work."

Mrs. Falconer rose swiftly.

"We must have tea together again some day. I am afraid your husband and I do not see eye to eye. I will leave now without causing you any embarrassment."

She sauntered off and casually went to the hotly contested side door, opened it, and walked up the steps without another word. Her use of the side door—more than that: the *way* she used it, as though she'd been doing it for years and would go right on doing so—was the crowning blow. Jessie's mouth was still agape with dumbfounded fury when Sam came in.

"What a day!" Sam said, throwing off his coat, his tie, and unbuttoning his shirt as he collapsed on the recently vacated sofa. He did not notice the tea service or even the candles, now burned low and beginning to flicker and gutter brightly. Jessica blew them all out.

"Say, where the hell were you . . . I kept trying to call you and you never answered the phone."

"It's a long story, I'm afraid. Can I get you something? You look exhausted."

"Christ, it's after eleven. And I *must* get into the office early tomorrow. Pierre is really putting the pressure on. I'm just hanging in there, Jess. We need that paycheck. I spent the entire day going over his bookkeeping system with two of the ugliest, nastiest, most irritating old broads. If I tried to describe one of the petty little scenes . . . well, you wouldn't believe it." He paused to yawn and scratch his head vigorously. "You know what would be nice, though? A good cup of tea." Jessie muffled her cry of dismay.

As he sipped his tea, Sam explained his stopgap strategy to Jessica.

"I'm going to give Pierre everything I've got, Jess. Just on the off chance that I may have misjudged him. I'm going to be everything he claims he wants me to be. I'm going to come in early, leave late, and work weekends, too, if need be. Even so, I don't think this job is going to pan out. But the longer I stick with it, the better off we'll be. Any other job I might get now would mean quite a drop in pay."

"Who knows, Sam, maybe you two are just having an adjustment problem . . . it may all blow over. Why, you could be there for years and years." In her eagerness she'd overstated the case.

"God! I don't think I could stand it!" They both laughed.

"Poor baby—you never should have left the theater."

"Poor baby, yourself—you never should have married an actor." It was not until Sam was already half asleep that he turned to Jessie and asked once more, "Say, where in hell *were* you today?"

Jessica told him. She made the trip into the city sound smooth and effortless and put a rosy complexion on Dr. Weller's prognosis. She didn't say anything about the postcard or about her most recent scene with the old woman upstairs. As she described Dr. Weller's plan for Patience—"So, he wants me to keep a written record of everything she says and does . . . like a journal. He thinks she may give us some clues, unconsciously"—she heard Sam drop off into the measured, sonorous breathing that announced deep sleep.

Now why did I do that? she wondered. Tired, but hyped into sleeplessness by all those endless cups of tea, she spoke quietly into the darkened room. "Why didn't I tell him how the day really went? Why didn't I tell him that I'm scared out of my wits . . . that this place is a *nightmare* . . . that I want to get the hell out of here!"

Chapter 15

A man of his word, Sam left the house on Granite Terrace early on Tuesday morning. Jessica was still half asleep when he kissed her good-bye. But once he'd gone, she found she couldn't stay in bed. With the resilience normal to her twenty-four years, she felt pretty good. She enjoyed a warm shower, and her eyes still took delight in the charming Edwardian details of the bathroom. There was a tantalizing atmosphere about this place—as elusive as a wisp of fragrance that brings back an all-but-forgotten memory—an atmosphere of solidity and continuity. The very walls, with their lavish, well-joined moldings, the lovely parquetry on the floors, all denoted a congenial, civilized refinement. It was possible to forget her fears and worries for large chunks of time, and Jessica willingly allowed these interludes of contentment to ensnare her. After all, it wasn't the house she felt so threatened by; it was the crazy old woman who owned it. At some time in the past people had been happy here. She knew it. And at some time in the future she, too, would know that kind of happiness. That was her goal. A serene, elegant warmth would pervade her own home someday. If not here, well, then somewhere else. She went into the kitchen, to find the remains of last night's bizarre tea party. Oh, well. So this wasn't the place she'd dreamed of. Yet maybe their move here wouldn't prove a total loss. Hadn't it provided them with a glimpse of something worthwhile—something they'd both once wanted very much? Sam's new schedule meant they weren't seeing very much of one another these days. Perhaps that was why they hadn't had one of those awful quarrels in quite some time.

It was a mild late October day. The rain had cleared, and the air was fresh, with that smoky, leafy scent to it that Jessica found most appealing. The sparkling Hudson, now more visible than ever with so many leaves gone, caused her to walk out on the big porch just to gaze at it. Patience joined her. Jessica picked her up and let her share the splendid view.

"Isn't it a beautiful day! Let's go to the park early and enjoy it."

"Out!" Patience concurred.

Soon after nine o'clock she and Patience were walking cheerfully down Maynard en route to the park. It wasn't an average posh suburb, Wimbledon. What made it expensive, really, was a trick of fate. The river had been there all along; but in the days when New York City was a more acceptable place to raise a family, it had not been all that sought-after. These quaint little Wimbledon cottages, built at the turn of the century to suit a much earlier generation of bucolic types, had now become prized suburban real estate, valued far beyond such ordinary criteria as square footage or modern plumbing. Today the modest cottages exuded a sense of smug exclusivity. "We've made it," the glistening, carefully-curtained windows seemed to announce to passers-by. "Keep off the zoysia grass!"

As Jessica pushed the stroller along, she had the sense of walking through a deserted 1930's Hollywood set. As the movie opened, a window would be raised, dotted-swiss curtains would part, and a pert Rosalind

Russell (Jean Arthur?) would call a smiling greeting to dapper young Cary Grant (Fredric March?) as he came whistling briskly up the walk, wearing a rakish fedora hat, and swinging his briefcase.

That scene just didn't play anymore; if ever it had. Jessica saw only an occasional desultory toddler, riding a tricycle or digging quietly in a manicured play area. No chatty neighbors hanging the wash. No postman walking up the front steps, stopping for a bit of gossip. Just a few discreet delivery vans. Hudson House Cleaning Service. Davey's Dairy. Kurtz's Quality Meats.

When Jessica arrived at the park she saw that she was indeed early. There were few other mothers on the benches, few children on the playing fields. The tennis courts alone were heavily trafficked. Such energy! The women, already perspiring fiercely, were playing with savage intensity. They seemed comical to Jess, who had played the game with some skill at college. They had all the equipment and all kinds of determination. But they didn't play the game. They were just running around competitively, missing the whole point. *Slam! Plop! Whoosh!*

"Ooops, sorry!"

"My ball."

"Your serve."

"Nice shot."

They talked a lot, too. She sat back, brooding, watching a passive Patience playing dully in the sandbox. How long would she be like this? How permanent was the damage? She closed her eyes for a minute, to keep worse thoughts from forming. She sensed somebody sitting down heavily beside her. Mary? No. A stranger. The woman, tall and carefully dressed, had what Jessica was already calling "The Wimbledon Look." Two parts intelligence to one part naked greed. Educated women, who, having made ambitious marriages, spent the rest of their days competitively clocking milestones of progress among themselves. It gave their pursed mouths two little telltale lines, and their restless, darting eyes seemed perpetually alert for dreaded flaws that might threaten their game plan for the next fiscal year. Jessica knew the woman would talk—there were plenty of empty benches if she had wanted privacy.

"There they are again!" she whispered.

"Who?" Jessie inquired politely.

"Over there. They've taken over that whole corner of the park. The nerve! We pay the taxes, and they get the benefits."

"I don't know what you're talking about."

"They live in *Yonkers*. They have no business using our parks. This playground is for *Wimbledon residents only*. I thought once I'd gotten that sign put up it would stop all this. But you can see it doesn't do any good at all. They probably don't read English. Something must be done!"

"What harm are they doing?" Jessica really wanted to know. She'd never noticed the people who were causing such anguish to the woman. And if they hadn't been pointed out to her now, she probably never would have noticed them.

"Just look at them! They come for the whole day. Pack god-awful picnic lunches, sit there talking that hideous Spanish they talk. I moved away from the city just to avoid this sort of thing."

"Pity." Jessica decided not to say another word.

"Oh, you're one of those bleeding-heart liberals, huh? Well, you'll feel differently when one of those Spanish hippies knifes *you* down." When Jessica didn't reply, the woman turned to her disdainfully and tried a parting shot: "How much do you want to bet that when they get to the bottom of the Kelly murder, they find it's a Puerto Rican dope addict from Yonkers?"

Jessica decided to move to another bench. She gave the woman her best Girl Scout smile, stood up, and said mildly, "If you have any inside information pertaining to the murder, I think you owe it to the police to tell them about it." She left without a backward glance and selected another bench on the other side of the sandbox. Before long, to Jessica's relief, Mary and Violet Smith came through the gate and joined her.

"Beautiful day!" Mary greeted her. Violet joined Patience in the sandbox. Patience smiled at her but didn't speak. She wasn't getting any better! If only she would show a little of her old spark! Jessie realized that Mary was watching her with something approaching clinical concern. No wonder, she could feel the tears welling up in her eyes. To distract herself, she asked Mary, "I've been wondering, do they all go so nutty over tennis here because the place is called Wimbledon . . . or is it called Wimbledon because they happen to have so many tennis courts?"

"Neither. It's just a coincidence. I never thought of it before. Come to think of it, if I were a more dedicated tennis player, I'd probably have more friends. But it's not just Wimbledon, really. It's all over Westchester. Physical fitness, I guess."

"Now there's a good name—Physical Fitness-on-Hudson. I like it!"

Mary laughed. "So tell it to the Chamber of Commerce. What else is new?"

She meant with Patience, Jessica realized, but, alas, there was nothing to report. Instead she gave Mary a blow-by-blow account of her evening's misadventures. When she got to the part about the photos, she tried to convey how horribly Mrs. Falconer had aged.

"How strange! Do you think she was crazy even way back then?"

"And that cane, Mary, what did she mean about that? Do you think it's hollow and contains hootch?"

"Could be. Next time you're close to her, smell her breath!"

"Ugh! No, thank you." They were laughing again. But Jessica grew serious almost at once.

"We can laugh about her out here, in the sunshine, six blocks away. But I've about had it, Mary. What with Sam having his own problems with Pierre and all—I've never been so lonely and scared in my life."

"Why not give that creepy place a rest for the day, Jess? Come have lunch with us. It'll be a nice change for Patience, too. And if you're willing to consider it, I know of a vacancy in town ..."

"Well, yes, to lunch. As for house-hunting ... I don't know. Maybe later. We'll see. I'm still recovering from our last move, you know. It was only two weeks ago, believe it or not!" Jessica felt very tired.

"My God, you're right! So much has happened since then, it seems longer. By the way, have you heard the latest on the Kelly murder?"

"That charming creature sitting across the way just gave me her thoughts on the subject," Jessica replied, her voice rather sarcastic. "She's convinced it's 'one of those awful Puerto Rican dope addicts from Yonkers.'"

Mary looked across at Jessie's former companion. "Oh, her. She's one of those people who goes around with petitions to be signed all the time. I think that every time she has her period she discovers a new threat to her valuable Wimbledon real estate: two acres with river view, and the most ticky-tacky ranch house you've ever set eyes on. Seriously, I think they're getting close to solving the murder. With all your Falconer problems,

I haven't talked to you about the murder. But, boy, that's all anybody's been talking about all week!"

"Do they have a suspect now?" Jessica's interest was merely perfunctory, but she could see Mary wanted to talk about it.

"No, they haven't. That's just it. There's a lot of pressure in the village. The story is, there's a special police inspector been assigned to call on just about everybody Miss Kelly ever knew. Seeing as she lived in Wimbledon all her life—that means practically the entire older population."

"Wow. You'd think they'd have more than that to go on by now. Does George have any more theories?"

"He has a feeling they're actually getting close to making an arrest. Remember that computer business we were all talking about at your party? I didn't understand it—computers tend to intimidate me—but George says it's got to be somebody connected with Copper-Cable, somebody who was threatened by all these payroll records being automated."

"Poor old Nora Kelly . . . she was killed the first night we spent in Wimbledon. What a way to start out—with a gory murder! That alone should have warned me what we were in for. It was like an omen somehow." Jessica was growing morbid. .

"Enough of that! Come on now, we'll pick something up in town for lunch, and you'll spend the afternoon with us." Mary was concerned about Jess. She looked drawn and nervous, seemed to be overreacting to things.

Detective Sergeant Michael Patrick Orsini stood at the top of Maynard Street and looked down on the steps leading up from Granite Terrace. The Falconer name had come up more than once in his investigation of the late Nora Kelly. That made it twice as interesting to him as some of the thirty-odd other names on his list. They'd only come up once. If quiet, dignified Nora Kelly—mainstay of the CopperCable accounting department, paragon of the Wimbledon library committee— had had a secret life, one of the names on this list would know it. He'd been ringing the bell for several minutes now, off and on, and it didn't look as though he was going to be let in.

He had with him a fairly fat folder, filled with complaints lodged against Mrs. Frederick Falconer by a succession of hapless tenants who simply ended up breaking their leases and were never heard from again. The complaints made interesting reading. He sat down on a stump.

8/1/72 Complainant states Mrs. Frederick Falconer harrassed her four-year-old son. Ran after him with a garden rake and accused him of stealing her false teeth.

10/15/70 Tenant claims Mrs. Falconer sneaks into their rental apartment at night. When they turn on the light she disappears through a connecting stairway. Investigating Officer Murphy found stairway bolted on both sides. Mrs. Falconer, upon questioning, denied ever having gone to tenant's apartment. Claimed bad leg made stairs very difficult. Accused tenants of being drunkards.

12/6/69 Dr. and Mrs. Reeves of 38 Granite Terrace filed a formal complaint against Mrs. Frederick Falconer. Insist her mental instability poses a threat to safety of neighborhood. Asked especially that she be forced to undergo a special driving test. Investigating Officer Tremont discovered Mrs. Falconer's 1949 Pontiac had driven over Mrs. Reeves' prized bayberry hedge. Driving test was administered 1/5/70. Mrs. Falconer passed.

157

On and on. All the way back to the late fifties. Nobody ever seemed to pin her down. Obviously she was one very slick operator. And obviously she was as nutty as they come.

Detective Sergeant Orsini had been sitting on the stump in Mrs. Falconer's side yard for about ten minutes when he saw what he'd been waiting for. Mary Smith's big station wagon pulled up and deposited Jessie and Patience. Orsini watched Jessica and Patience grow from little to big as they mounted the steps to the porch door and went inside. He left his patrol car parked where it was and slowly walked down Granite Terrace and up the many steps. Detective Sergeant Orsini, an amateur photographer, admired the setting. He thought he could understand that pathetic parade of unwitting tenants who tangled with a crazy old lady just to live in a setting like this. When he reached the porch, the river view was nothing short of astonishing. The red, spiky leaves on the huge old Japanese maple tree, which were protected by the house and had not yet begun to fall, made the sergeant long for his Hasselblad. He noticed the old-fashioned key-shaped bell to the side of the door.

"Haven't seen one of those since old Aunt Zelma sold her place on Mulberry Street." He turned it.

The raucous summons almost caused Jessie to stick Patience with a diaper pin. Patience was in diapers all the time now. Jessie had bought a spiral-bound notebook with Mary—at Murphy's—and when they got to the Smith house, she sat down and filled six pages with notes about Patience's behavior. When she'd read over what she'd written, she had to accept the fact that Patience was not improving in any way. Indeed, it had seemed to Jessie that her passivity, speechlessness, and general lackluster attitude were getting worse. Especially when they were here in the apartment. The change in her seemed almost physical. She moved as though some invisible current made movement difficult. As soon as they got in the house, Jessie noticed the dark stain that announced a change of diapers was needed. Maneuvering the baby to change her was far from easy —she was stiff and cumbersome. So, when the buzzer sounded, Jessica jumped. She was upset enough already. Patience, startled, began to howl.

Jessica dropped the diaper and picked up the baby. "There, there! It's all right." So, carrying the bare-bottomed, wailing child, Jessica opened the porch door for Sergeant Orsini.

"How do you do, ma'am. Detective Sergeant Orsini, Yonkers Third Precinct." He flashed his badge. "I was wondering if you could tell me how to get in touch with your landlady, Mrs. Falconer. Does she still reside on the premises?"

"Come in, please. You startled us ringing that old bell." As it was still mild, they sat down on wicker chairs on the screened porch.

"Beautiful view," Orsini remarked.

"Yes, it is," Jessica agreed. Patience, still bare, wandered off into the apartment. "Why do you want Mrs. Falconer?" Before he could answer, she added, "The reason I'm asking is that I almost went to the police myself yesterday but had to take my child to the doctor instead."

"She's giving you trouble, huh?"

"I don't even know how much of what has gone wrong is her . . . I—oh, it's a long story, and rather muddled —maybe you'd better tell me what you're after, first; you'd probably just think I'm some kind of a nut case. . . ."

"This has to do with the investigation of the Kelly murder, Mrs. . . ."

"Porter. Jessica Porter."

"I want to ask Mrs. Falconer a few questions, that's all. It was Mr. Falconer who was acquainted with Miss Kelly; but we're checking everyone who knew her. Mr. Falconer died more than ten years ago, I believe?"

"Sergeant, er, Orsini, we've only been here for two weeks. In fact, poor Miss Kelly must have been killed the first night after we moved in. I don't know anything about Mrs. Falconer except that she's completely mad, and frankly, officer, I'm afraid of her."

Jessica found the whole erractic story of their two weeks as tenants tumbling out of her. Part of her felt that the police officer must think she was hysterical, but once she'd begun, she found she couldn't stop. Orsini, quite the contrary, primed by the accounts he'd just read in the fat Falconer folder, felt sympathy for Jessica and wished there was something he could do to help. Her story made little sense, it was true; but a child's welfare was obviously at stake.

"Mrs. Porter, I can only suggest you file a complaint and start looking for another place to live." He indicated the folder. "This is full of other complaints against Mrs. Falconer. She hasn't broken any law that we know of, if that's any help. This apartment has passed inspection time and time again. I would like to question her about her husband's old friendship with Miss Kelly. Does she ever answer her bell? Is she a recluse or what?"

"Try phoning her first. That's what I did when she locked us out of the house with those damn bolts and locks of hers. But I don't think she'd agree to talk to the police—she's really crazy . . . paranoid, maybe. Good luck. Thank you for listening to me, although I don't think I really told it right. I hope you solve your murder." Jessica's voice was trembling; she was far more shaken than she herself realized. The officer looked at the slight, pale, pretty young woman and wondered, absently, what she looked like when she was happy.

"Well, we've got quite a few men on it now—I won't solve it all by myself, that's for sure."

"I've been so upset by what's happened to us since we've moved here, I keep forgetting there's a murderer loose."

"Thank you for your help, Mrs. Porter. And, look, if Mrs. Falconer gives you any more trouble, you might get in touch with old Ralph Newcomb. He serves as the Wimbledon building inspector, even though he has a full-time job in the city. Here's his number; he lives close by, on Riverview." He wrote down Newcomb's number and address and handed it to her. "If she's as old and crazy as you say, and as all these complaints attest, there may be some legal means to prevent her from renting this place again." He departed briskly down the steps.

Jessica, rattled by the way she'd tried to enlist the police officer's help, sat down once again on the wicker chair. "I didn't get any of it right! I didn't show him the cigar stub . . . when I said 'Tweetie,' he probably didn't know what on earth I was talking about. And I never even mentioned that sordid pornographic doll we found in Patience's crib!" Where was that awful doll now? What had they done with it after the party? She couldn't think. Patience's illness was affecting her normally logical, well-ordered mind. She couldn't, for the life of her, recall what she or Sam had done with the hideous doll that had, in fact, begun the whole fearful series of events. She herself had all but forgotten it, until just now. Repressed it, most likely. The more she thought about it, the more convinced she became that every single unlikely episode that had occurred since they came to this place was in some way connected. There was a thread linking everything together. And somewhere behind it all, she was certain, loomed Mrs. Frederick Falconer. "We must find that doll." She couldn't wait for Sam to come home to question him about it. They would put it, and the cigar stub, together. Exhibit A and exhibit B. And whose case would it be, finally? Officer Orsini's or Dr. Weller's?

Chapter 16

THAT night Sam managed to come home at a reasonable hour. He walked up Maynard Hill feeling a hint of his former enthusiasm. He hadn't even stopped for a drink. The little hilly streets were dark, but now that they were more familiar to him, the few lights that peeked through the shrubbery and hedges and the metallic, luminous sheen of the omnipresent Hudson gave him all the light he needed.

He'd be home by seven. They would eat dinner together like a family. Jessica would be pleased. And Patience, his own dear Patience, poor thing, she'd be pleased to see her daddy.

The porch door was open, every light in the place on.

"Jessie? I'm home." No answer. Sam looked around, conscious of a peculiar disorderliness. Every drawer and cabinet had been left open; old packing boxes were out of the closets into which they'd been stored. Good God! Had they been robbed?

"Jessica? I'm home! Are you all right? What's going on?"

Jessica scurried into the room, smudged, harried, preoccupied.

"Sam, you're home early. Thank goodness. I've been going out of my skull trying to find that awful Kewpie doll. It should be our exhibit A. That cigar butt is exhibit B. I've looked *everywhere*. What did we do with it the

163

night of the party? I can't remember seeing it again after it jumped at Dorcas. I remember cleaning up the kitchen with Sarah and Mary—we put everything away, but I don't recall seeing the doll. Did you put it somewhere? It's important."

"Exhibit A, exhibit B? What in hell's been going on here? How long have you been looking for it?" Jessica explained about Detective Orsini's visit and how she'd tried to enlist his assistance.

". . . and it wasn't until after he'd left that I remembered about the doll, Sam. All of a sudden I realized it was important. I have this weird feeling that it can prove something—God only knows what. Then I couldn't find it, not anywhere. I've gone over everything. It's simply not here."

"Jessica, give me a moment, huh? I just got home, and I'm a little tired. I don't know what it is about you and Patience; it seems like every time I turn around one or the other of you is missing a doll."

"That's not funny, Sam."

"I'm sorry, I guess I need a drink. What do we have?"

"There's just enough gin left for one good martini. I'll fix it for you. Why don't you go change and let your subconscious mind work out what you did with the doll, okay?"

They didn't find the doll. Sam vaguely recalled placing it on top of the refrigerator the night of the party. Sam, who was over six feet tall, found the top of the refrigerator a most convenient surface to put things down on. This irritated Jessica, who was five feet three and thus could never see what was up there. Often the only way she discovered that Sam had once again booby-trapped the fridge was when the object—a melon, perhaps, or a thick cookbook or, on one painful occasion, a ketchup bottle—hit her resoundingly on the head as she innocently opened the door.

It would have been perfectly possible for the doll to have remained on top of the refrigerator all this time, unnoticed and undisturbed. But it was not there. Jessie thought she knew where it was. But she said no more about it to Sam. A plan was forming in her mind that frightened her.

Sam, exhausted from his day's work, went to bed right after their rather meager supper of salad and soup.

Jessica was still thinking about her plan the next morning. She was amazed at the stubbornness with which it adhered to her startled imagination. She knew that sooner or later she would be bound to follow it; but fortunately she wasn't compelled to do it just yet.

Mary called and once again mentioned that there was a house in town that would be available soon at a reasonable rent, if Jessie were interested. Jessie told her she'd think about it. They agreed to meet at the park that afternoon. It was another splendid fall day. Sam called, saying he'd been given an evening assignment and would spend the night with the Tarpinians, rather than try to catch the last train to Wimbledon. Jessie agreed mildly. The prospect of being alone in the apartment didn't seem to worry her. Sam's troubles were so different from her own these days that they simply weren't on the same wavelength. Maybe a night with the Tarpinians was just what Sam needed to cheer him up.

Patience followed her about the house as she did a cursory cleaning up. She put some laundry together to do at the village laundromat, packed a lunch for Patience, and was getting ready to leave, when, at noon, the phone rang.

It was her brother, Tom. He was leaving for his new European job Saturday, could he drive his Volkswagen up for them today?

Jessica was thrilled. Wheels at last. She gave him careful directions to Wimbledon and 33 Granite Terrace.

"I can be there by four, Jess, it'll be nice to see you again."

"Will you stay for dinner?" As she extended the invitation, she wondered how she could keep from confiding all their troubles to him over dinner. He was only two years younger than she was, and they'd always been close. One drink and she'd spill the beans for sure . . . and what would Tom be able to do about any of it? Not a thing.

"Gee, no, Jess. I'd have liked that, but with only three days in New York, I'm booked solid already, you understand." Just as well. Let him start his own life without any of her unsettled questions gnawing at him. And the car would be wonderful to have! She looked at the pile of laundry she'd been about to push downhill in Patience's stroller and grinned. From now on, all those errands could be done by car.

Tom arrived at the dot of four, just minutes after Patience and Jessie had returned from the park. They must have looked the picture of brimful health, eyes sparkling and cheeks reddened by the brisk fall air. It was so good to see him again! Jessica and Patience babbled excitedly and Tom, a genial extrovert, accepted the fuss as nothing more than his due. The only other time he had seen Patience was when she was a tiny baby, so her new condition was not apparent to him. Jessica said nothing about it. Over two beers Tom described his new job, chided Jessica for not writing often enough to their parents in Ohio, and inquired about Sam.

"Is he still acting, Jess?" There was an edge of condescension in his voice.

"No. He gave that up, Tom. When Patience was born. He has a new job at the moment; it's too early to tell whether it's the right one, yet." Jessica was defensive.

"I like Sam. He's a lot of fun. But, you know, when the two of you got married, I was never more surprised. I'm glad to see you're making a go of it—this certainly is a terrific place you've got here. Maybe all Sam needed was a sensible little sobersides like you to make him settle down." Tom smiled.

"Sensible little sobersides! Why, Thomas Vernon Ludlow—how dare you! That's how you see me, is it? I guess you figured I'd marry an accountant."

"Yeah, or an orthodontist."

She threw a pillow at him, and his beer glass tipped over. No harm. It was empty. He got up, laughing, protesting his good intentions.

"Hey, I've got to go. Let me tell you what you need to know about my dimpled darling in the driveway. She's got at least another thirty thousand miles in her . . . and you can have them all. If the car expires while I'm gone, never mind. I hope to pick up a Porsche on my return trip."

"Gads! To be young, good-looking, and rich all at the same time—how you can stand yourself, I don't know." Jessica loved the car on sight: from its rusty front fenders to its dented rear. The car definitely had personality. She and Patience drove Tom to the Wimbledon station, joking all the way. Much of the laughter had to do with Jessica's awkwardness with the manual gearshift, but she remembered it all soon enough. Jessica was so glad to have the car and happy to have seen her easygoing, familiar, dependable brother. For the first time in months she felt as though her feet were touching solid ground.

Their return to 33 Granite Terrace, though, was a terrible letdown. Jessica wished Sam were coming home. She wanted to show him their car, tell him her brother's news. The house was very empty. When she heard Mrs. Falconer clumping upstairs, Jessica remembered the brave plan she'd been formulating earlier and was appalled. She could never do it. What could she have been thinking of! That doll could just stay up there. Never mind about it. Tomorrow, she'd take Mary up on her suggestion and look at that house for rent. The sooner they left this place, the better.

While Patience sat placidly in her high chair eating dinner, Jessica took out the spiral notebook she was keeping for Dr. Weller and began to bring it up to date.

Oct. 20th: Patience played contentedly in the park. She is still wearing diapers. I have made no effort to get her to use the bathroom again. She eats well. Her eyes have a guarded look. She seems to stay closer to me every day. She does not play alone in her room the way she used to. The new Tweetie is with her all the time, but she doesn't play with her. It's just an object, like a security blanket. She likes to laugh, and will laugh whenever I do—but there doesn't seem to be much comprehension, just a kind of nervous release of tension.

Jessica paused. The house was so quiet. The only sounds she heard were distant cars and the gentle rustling of nearby trees in the light evening breeze. She hated keeping this journal. It forced her to think about things the pressure of daily living made it possible for her to ignore. She wondered, guiltily, whether this distaste for the job was interfering with the accuracy it called for. Would any of these pages contain a significant clue for Dr. Weller's hocus pocus?

It was nearly seven. She'd better put Patience to bed and go over the journal again later. As she rose to lift Patience from the high chair the noise of their ridiculous porch doorbell shattered the air. Jessie, taut as a drum, reacted with a violent thudding of her heart. *Who?*

The bell rang again—this time in the familiar dot-dot-

dot-dash rhythm that told her disbelieving ears it must be Pierre. But why?

"Pierre. Dorcas. What an extraordinary surprise! What in the world—"

"Ah, Jessica, *ma petite* . . . we were in the neighborhood . . ."

"You see, Pierre, I told you it would have been considerate to call. Jessie, he simply insisted. It was such a beautiful fall day that Pierre decided to take off into the country. We've rented this enormous American car and have been all over the Catskills. Frankly, I'm simply exhausted! I must look a sight, too, do you mind if I use your . . ."

"By all means, Dorcas, it's right down the hall, next to the kitchen."

"Ooh, yes, your kitchen. I'm not about to forget that in a hurry, am I?" Dorcas giggled and rushed out of the room.

"Dear Jessie, I do hope we're not inconveniencing you. But as we saw the Wimbledon exit on the Saw Mill River Parkway, I thought to myself, 'Jessica is just over the hill, there, all alone. Why shouldn't we drop in?' We bought some beer, and sandwiches, and here we are! There are such terrible places to eat along the way. These awful mass-produced foods. I really cannot bear them. See, I've even got some caviar for you. I thought it would cheer you up to have some company when your hardworking husband has to spend the night in town."

"Well, that's a sweet thought, Pierre. Actually, Patience and I have already eaten. But, I'll tell you what, just let me get her off to bed, and I think I can find some room for that caviar!" Jessica hoped she didn't appear downright hysterical. But then, Pierre was never known for his perception. He probably did this to people all the time.

She accepted his proffered six-packs of Heineken's and

169

several parcels wrapped in butcher paper and took them off to the kitchen. Patience walked over to Pierre and smiled at him.

"Ah, Patience, *comment ça va?* Such a beautiful child." He sat down expansively in the black wing chair and took off his shoes. Jessica had never seen the dapper Pierre in country clothes. He cut quite a dashing figure in well-worn British tweeds and a Fair Isle sweater. Both he and Dorcas had tanned faces. Boy, what a life—just take off when the whim hits you. As long as you've got somebody like Sam to do the grunt work, why not? Jessica wasn't usually bitter. She consciously put a friendly smile on her face and went to collect Patience.

"We won't be but a minute, Pierre. Dorcas, perhaps you'd like to pour the beer while I'm busy with Patience? Oh, by the way, Dorcas, that was a lovely card you sent. Thank you for the thought." As she said it an image of the card's mysterious placement in Patience's window flashed through her mind . . . what would Dorcas have thought of that? Jessica noticed how often, lately, her thoughts were at variance with her actions. It was a strain. Normally she never felt the need to withhold things.

While Jessica busied herself in the baby's room, Dorcas handed Pierre a beer, and he sat back and relaxed, taking generous, thirsty drafts. There had been a reason behind his apparent spur-of-the-moment visit. He was hoping he might yet be able to save a friendship that he'd come to value. Sam's unpredictability at the office and his curious lack of interest in learning the basics of the business had created a painful situation. Pierre could see that having taken on a friend as a business partner might well leave him without the friend—and without a business partner. He'd miss the friend more. Jessica, too. He could see that Dorcas liked her. They might have had such amusing times together. Two couples . . . evenings on the town . . . dinners at each others' homes. He sipped his beer more slowly, now, the first thirst satisfied, and wondered whether the friendship could be saved. He could hear Dorcas and Jessica chatting in the hall.

"Is there anything else I can do to help?" Dorcas was saying. "Would you let me tell your dear little girl a bedtime story?"

Ordinarily Jessica would have jumped at the offer, but now that Patience had changed so much she hated to expose her to strangers.

"What a kind thing to suggest, Dorcas. Only, I think Patience is very tired tonight; we've had quite a day." She hurried Patience on to bed. Dorcas returned to the living room to join Pierre.

Then, as she was tucking the child in, Pierre entered the room.

"Charming!" he declared. He was a large man, and his presence in the room was awkward. Not that he noticed. He sat down in the rocking chair, lit up a Dunhill cigar, and smiled at them both.

"Since I have become a bachelor, I cannot tell you how touching a sight you two present to me. Such gentleness! Such beauty!" He didn't budge.

Patience regarded him levelly. She did not smile; but she seemed fascinated. Pierre, flattered by her attention, walked over to the crib and peered down. His face wore the most excruciatingly inane smile Jessie'd seen in some time.

Pierre leaned over some more, holding the cigar in one hand. With the other he poked at Patience's little middle and began to tickle her. He actually said, "Kootchie coo! Kootchie coo, you adorable little girl!" His tickling continued, as Patience began to scream. Her face grew pale, her eyes popped with terror, and her scream gathered momentum with blood-curdling intensity.

Jessica all but knocked Pierre down in her effort to reach the child.

"Oh, my God," she murmured, "it's starting again!" Pierre, dumbstruck, stepped aside. Patience still screamed. No words, just screams. In Jessica's arms, with a blanket wrapped around her, she began to sob. Her behavior was very much the same as it had been on the awful night her illness had begun.

"What have I done?" Pierre muttered. "What have I done to that poor child?"

"Pierre, it's a complicated story. Patience had a kind of attack last week. I've seen the doctor about it. It's hard to diagnose. I'm sorry this had to happen while you were here, truly. Please don't blame yourself. This may be some kind of breakthrough. Come, let's go into the living room. I'll try to calm her down." The baby's sobbing was so plaintive and noisy Pierre barely understood Jessica's words, but he nodded seriously and headed for the living room.

Dorcas looked miserable. She didn't know what the screams meant. She looked to Pierre for guidance as he entered the room.

"All I did was tickle her. She screamed as though I were beating her. Never in my life have I felt so helpless!" He reached for the fresh glass of beer Dorcas had poured for him and drank it down.

"I'm going to call the doctor. Please don't feel responsible. You're not. She'll be all right. I know this isn't the way you planned it, but won't you just eat your sandwiches now, while I call? She should calm down in a little while; I'll try to explain then. All right?" Though she didn't know where her strength was coming from, Jessica seemed by far the most rational person in the room at that moment. Still carrying Patience, she went to the telephone and dialed Dr. Weller's number. It was seven forty-five, and she got the answering service.

172

"Dr. Weller is out of the office. His hours are Mondays, Wednesdays, and Thursdays from two to four. May I make an appointment?" The mechanical-sounding voice did not seem in the least approachable, but Jessie tried, anyway.

"Where can I reach him *now*? It's important!"

"This is a recording. You may record a message when you hear the beep."

Jessica was so flustered she listened to the silence that followed the beep, realizing that she'd missed her turn. After a while, the message repeated itself.

"Dr. Weller is out of the office. His hours are Mondays, Wednesdays, and Thursdays from two to four. May I make an appointment?" This time, when the beep came, Jessica was ready.

"Dr. Weller!" She fairly screamed into the phone over Patience's cries. "It's Mrs. Porter. Patience is having another crying attack. A visitor's tickling her seemed to bring it on. What should I do for her? Please call me. My phone number is Greenland 7-6342." Exhausted, she hung up. "He may not call the service for hours. What will I do now?" She decided to try Dr. Norris. Dr. Norris used a live answering service, but the girl did not know when Dr. Norris would return from out of town. Would she like the name of another doctor?

"No, thanks, I'm calling from out of town myself." Jessica hung up.

"Jessie, do you have a tranquilizer for her?" Dorcas put her arm around Jessica in kindness and sympathy.

"Well, the last time I used some Phenobarbital drops she'd had since she was a baby, but my doctor said those were no longer right for her and I threw them away. I think you're quite right, Dorcas; she ought to have something to help her."

"Do you want us to stay, dear? Or would you feel better handling this on your own? We'll be glad to drive you

173

to a local doctor, if we can find one that's available. Or maybe you'd like to take her to the hospital?"

"Oh, God, no, I don't think so. Dorcas, I'm so sorry you've had to become involved in this. She did calm down, finally, last time. Maybe you and Pierre had better just get back to the city. I can't tell you how sorry I am your visit turned out so badly. Really, it's nobody's fault." Patience's cries were not letting up. Jessica carried her back into the living room. She'd never seen Pierre look so serious; he looked as though he might cry himself. Jessica couldn't think anymore. She really didn't know whether to ask them to stay and try to help or just to tell them to leave.

Pierre misunderstood her indecision. She'd been standing in the middle of the room, holding the screaming child, when he came over to her and tried to take the child from her, to ease the burden. His gesture toward Patience—and a gesture was all it was, he had not in fact got hold of her—was enough to get her screaming with even renewed force. It was just as horrible as it could be—the child was now screaming directly at him, and it was possible for Jessica to make out some words. Whether or not Pierre understood the words, he did understand that the screams were being directed at him. His Gallic pride was affronted, and misery became outrage.

"Dorcas. It is obvious we are in the way here. There is something wrong in this house. I have wondered about Sam, and now I see there is something to wonder at about the whole family. Come, Dorcas, we must leave."

Dorcas flashed a pathetic, well-meaning smile to Jessica.

"Oh, Pierre, surely you can see that this child is suffering from something that has nothing whatever to do with you. You mustn't take it personally. Jessica, dear, I couldn't be sorrier. This is damned awkward. I think

174

we'd best go. Is there anything we can do? Would you like us to contact Sam for you in the city?"

In the middle of this nightmarish scene, part of Jessica was listening very carefully to Patience's choked screams. She could make out the words. They were what mattered. She mustn't miss any of them. Her intent listening gave her a mad, vacant look. She knew Dorcas was trying to mend fences, but she couldn't divert her attention from Patience even for a minute.

Dorcas hesitated, looking now as though perhaps she might agree with Pierre's "something to wonder at about the whole family." Jessica turned briefly to her and said hurriedly, "Dorcas, I'm sorry—I'm trying to make out what she's saying. Do go. We'll be all right, it's just a matter of time before she calms down. Don't trouble Sam with this—I'll tell him about it when he comes home tomorrow. I'm so sorry." She continued to pat the sobbing child as she spoke.

Pierre whisked Dorcas out of the room. Jessica heard the porch door slam, the big car starting up. And she stood there, in the middle of the living room with her screaming child, wondering when she'd hear from the doctor. Wondering *if* she'd hear from the doctor. And wondering at the meaning of the words she could make out among the cries.

Chapter 17

THE words were: "Bad man. Bad man smell bad. Took Tweetie. Thing on Tweetie. Bad man. Thing out. Gar smell bad."

They didn't all make sense. Jessica was sitting down at the table with the notebook in front of her. Patience, still crying, but possibly not as hard—or was Jessica merely becoming accustomed to it?—was cradled in her arms. With one hand free, Jessica began by putting down phonetically the sounds that Patience made. She was sure about "bad man" . . . "smell bad." "Thing on Tweetie" was a guess. "Thing out" was fairly clear. There was one more phrase she simply couldn't make out. It sounded like "Thing Ween Yog." "Yog?" Perhaps "Yeg?" Anyway she'd recorded it. No more than two or three minutes had passed since she'd sat down.

It had been easier, somehow, the first time. Sam had been with her. And that time it had been in the middle of the night—it seemed more like a nightmare, something that could be safely forgotten by morning. Jessica turned Patience over on her stomach and caressed her back. It was now after eight. She'd been crying for twenty minutes. Would Dr. Weller never call? The way Patience was crying and gasping made Jessie fear she'd literally tear something inside her. The child had reached a stage beyond tears now; there were just spasms of dry, rasping sobs that shook her violently.

The telephone rang.

It was Dr. Weller.

"Jessica. I've just come in. My God, I can hear her crying over the phone. Are you all alone now? Did your visitor leave? How long ago was all this?"

She told him.

"Can you get to a drugstore?"

"Yes."

"Have them telephone me here at home: Tarrytown 4-2268; I'll give you a prescription for a tranquilizer. Give her two tablets dissolved in her milk. She'll sleep. She'll be okay in the morning. Did she say anything you could understand?"

"I wrote it down in the book."

"Good. Come see me with her tomorrow at one. And try to get a good night's sleep yourself." He hung up.

Thank God for the car. Jessie grabbed Patience and threw on a coat. She went tearing down the steps. She'd be at the drugstore in no time. When she reached the car in the driveway, she'd placed Patience firmly in her lap and buttoned her own coat over the child, forming a kind of seatbelt. She hoped that maybe the distraction and the noise of the motor might lull the child. When they reached Main Street, the crying did seem less intense. Patience seemed to be taking some notice of her surroundings, aware she was in the village, and that the darkness made things look different.

When Jessica stepped into the brilliantly lit drugstore, with Patience still sobbing and gulping away, she felt horribly conspicuous. There was only one other person in the store, and the pharmacist was just handing a wrapped parcel to him.

"There you are, Dr. Wright, and will that be all for tonight?"

"Yes, thanks, John—and what have we here?" He

turned, curiously, but with concern, to Jessica and Patience.

Jessica's voice was unsteady. She was out of breath.

"My child needs some pills. Here's the doctor's number. He's waiting for you to call him."

The pharmacist took the number and moved swiftly to the rear of the store. Dr. Wright looked at the child with what seemed like Jessie like professional interest. She found herself babbling. "Some kind of fright. It happened last week for the first time. She regressed. This is the second crying spell. She just needs to sleep now."

"Let me hold her for you, Mrs. . . . You look worn out."

Without hesitating even for a moment, Jessie handed Patience to Dr. Wright. He looked young but competent. She sat down on a stool by the cosmetics counter. Her legs were weak, and her hands were trembling. She'd been carrying that baby continuously for nearly an hour.

The pharmacist reappeared.

"Your doctor said to give her two right now, before you get home. Here, let's take a bottle from stock; we'll put some milk in it for you." He grabbed a baby bottle from a display shelf and disappeared again, returning with a blue plastic bottle filled partially with milk, which he handed to Jessica.

"I dissolved two of the tablets in it. Let her have some now; see if she'll calm down enough to drink it." The pharmacist stood by, watching benevolently, as Dr. Wright handed Patience back to Jessica. Both men watched as Jessica put the bottle to Patience's mouth. They held their breaths. Patience took a tentative sip. She choked a little, gasped, and then took another sip. She was drinking, and her eyes began to flutter. It worked with incredible rapidity. Before she'd had even four ounces, the child's mouth let go of the bottle, her eyes closed, and her breathing became as regular as a cherub's. Beautiful.

178

Jessica looked from one man to the other with heartfelt gratitude.

"Boy. That really did the trick. I can't thank you enough."

"It's a good thing Doc Wright was here, young lady. We usually close at eight. But Dr. Wright had a little emergency, and we like to oblige him when we can." The druggist began to turn off the lights, one by one. Jessica picked up the little tube of pills, and asked, "How much do I owe you for these?" She was still unsteady; without thinking, she handed Patience to Dr. Wright once more, and he accepted her matter-of-factly.

"That's six forty-nine. Glad it helped."

Jessica handed him a ten-dollar bill and got her change. She turned absentmindedly to leave. As she got to the door, Dr. Wright said, very quietly, so as not to waken the baby, "Hey, Mrs. . . . you forgot this!" He smiled. It was an understanding smile.

"Thank you. You've been so helpful. I'm still a bit rattled." She took Patience back into her arms and began to walk to her little VW. Dr. Wright headed in the same direction. They walked companionably down the street.

"I'm Jessica Porter," she said, "and this sweet, sleeping baby is called Patience. We were all alone tonight, and I can't tell you how much I appreciate your help, Dr. Wright."

"It wasn't anything at all. Tell me, are you sure you can make it home? How far do you live?"

"Oh, we're just off Maynard. I'll be all right, really." She looked at him once more and managed a tired smile. He had a nice face. He opened the car door for her. She got in, trying to adjust Patience on her lap as she had done on the way down. But now that the child was asleep, she couldn't get her to stay upright, coat buttons or no coat buttons.

"Say, you've got a problem, there. Don't you have a baby seat for her?"

"No. We just got this car today—although it seems like a million years ago."

"Look, I live over on Edgewood, Maynard's an easy walk for me. Let me hold her for you while you drive home."

"But what about your car?"

"Mrs. Porter, pardon my saying so, but you're punchy tired, and everything seems like a big problem. Relax. All you have to do is drive home. I'll hold the baby. And in case you're really worried, my car is parked right off Main Street by my office, and I can use my other car to get to work in the morning. Okay?"

Jessica smiled sheepishly. "Thank you. I guess you're right."

When they got to the driveway and the doctor saw all the steps, he shook his head in wonder.

"You go up these every day?"

"Sometimes two and three times."

"No wonder you're so trim! It's probably very good for you. But not tonight. Not in the state you're in. Here, you hold onto my arm, and I'll carry Patience."

"No, you've done quite enough, really!"

"Don't argue with me. You're too tired, remember?"

He led them both slowly up the steps. At the door he solemnly handed the sleeping Patience to Jessie.

"Take good care of her, now."

"Oh, I will! And thank you so much, Dr. Wright."

"Take good care of yourself, too, Mrs. Porter. You're under quite a strain."

"Yes. I am. Thank you again."

When she closed the door, she realized she'd behaved a little awkwardly; but that nice young doctor seemed very understanding. She'd make a point of thanking him again one day, when all this was behind her.

Jessie managed to put Patience to bed without waking

180

her. She'd sleep through until morning—no doubt about that. She opened the window a crack. Tomorrow, they'd have to go into the city and see Dr. Weller again. She'd better get to bed, herself. She took a warm, relaxing bath, and put on a cozy flannel gown her mother had given her years ago for Christmas. Before she went to sleep, she picked up the little spiral-bound journal and studied the words she had recorded. "Bad man. Smell bad. Gar smell bad." *Gar—cigar!* Pierre had been smoking a cigar —and then he'd leaned over the crib and tickled her. Could it be, then, that somebody—some "bad man" had been in Patience's room, smoking that cigar they'd found the butt of, and had tickled her or touched her in some way? Tickled her . . . what was it Mrs. Falconer had said, the next morning?

"I thought I heard a child laughing."

But who? Who would appear in Patience's room in the middle of the night. And why take her doll? "Thing on Tweetie." What thing? What dreadful mischief had this unimaginable intruder committed? What terrifying act caused this bright, outgoing precocious little girl to close so many psychic doors . . . try so hard to build a wall to hide behind? She'd have to tell it all to the doctor tomorrow. She turned off the light and tried to sleep. She wondered how Sam was, wondered if he'd called her to say good-night. Would he be with the Tarpinians by now? Perhaps it was just as well. It would be easier to tell him about Patience's latest crying spell after she'd talked it over with the doctor. Then she remembered the state Pierre had been in when he and Dorcas left. Oh, God. He was bound to hear about it all soon enough. "Something to wonder at about the entire family," Pierre had said. She found she had to agree with him.

Though Jessica fell asleep, her sleep was disturbed, agitated, and she kept waking up. And even while she slept, there was the gnawing awareness of the empty space in the bed next to her. At one point during the seemingly endless tossing and turning, she entered into a terrifying dream. The terror, at first, seemed all out of proportion to the actual situation. It was a kind of schoolroom or lecture hall. But everybody was sitting on the platform, and only Jessica was sitting in the audience. A spotlight made a swift arc over the platform, and she recognized her mother and father; her eighth-grade teacher, Mrs. McNeill; Pierre; Dr. Weller; Mary Smith; Detective Sergeant Orsini; and that nice Dr. Wright. . . . But even as the light moved over them, their friendly expressions—weren't these all people whom she liked and trusted?—changed, to become fiercely accusing. They scowled at her and in unison pointed their fingers directly at her. The spotlight hit her, then, and stopped. They were about to tell her the truth about herself, and her clammy hands told her it would be vile.

"You! Don't you know yet that you can't hide behind that mousy manner forever? You can't stand being looked at—why? Don't you want anyone to know what you're really thinking? You'd better speak up . . . speak up before it's too late!"

It didn't make any sense, yet Jessica felt exposed, threatened, transparent in a shameful way. Then there was a hideous cackling laughter. The rather staid group swelled up and became an enormous crowd . . . and the platform turned out to be the Wimbledon train station. All were laughing, jeering, pointing fingers at Jessie. The spotlight continued focusing on her, cruelly, and she looked down at herself and saw, to her consternation, that she was wearing diapers—and nothing else.

"Oh, baby, baby!" the voices said. "Baby, baby!" and laughed some more. Jessie woke up.

"Oh, baby, baby!" she heard. A single, gravelly voice —not a jeering crowd. Cackling, phlegmy laughter, and

182

the slamming of a door. But that had been real. She'd heard that after she woke up . . . it was the sound of laughter that had awakened her! She leaped out of bed and ran out to the hall. All was quiet. She groped along the wall for a lightswitch. Just as she found it, she recognized the smell of cigar smoke. And, as she turned on the light, she saw the gray wisps of fetid smoke curling menacingly around her. For a second Jessica froze. A wave of nausea threatened to overwhelm her; but before she could do anything to quell it, she was taken by a fit of trembling so severe she had to cling to the wall to force it down. She had to think. She had to keep in control. She swallowed. She took a deep breath. Then she walked to the back door and opened it. She saw, in the vague moonlight that penetrated the small barred basement window—nothing. The moonlight cast eerie shadows over the trash cans, the familiar Borden's milk box, and the mops and brooms—but there was nothing more to see. Nor did she smell the cigar out there. She shivered, but merely because of the chill of the back entrance. She closed the door again. The door she heard slamming must have been the side door. She walked to it. She opened it—it was not bolted. She peered up the stairs that turned a corner halfway up. At the top there was a dim light, very dim. But enough to show up the cigar smoke, though the smell alone had already told her all she needed to know.

Try as she might, she could not gather up enough courage to mount those steps. She closed the door, and she bolted it.

"Oh, baby!" the voice had said. *Patience!*

"Oh, my God." She ran to Patience's room. The child was in her crib, soundly sleeping. The window had been opened wider from the bottom . . . the curtains were billowing wildly. She closed it with a slam. Jessica turned on a lamp and examined Patience closely. This time she had come to no harm. Perhaps the drug had kept her asleep. In the crib, next to her, one on either side, lay two Tweeties. The new Tweetie was on Patience's left. On her right, looking very much the worse for wear, lay her old, vanished friend.

"She must never see this," Jessie decided at once. She picked the poor old doll up, turned off the light, and left the room. The old Tweetie was sticky all over with a kind of slime. "Exhibit C, Officer Orsini." Jessica wrapped the doll in a napkin, and washed her hands with very hot water.

She returned to the bedroom and turned on the light. It was four in the morning. She'd never sleep now. She put on her robe, and sat by the window. There they were—Mrs. Falconer's clumping footsteps. Directly overhead. It was too much. Jessica began to cry. What could she do? What if the intruder came after her? The laughter. The smoker of cigars, the violator of babies' bedrooms. Who was he? Or it? What was the connection to Mrs. Falconer? She felt herself losing control. If only Sam were here! Would it help if she called him? The Tarpinians loved her. Surely they'd understand if in her terror she called them up at this hour. All three of them would comfort her . . . get her through this cold, agonizing, brutal fear. She still knew the number by heart. She walked over to the bedside phone and calmly, purposefully, even remembering to dial 212 first, rang the Tarpinians' number in the Village. The phone rang twice before she heard Sarah's groggy "Hello?"

"Sarah? It's Jessie—I'm sorry to call in the middle of the night, but I'm so scared. . . . Somebody—a prowler —was here . . . I'm so scared! Could I speak to Sam, please?"

"Jessie? What? Sam? But why are you calling us? Isn't Sam with you?"

184

"No, no, Sam's with you. He's spending the night with you!"

"Jessie, believe me, he's not here. I haven't seen Sam since the night of your party."

Chapter 18

VICTOR picked up the extension, and both Tarpinians began talking to Jessica at once. They said vague, comforting things that helped her merely because they sounded so normal—she didn't really take much in. More important, they listened to her. She told them everything that had happened, and they soothed her, agreed with her, cautioned her just to try to get through the night.

"You'll be all right when morning comes, dear," Sarah promised.

"Play some music, Jessica," Victor advised. "Don't even try to sleep anymore."

"Watch the dawn come up," Sarah suggested brightly.

"Keep the doors locked—don't let anybody in."

"It's only a few more hours until daylight. You'll get through."

"Everything will sort itself out soon. You'll hear from Sam, and there's bound to be a perfectly logical explanation for his not being here with us."

"Make yourself some tea—and wait for the dawn."

"Take care—and call us tomorrow. Let us know what the doctor has to say!" Thus, still babbling sympathetically in tandem, they hung up.

For a moment Jessica sat holding the dead receiver in her hand. Then, with careful deliberation, she replaced the receiver. She stood up, went into the living room, and rummaged through her phonograph records. The Beatles. Simon and Garfunkel. Sentimental leftovers from her college days. She stacked them on the player. The clumping was still going on upstairs. The music would drown that out anyway. She made a pot of tea. She wrapped a blanket about her shoulders, sat down on the sofa, and gave her full attention to the poignant words of a Beatle song she hadn't played in a long, long time. She could feel her panic begin to ebb.

She lapsed into a dry-eyed nostalgia for the person she so recently had been, and would never be again. For the marriage she had dreamed of that had, in fact, been just a dream. Where would she and Sam be when they were sixty-four? Together? Apart? Needing and feeding— that's what it all boiled down to, in the end.

Almost imperceptibly, a cool gray Thursday late in October made its modest appearance. The only movement, as black night became leaden dawn, came from a light veil of ground fog circulating among the bare trees. Jessica had never seen anything more beautiful. She discovered she had the strength she needed to face the day.

Just before seven, Patience awakened, crying.

"Mommy!"

Jessica ran to her.

"Here I am, love, what's wrong?"

"Mommy! Bad man took Tweetie. Scared me. He laughed. And then he— Don't let him come back!"

"I won't, baby, I promise!"

Although Patience was crying, her voice was so much clearer than it had been, her words so much more like her old self, that Jessica couldn't help being overjoyed. She'd made progress! Dr. Weller would really be able to get somewhere today.

"Mommy?"

"Yes, love."

"Can we go 'way?"

"How would you like to spend tonight with Violet Smith?"

"Okay."

"And today we're going to drive Tom's nice car to New York and visit Dr. Weller. When we get back, I'll drop you off at the Smith house. Tomorrow, I think I'm going to find us a new place to live. What do you say to that?"

"Okay!" She gave a little smile, and her tears stopped. Jessica hugged her.

"It'll all work out, Patience; just you wait and see."

A hopeful smile lingered on Patience's face through breakfast. She said little more, but there was no doubt in Jessica's mind that a major breakthrough had indeed occurred. If only poor Pierre could know that he'd actually done them all a favor. Maybe she'd call him later and explain.

They were still sitting at the breakfast table when there was a knock at the back door. The smile left Patience's face; a closed, dull look replaced it.

"Just a minute!" Jessica called. She hadn't heard the old woman's footsteps on the back stairs—who could it be? She opened the door, and it was Mrs. Falconer, after all, dressed in an ancient black alpaca overcoat strung with a grotesque collar composed of three little dead foxes. Long dead.

"Ah, Mrs. Porter. I felt certain I'd catch you here at this hour. It is my custom to market on Thursday mornings. Imagine my surprise when I passed Granite Terrace in the Pontiac just now to see a small foreign motor car parked in your driveway. You made no mention of a car when you rented this flat from me. As you know, there is a fine garage at the end of the driveway. Frederick had it built at considerable expense . . ."

Jessica looked at her. She seemed very agitated, out

188

of breath. Why had she turned around and driven back up the hill, just to tell her this?

"The use of this fine garage, built at considerable expense for the convenience of our tenants, will be fifteen dollars extra a month, Mrs. Porter. I require payment in advance." She held out a gloved hand, as though Jessica would fork over this amount there and then.

"But, Mrs. Falconer, I really don't think that old car needs a garage . . . the driveway is just fine."

"Don't you try to play games with me, young woman! Sneaking a car in behind my back, just to cheat an old lady out of a few dollars . . ." The fierce blue eyes bulged, and the mouth sputtered, as she prepared to summon a fresh barrage of words.

Jessica spoke first. "Mrs. Falconer. I have no intention of paying you anything at all. I have no intention of staying here another month. This place is a nightmare! We've been harassed and terrorized since the day we moved in. I don't feel safe here! I may as well tell you that there's been a prowler in this apartment . . . I heard him again last night. He smokes a cigar; and he went up those side steps you claim to keep bolted. Talk about playing games, Mrs. Falconer . . . just exactly what is *your* game?"

The old woman, though startled at first by Jessica's attack, became instantly very calm. She replied at once, airily and with a certain glee, "Poor dear. Hubby drinks. Stays out all night. Makes the little woman nervous being all by herself . . . starts imagining things. Tut-tut, my dear. It happens all the time. You must get hold of yourself, you know. There are worse things in life than hubbies with a roving eye. I shouldn't babble my fancies about, if I were you. People might think your head's not screwed on quite right, don't you know?"

"Isn't that a coincidence, Mrs. Falconer—that's just what the police inspector said about you! I hope he reached you; he seemed most anxious to question you the other day!"

Jessica was delighted to have come up with this retort. She'd planned it as an exit line, and meant to close the back door in her face. But it didn't turn out that way. At the word "police" Mrs. Falconer's face underwent another change. Her features fell. All the wrinkles became slack, the mouth hung loose and flaccid. She grasped the doorknob tightly and muttered, "Police? What're you talking about?"

"There was an inspector here, Mrs. Falconer, the other day. He rang your bell and couldn't reach you, so he spoke to me. I told him all I knew, but he was determined to see you, too. I expect he'll be back."

"Police? Why should I talk to the police? I am an old woman. All I ask is a little privacy. . . ." She began to whine. "I'm too old to be of interest to the police. I don't know anything about what goes on here anymore. How should I know who killed Nora Kelly, anyway? What could they want of a poor old woman like me?" Her eyes, blue and piercing just seconds before, looked washed out, rheumy. She turned them on Jessica and pleaded, "If he comes back again, Mrs. Porter, won't you please just tell him to go away? I'd be much obliged." She turned away and, leaning heavily on her walking stick, looking for the first time as though she needed every bit of support it gave, walked out the back door.

Yet, when she left, Jessica felt no relief. She was suddenly more frightened than ever. All those chameleon changes, a kind of trademark of Mrs. Falconer's, hadn't provided the smokescreen they usually did. Jessica had said nothing about the police wanting to talk to her about Nora Kelly's murder. But Mrs. Falconer knew. It had never occurred to Jessica to connect Mrs. Falconer with the Kelly murder. There was no reason to suppose a connection existed. But now that the idea had lodged itself, she doubted she'd be able to shake it off. She'd have to act fast. They had to get out of here!

The first thing she did was telephone Mary Smith.

"Mary, an awful lot has happened, and I don't have time to tell you all of it. First, Patience had another crying attack. But she seems to have improved as a result of it. Second, the cigar-smoking prowler was here again last night. And third, I can't let Patience spend another night in this god-awful place—can she spend the night with you?"

"Of course, Jessie. You're all out of breath—are you all right? Is there something wrong this very minute that you can't tell me about?"

"You mean, is *she* here? No, no, nothing like that. Still, I think we may be in real danger. I think Mrs. Falconer may be . . ."

"May be what?"

"Nothing. Look, I'll talk to you later, okay? I've got to take Patience in to see Dr. Weller. Did I tell you about my brother's car? He left it with us yesterday."

"Yes. You told me yesterday, at the park, remember?"

"God, that seems like days ago. So much has happened. Before I hang up, though, Mary . . . that house you've been telling me about all week—the one that's up for rent—is it still available? I've got to get us out of here!"

"Yes, Jessie, I think it's still available."

"Do you think you could arrange to have us look at it tomorrow morning?"

"I'll arrange it, Jess. First thing. Look, you really sound upset, are you sure you'll be okay? Do you want me to take you into the city?"

"Mary, I'll be okay just as soon as I get out of here, honest!"

"Well, let me know if there's anything else I can do."

"It just seems like everything's happening at once, that's all. I haven't even told you about Sam. Or Pierre. But the good thing is Patience—I really think she's started to recover. I've got to run. I'll see you late this afternoon, and drop her off, thanks!"

She had to get out of the apartment. By the time she and Patience were ready to leave and Jessie'd gathered up her notebook and exhibits B and C to show to Dr. Weller, it was only ten fifteen. Why was she in such a hurry? Their appointment wasn't until one. They'd stop in the village for a snack. She just wanted to be out of there.

They didn't go to Murphy's. Jessica didn't feel up to making conversation with Mrs. Murphy, who'd be sure to remember her. She wanted to be anonymous, let her mind wander, stare into space over an anonymous cup of luncheonette coffee.

With Patience cheerfully in tow, Jessica entered the Starlight Diner, feeling as anonymous as years of living in New York had taught her to be. It was exactly what she had in mind. She picked up a copy of the *Times* from a rack and moved over to one of the pink plastic booths.

"Why, Mrs. Porter, we meet again! May I buy you a cup of coffee? Hello, Patience, you look just fine this morning." Dr. Wright, a broad grin on his good face, was genuinely pleased to see them. Jessica's heart sank. But she couldn't avoid sharing his booth, not after his help the night before.

"Dr. Wright. What a nice surprise! I'm on my way into the city. . . . Patience has a one o'clock appointment with her doctor. I'd love a cup of coffee, thank you!"

"I hope you'll get a car seat for her; that's quite a trip into town."

"You're right—I almost forgot. Is there somewhere here in Wimbledon I can buy one?"

"The drugstore has 'em. You know, the only reason I popped by there last night is that my assistant has been sick and I ran out of supplies. I had some complicated root-canal work scheduled first thing this morning, and I found I was completely out of the right type of analgesic. I'm glad it happened, though. You were really a lady in distress, if I ever saw one. An old boyhood fantasy of mine—coming to the aid of a fair damsel in distress. Somehow, growing up here in Wimbledon, I never thought I'd meet up with one. . . ."

"Root-canal work? You're a . . ."

"Max Wright, Jr., DDS, son of Max Wright, Sr., DDS. . . . You thought I was a doctor."

"Well, you were introduced as Dr. Wright. It's a natural mistake." Jessica was acutely embarrassed. She was afraid she'd looked disappointed when she'd realized her mistake. "I'm not disappointed you're a dentist!" she blurted. "I mean, I make no value judgments that way. Please forgive me, I'm being stupid. Last night was even worse than you know."

"Mrs. Porter, I get that all the time. I don't mind. I love my work. I'm proud of it. Nobody ever dies in a dentist's chair. I put people's mouths in order, and they're always so happy and filled with a sense of their own virtue when they leave me that I get to see humanity in an excellent light."

"You're a nice man, Dr. Wright."

The waitress brought coffee and danish and a glass of chocolate milk for Patience. They chatted neutrally about Wimbledon, and Dr. Wright told her about taking over his father's practice.

"I tried medicine, and found I couldn't take the

grief. I went to dentistry school in California, settled down there, and found I missed Wimbledon. So, when Dad retired, here I was, the prodigal son, returning. I have some patients that first came to Dad back in 1927. He's taken care of most of Wimbledon for more than forty-five years."

"He probably put in Mrs. Falconer's china teeth. The ones she accused the poor Teel boy of stealing. . . ." Jessica thought out loud.

"Falconer?" Dr. Wright asked, as he threw a dollar and some change on the table.

"Yes. Our landlady. Quite mad. That's why I'm so upset. Why Patience had this attack. We're renting from a crazy woman, and ever since we moved in, it's been one damn fright after another. Do you know anything about her?"

Jessica rose, and all three walked out of the diner together.

"Falconer, yes, I think there's a file with that name. I don't recall her personally, but I bet Dad will. Giving you a hard time, eh? Well, look, you'll get out of it. I can tell. You may think you're a nervous wreck; but I bet the next time I see you, you'll have solved all your problems with this Falconer lady. See you around, take care!"

Jessica went straight to the drugstore and bought Patience a car seat. Patience loved it. Jessie settled the child comfortably in the seat next to her and headed for the Saw Mill River Parkway. She'd get into the city early; but that was all right with her. Maybe there'd be time to drop in on Sam at the office. He'd have to tell her where he'd spent the night.

As Jessie drove once more through the crowded, dingy hills of Yonkers, Sam was being summoned to see Pierre, by Gloria Payne, his formidably unappealing secretary.

You give me such a glorious pain, Miss Gloria Payne, Sam thought to himself as he followed her steely back down the corridor. He knew that whatever his upcoming interview with Pierre was about, it was bound to be unpleasant. When Pierre walked into the office that morning, he'd given Sam a look that chilled him through and through. No "good morning," just a look. Sam, still wearing the same clothes in which he'd spent the night, felt scruffy and disreputable, though he'd managed to shower and shave. Still, the night had been worth it. For the first time in years, Sam felt a surge of real enthusiasm toward the future. If he hadn't bumped into old Chris Banning right there in the middle of Park Avenue last night, he'd really be scared now. As it was, he squared his shoulders proudly and strode into Pierre's discreetly opulent office with all the confidence in the world. He wasn't going to let this phony intimidate him! No way.

"Ah, there you are, Sam; come in, come in, *s'il vous plaît.* How are you today?"

"Just fine, Pierre, thanks."

"How was your night in town?"

"Just fine, Pierre, thanks."

"Uh, Sam, I was in Wimbledon yesterday. Just passing through, *n'est-ce pas?* But Dorcas—she was with me, we were enjoying a ride through the countryside—Dorcas insisted that we drop in on your charming wife. I don't know how to put this, Sam, but your wife was, uh, very upset about your leetle baby. I don't understand such things, but it seems to me that you have, uh, quite a serious, uh, domestic problem . . ."

"Pierre, what in hell are you talking about?"

"Let me finish, Sam, please. My point is simply this. I may not understand much about, how-you-say, *mental* irregularities, but I know this much: There is something very wrong in your leetle household, Sam. And until

105

you solve these domestic problems, you will be of no use to me—that, I can promise you. I was shocked at how, uh, distracted and unreliable you have been since you joined this beeznezz. Now, *peut-être*, I have discovered why." Sam started to speak again, but Pierre held up his hand and continued, "Before either of us says anything we will regret, may I suggest that you resign? It is not good beeznezz to employ somebody who is in a state of distraction caused by serious domestic problems. I am sorry, Sam, but I have no choice. . . ."

Even prepared for the worst, as he had been, Sam was not prepared for the bluntness or the callousness with which this erstwhile friend had chosen to dispose of him.

"Pierre, you're not getting any resignation out of me. You're going to have to fire me. And I expect a full month's severance pay. I doubt whether you'll ever have the insight to regret this; but I, at least, know you've made a gross error in judgment. I expect a check for a month's salary on my desk before noon. I'll be out of here as soon as I get it." Pale, hands clammy, Sam nevertheless turned calmly on his heels and left Pierre's office. Very quietly, he shut the big door behind him, until he heard the discreet click that concluded yet another chapter in his checkered business career.

And that was why, when Jessica and Patience appeared brightly at the receptionist's desk of Manhattan Office Maintenance Corporation and asked for Mr. Samuel Porter, Jessica was told, "I am sorry, madam. He is no longer with this company."

"Surely there's some mistake? May I see Monsieur Villard, then? He's a personal friend of mine. Tell him Jessica would like to stop in to say hello."

The receptionist buzzed Pierre's office.

As she relayed Jessica's message, Jessie could actually

hear the sound of Pierre's accented voice on the other end.

"I am sorry, madam," the receptionist said in a voice that sounded not at all sorry, "but Monsieur has already left for lunch."

Chapter 19

THERE was nothing for Jessica to do but go directly on to Dr. Weller's office with Patience. They were early, and Jessie sat down with the child on her lap and made a big show of going through some *National Geographics* with her. Her animated, glassy-eyed delivery of such remarks as, "Ooh, look at Auckland, New Zealand—isn't that nice!" and "See that? It's a strip mine in South Dakota!" cut no ice with Patience.

Sam's latest fate had Jessica beside herself with anxiety. She'd been concerned enough last night—hurt, indignant, even. Now she was completely undermined by a sense of unreality and loss. Sam had been fired. But why? What had gone wrong? How would she find him, now? Would he return to Wimbledon tonight; or would he go get drunk somewhere instead? What would they do for money? She was frantic.

"Look, Patience, that's how Japanese ladies dive for pearls."

Dr. Weller arrived. He took one look at Jessie, and said, "My God, Jessica, come into my office, won't you? You look awful—has something else gone wrong since last night?"

Jessie walked in with Patience, and all her misadventures and anxieties rattled out of her like so many marbles spilling from a bag.

"Am I losing my grip, doctor?" she asked. She'd been

undressing Patience as she spoke to him, removing everything except her underwear and shoes and socks.

"I have to go to the bathroom," Patience said.

"Well, Jessica, you may be deteriorating, but I'd say Patience is staging an impressive comeback. It's right across the hall."

When they returned, Dr. Weller was sitting at his desk, writing a presciption. He was a dry, metallic sort of man, and though his hair was stylishly long and his eyeglasses had the latest sort of steel rims, he reminded Jessica of Robert McNamara. He smiled now, and it lit up an otherwise forbidding face.

"This is for you, Mrs. Porter. I want you to have this filled right away. You're under quite a strain, and I definitely don't want you losing your grip, not when my young patient is on the verge of making a remarkable recovery. From what you've been saying, there seem to be some very strange things going on up there in Wimbledon that have nothing whatever to do with you and Sam. And then, too, there's a crisis building up between the two of you—and you're going to have to be very clear in your mind just what your goals are, because a commitment one way or the other will be required of you—and soon. As for the other; damned if it doesn't sound to me like a police matter. By all means see if you can find a different place to live tomorrow; and then maybe you'd better tell the police about your prowler. That's my advice, for what it's worth. Now, we've already used up fifteen minutes of the forty-five I can spare you today. I'd like to devote the rest to my patient, okay? Why don't you go downstairs and have that prescription filled?"

Jessica protested. "But I had some things I wanted to show you. Exhibits B and C, I call them."

"Later. Okay?" Still, he couldn't help asking, "What happened to A?"

"Ah, but that's the crux of the whole thing, Dr. Weller. I'm sure of it." She was about to elaborate, when Dr. Weller took her by the hand and ushered her kindly but firmly out of the room.

"Later, Jessica. Later."

"Now, Patience, let's have a look at you." First, Dr. Weller examined her superficially: heart, lungs, muscle tone, eyes, reflexes.

"You're as sound as a dollar, young lady. Even better; make that as sound as a deutsche mark." He helped her back into her polo shirt and overalls.

"Tell me, Patience, what's the first thing you remember about the bad man?"

Patience looked at him solemnly. She didn't want to talk about it. She wanted her mother.

"Where's Mommy?"

"She'll be right back. I want to talk to you alone for a few minutes. Try to help me, won't you? You see, I'm trying to picture what it was like, that night when this man came into your room. . . ."

"He took Tweetie!" Patience accused.

"Oh. I see. And then?"

"He laughed. He pushed me. He took Tweetie, and he—" Patience stopped.

Dr. Weller could see her reexperience the event, but the child's vocabulary, precocious though it was, failed her.

She gestured instead. The gesture confirmed Dr. Weller's suspicions.

"He didn't touch you anymore, then?"

Patience shook her head no but began to cry. "Thing out," she said. "Thing on Tweetie."

"It's all right, dear. It's all right now. Is there anything else you can remember about him that you can tell me? It's important."

"He . . . he . . ." She gestured, holding herself, and circling her arms around her little chest.

"He tried to hold you?"

"Yes . . . and, he—" She lifted up her shirt.

"He tried to take off your clothes?"

"Yes."

"And you screamed, right?"

"Yes. He smelled bad. I wanted him to go away."

"Did your screaming make him go away?"

"He ran out. He took Tweetie with him!" She said this very loud. Taking Tweetie was the worst crime. Patience did not consciously comprehend the sexual nature of the intruder's attack. But unconsciously? Dr. Weller, though delighted to see—for the first time—the precocious child he'd only heard about before, was immediately sobered by the thought of the enormous network of ancillary symptoms that could lie dormant until this child reached puberty. Although the regression seemed to be resolving itself, both she and her parents would require further observation and counseling. He wondered how much of this her mother suspected but had avoided facing. He would have to make her understand that although the child had apparently not been molested physically, she had been forced to witness a rather bizarre form of sexual perversion; and they'd both have to keep an eye on Patience to prevent a deep-seated neurosis from crippling her in later life.

Still, he was gratified at how quickly the child shook off the symptoms of her regression. She was a tough little customer, and she had a good, clear mind.

"Now then, Patience, let's see if your mommy has come back."

While Patience played quietly with an elaborate dollhouse in one corner of the office, Dr. Weller went over the material in Jessica's notebook and examined the two exhibits. He decided, intuitively, not to divulge his reconstruction of the intruder's visit to Patience's bedroom. Mrs. Porter was too high-strung today. Instead, he said, "You can keep the cigar, but let me do a lab analysis on this doll." He spoke quietly. Jessica had explained to him about the substitute Tweetie they'd given to Patience. "I'll return it to you. I'll let you know the results tomorrow. Did you have that presciption filled?"

"Yes."

"Good. Take one of these four times a day until your life settles down. And, Jessica, good luck with your husband tonight."

"You mean, if he comes home?"

"He'll come home—where else could he go?"

"Wherever he spent last night?"

"Well, you know him; I don't. But I think he'll be home, and I hope you both are mature enough to resolve this new setback. I'll see Patience again in two weeks, unless there's a change. Okay?" He handed her an appointment slip, and minutes later Jessie and Patience were battling the afternoon traffic on their way back to Wimbledon.

Jessica and Patience arrived at the Smith house by four. Jessie was exhausted; Patience more her old self than would have seemed possible. Mary noticed the change right away.

"Wow! Now that's the Patience I used to know. She seems all better—is it true?"

"I think she's especially happy to be spending the night with you all, Mary. That's all we talked about on the ride back. But you're right, of course, she's just about recovered from the regression. Dr. Weller was very impressed." Jessica plunked down noisily on one of the Smith's two camelback horsehair sofas.

"Whew! I've about had it."

"You don't look well, Jess. Would you like some tea, or maybe some sherry?"

"Tea." Jessica leaned back and closed her eyes for a minute. Then she reached into her bag and took out the pills Dr. Weller had prescribed.

Might as well take one of these now, she thought.

Over tea Jessica told Mary about Sam.

"So, just as one problem seems to be solving itself, I've got another. This one's a doozy, too. I mean, we've been living from paycheck to paycheck right along, which is bad enough in its way. But what do you do when the paychecks stop altogether?"

"Don't worry about that just yet, Jess. If Sam really was fired, he'll have received some kind of severance pay; and surely, as an actor, he must have been on unemployment before?"

"Not when we were together, he wasn't. Oh, Mary, he's really rather odd. See, on the one hand, he's always had this straitlaced, old-fashioned idea of stability and propriety; you know, all those kind of 1940's goals. And yet, on the other, the only thing he's really ever been good at has been acting. And there's nothing less stable or straitlaced than that! In his business dealings he often seems to be on the wrong wavelength, has a way of getting all tangled up in these colossal misunderstandings. I never asked him to give up acting, when Patience came along. He seemed eager to do it. Like he was telling the world, 'I'm a grown-up, solid citizen, now!' Sometimes I think the reason we seem so well matched to people is that we're both acting out our fantasies of what married life should be like. Fantasies straight out of the Late Show! And, come to think of it, who's to say that's wrong? As long as it works."

"How're you going to make it work now, kid?"

"Tonight I expect we'll have a totally unrehearsed knock-down and drag-out brawl."

"Well, may the best man win. Let me know what happens, huh? And tomorrow, as soon as you can, come by and we'll take a look at that house. Have breakfast here, why don't you?"

Jessica got up to go, kissed Patience, who was so engrossed in the game she and Violet were playing that she gave her mother a most perfunctory kiss.

As she turned to go, Jessie said to Mary, "Look, if Sam doesn't come home, could I stay here, too? I don't think I can face that place all alone."

"Of course, Jessie, we've got lots of room. But you'll see, Sam'll come home. Good luck!"

During the short drive to 33 Granite Terrace, Jessica could feel the tranquilizer Dr. Weller gave her begin to work. She rarely took pills of any kind. Not even aspirin. Now all her tension and anxiety seemed magically to be moving away from her. Almost as though all of the stresses and pressures were being carefully wrapped in cotton, in preparation for a long journey. They didn't disappear altogether; they simply became less threatening.

She found it a great comfort. For the first time in her life, she had a glimpse of what alcoholism or narcotics addiction were about. She shuddered. Not for her! But for the moment she was grateful for the help.

Jessie parked her "small foreign motor car" in the driveway. She noticed the ramshackle garage at the end of it. It was green and grimy with moss along one side; and the swaybacked roof was a patchwork of lost shingles, corrugated tin, and dozens of years' worth of fallen leaves and twigs. There was not a pane of glass remaining in any of the windows. Fifteen dollars a month for that! The woman was crazy, true; but maybe the lack of money was making her worse. She probably had a fixed income from some pension or other—those never changed. She'd been on her way shopping, worried about the high cost of food, and decided the new car in the driveway might produce an extra fifteen dollars for her. Well, it was no problem of Jessica's—not anymore. The sooner they got out of here, the better. She looked up at their apartment and saw the living-room light was on. Sam—home? How would she greet him? She had all those steps to prepare a face for him. She took the steps slowly. Nevertheless, she was at the porch door in no time at all. She took a deep breath and walked in.

"Where have you been? I've been trying to reach you all day!"

"Well, I'm here now. What did you want to tell me?"

"Look, Jess, I've had a rough day—don't play games with me. It seems like every time I try to call you, you're not at home. You could at least give me a straight answer to a direct question."

"That's really funny, Sam." Jessica found herself laughing. That damn pill seemed to be making things go out of kilter. Everything was ludicrous. She went on.

"Considering that you've been the man who isn't there for the last twenty-four hours."

"I was working last night!"

"Yes, well, where did you go after work, Sam?"

When he hesitated, Jessie continued calmly, "And then, of course, when I decided to look in on you at the office this noon, you weren't there, either. 'No longer with the company,' the girl said. Patience and I were a bit put out by that, Sam."

"You know, then!"

"Well, I know you've been let go. I don't know why. Or where you were last night. You see, I tried to reach you at the Tarpinians. Imagine my embarrassment when you weren't there. Oh, the Tarpinians were very nice about it, of course. But I did feel that at four o'clock in the morning, when a woman's been scared out of her wits by a prowler, it would be better if she could talk to her husband. I didn't want to tell you about Patience's second crying attack. (Your ex-employer, Pierre Villard, brought that one on, by the way.) But, somehow, a prowler . . . I really wanted to talk to you then."

"I was with Chris Banning. What happened? Are you okay? Where have you got Patience now, anyway? She's not in the—"

"No, Patience is fine. She's not in the hospital; she's with the Smiths. But she could be in the hospital, couldn't she—and this would be the first you'd know about it, wouldn't it? As a matter of fact, Patience is much, much better. The second attack seemed to bring her around. Dr. Weller's prognosis, this afternoon, was very encouraging. Who is Chris Banning?"

"That agent. You remember. Used to be with William Morris. Went out to the coast last year. We bumped into each other on Park Avenue, just as I was leaving work. It seems Chris had been looking for me all over town—and then we bump into each other like that, right—"

"Yes, I know, right in the middle of Park Avenue."

Jessica's lack of enthusiasm did not deter him.

"I went over to Chris's hotel room to talk. See, there's this new TV series, a detective thing, really first-rate. Excellent writing. Chris says I'm perfect for it. We talked until all hours. I got so excited, I finally agreed to fly out to L.A. to meet the producers. Jess—I *am* perfect for it. The guy's sort of a throwback, see. A gentleman of the old school, courtly, Victorian, you know? But it's set right now, in fact, maybe a little in the future. It moves very fast. Yet the main character, this detective, he moves very slowly, very deliberately cutting through all the crap. You know what I mean? I read the pilot, and it was like I was meeting a long-lost friend. I know this character! I can really sink my teeth into this. And, it doesn't matter how I photograph, because it's a character role. That's what I like best about it. No more groveling around for the Paul Newman discards!

"I couldn't help myself, Jess. Really, Chris was absolutely right. When we finished talking, it was nearly three in the morning. I saw no point in going on to the Tarpinians. So, I just spent the night on Chris' sofa."

"He didn't mind?" Jessica asked.

"*She* didn't mind. Don't you remember Chris Banning? You met her at that last big show-biz party we went to . . . just before Patience was born."

Dizzily Jessica remembered Chris Banning and the awful show-biz party when she'd been nine and a half months pregnant. She had just stood around, feeling drab and huge and miserable. Chris Banning, of course, was sleek as a fashion model and managed to spend the entire evening lionizing Sam. The two of them had ignored her so completely that Jessica found herself hoping the baby would come then and there—just to get a little attention.

So that had been Chris Banning, huh?

"If you were so sure I remembered her, Sam, how do you explain your remarkable reluctance to make use of even one personal pronoun just now . . . until I forced you into it?"

Chapter 20

"CHRIS BANNING happens to be an excellent agent —in fact, I wish she were mine. Jerry Wolfe never hunted all over town for me with a hot new pilot in his hands."

"I guess Jerry is just the wrong gender."

"Now, look here, Jess—you want a fight? Okay. You think Chris has the hots for me? Maybe she does. I don't care. I do care about that part, though. And I'm going out to Los Angeles first thing tomorrow to discuss it with them."

"How're you getting to L.A.—hitchhiking? Stowing away? Roller skating?"

"Don't try to be funny. It's not your style. Chris is picking up the tab. It's nothing for you to worry about."

"But I do worry, Sam! You've just been sacked. I'm worried about money. Patience has been seeing a child psychiatrist—they don't come cheap, you know. I'm worried about a lot of things. We have to leave this place. Patience is afraid to stay here. Let's face it, so am I. So, we'll have to move again. That's not cheap, either. And since when does an agent 'pick up the tab' for an unemployed ex-actor's flight to L.A.?"

"I guess Chris is pretty sure I'm going to be an employed actor and an ex-businessman, bless her. She says I can pay her back as soon as we sign the contract."

"You really believe all this is going to happen, don't you?"

"Why shouldn't it, Jess? Why the hell shouldn't something good happen to me for once?"

"Sam, I don't mean you're not good enough to get the part. I'd never say that. I just know how often these things fall through. Certainly you of all people should remember how often these terrific deals you spend half the night talking about are dead as ashes twenty-four hours later. My god, Sam. Use your head! There's probably twenty able-bodied actors out there right now, garroting each other behind the scenery, scrambling for this part. And another dozen flying over from London. Don't you remember what it's like? You fly out to the coast, and the chances are ninety-nine out of one hundred that all you'll have to show for it is an IOU to Chris Banning for your round-trip fare. And if anything cures a case of the hots faster than an IOU like that, I'm damned if I know what it might be."

"God damn you!"

"Well-spoken."

"God damn your good gray caution! God damn your Nice Nellie realism! You can't *survive* in this business by looking back—remembering disappointments. You've got to keep your enthusiasm or you may as well give up."

"Well, forgive me, then, Sam, but that's exactly what you persuaded me most earnestly you *had* done, not too long ago."

"Well, forget it, I'm going out there. And I'm going to get that part. If it had been written for me, it couldn't suit me more. And if you don't like the way I earn my living, you can just go find yourself some other bloke and settle down to your own kind of brittle domesticity with all the child psychiatrists you need and the constant smell of cooking cabbage."

"Why, Sam, bravo! You sound just like Leslie Howard

did in *Pygmalion*, telling Wendy Hiller to 'marry Freddie.' And you know what? I'll bet we'll be very happy, Freddie-the-reliable and me. And every Saturday night, right after *All in the Family* we'll sit there in our cozy little basement playroom, with the plastic logs glowing electrically in the plastic hearth, and catch your very latest episode. I'll call Patience and say, 'C'mon down, kid, show time! Time to catch your ex-daddy's act on the old boob tube!'"

Sam slapped her. Then, shocked by what he had done—it had never happened before—he apologized.

"I'm sorry, Jessica!"

"I'm sorry, too, Sam."

"Jessie—I don't know you anymore."

"Sam—I think maybe if you knew me better, you'd like me even less." Two enormous tears slid down her cheeks.

"Christ! Don't you even want to make up?"

"Not if it means making believe, Sam! I can't keep that up anymore."

"Jessie—we never made believe. What're you talking about? What about Patience and the way we feel about her—is that make-believe? You're trying to make things worse. I'm trying to make them better."

"So, okay. Let me be the villain, then. I know you love Patience. I know you try hard to earn a living for us. I know you mean well. But it's all make-believe. Patience's regression—that's been real. How much attention have you paid to any of it? You acted as though this weird nightmare she's been going through were some kind of unpleasant skin rash that just might be catching. Well, that was the real Patience. And she was scared right out of her wits—by a prowler. A prowler and a pervert, Sam."

"What's that?"

"You heard. What's more, you'd have guessed it by now, too, if you'd given it any thought. What about that pornographic Kewpie doll? How come you were able to treat that so lightly? That's the tip-off to the whole thing. And your beautiful, smart, lovable little daughter's been mixed up pretty thick right in the middle of it. Couldn't you face it—or didn't you even notice?"

"Now you're really being unfair. The night we found that doll—who went right back to sleep—and who was up half the night trying to figure out what to do?"

"The night the prowler came back—where were you? When I tried to talk to you about my visits to Dr. Weller—you didn't even stay awake to hear me out! I could have told you Patience was paralyzed in both legs and you wouldn't have noticed! You've been so preoccupied these last weeks I found myself making all kinds of decisions without even thinking to consult you. And you know what? I don't feel any the worse for it. I've never had so many bizarre things go wrong before in all my life. But I've discovered one thing: I don't need you, Sam! I can get along just fine without you. So, if you want to go to L.A. . . . well, go. And, good—" She hesitated, in another second she would have said "riddance," and she didn't mean that.

"Good luck, Sam. I really mean it."

"You may think you don't need me now. But I know you better, Jess. You scare easy. You like decisions made for you. You like somebody to huddle up to on cold nights." Jessica shook her head no, vigorously, to the first three statements. The last one she passed on.

"I get the impression, Jess, that you're so afraid our marriage will break up that you've decided to help it along; the suspense is too much for you. Well, don't do it. Give it a chance. It can still grow. You've been growing, too, lately. After all, you were very young when we got married. It's only natural that you'd keep right on growing and changing afterward. So, okay. Maybe you're not the adorable, fragile little muddlehead I thought you were. I'm willing to accept a more mature, liberated type than I bargained for. What do you say?"

"Well, I'd like to get a more mature, liberated type in the bargain, too, damn it! You never change at all, Sam! You're exactly the same!"

"Jessica, I'm thirty-three years old. This is me. This is all the me there's ever going to be. Maybe I'll make some money someday. Maybe I won't."

"It's not money."

"What is it, then?"

"It's the make-believe. The role-playing. The fact that all the so-called magic between us is really kind of a put-on. We don't cope with reality together at all." Jessica's voice broke.

"This last episode, here in Wimbledon, is an exception, Jess. Surely you can tell that much. I was up against something just as bad in the city as you were here. I came home so exhausted and scared and confused I didn't have enough energy left to see how serious the situation had become. I'm sorry. I didn't understand what you were going through. I apologize, really! As soon as I get back from the coast, I'll spend more time with you and Patience, and we'll get back on the same wavelength again. You'll see."

Jessica did not appear convinced. Sam went over to where she was standing, rigidly. He put his arms around her. She did not relax.

"For Christ's sakes, Jess! What do you want, blood? I apologized, didn't I?"

"I can't help it. I'm numb. Let's leave it for now. You're right about my worrying that our marriage will break up. I worry about it a lot. Patience loves you so much. And she means everything to me, you know that. She's going to need extra-special care and attention. Dr. Weller didn't come right out and say anything; he probably thought I was too high-strung already. But this whole regression thing was the direct result of a sexual assault—"

"You mean she was *attacked?*" Sam didn't recognize his own voice.

"No, but something bizarre, something really kinky, happened in her room; and she saw it."

"Christ!"

Sam was pale. He sat down. It was obviously a whole new thought for him. He'd never considered the possibility before. Watching him, Jessica had a sense of the separateness of their lives. He'd had no idea of how serious a symptom Patience's regression had been. She knew then the signal she'd been waiting for from Sam. And she knew it was probably an unreasonable demand on her part. She wanted Sam to postpone his trip to the coast. He wouldn't have to cancel it—just to delay it a day or two. If he offered to do that, she'd feel that his commitment to her and Patience was solid. If he didn't, she wouldn't feel that way, perhaps never could feel that way, again. She waited for him to speak.

"Jess, I had no idea it was anything this bad." He got up and put his arm around her.

"Look, hang in there for another day or two. When I come back from L.A., who knows, maybe we'll be in line for a move to California! And, if not, I promise I'll get you and Patience settled in a good, safe place. We'll do everything we can to see she recovers from whatever awful thing it was she saw. Okay?" Jessie remained silent, sensing her demand—silent though it had been—had probably been excessive. She certainly wouldn't ever let him know about it. She moved away from him, walked to the hall closet, and said, "Well, I guess you'll need to pack some things, then."

"Yeah, here, let me help you get that bag down."

Chapter 21

"SO, where is this house you've been advertising all week?" Jessie was sitting in the Smiths' large, old-fashioned kitchen. Sunlight was pouring through the tall windows, bordered on all sides by neat squares of pastel-colored glass, and casting beautiful, watery shadows on the white linoleum floor.

At seven thirty that morning, she'd driven Sam to the crossroads where the airport limousine sat and waited for that day's contingent of Wimbledon's Kennedy-bound businessmen. That had been the first Sam had seen—or even heard of—the little yellow Volkswagen. Even then Jessica doubted how much he was taking in. His manner had been mild, apologetic, distracted. He told her he really had had no choice but to go to the coast that day. He would regret it for the rest of his life if he didn't. He told her he'd call her that night. He kissed her very sincerely, as the three other men already in the limousine sat and watched. Now it was after nine, and she'd enjoyed a hearty breakfast with Mary. She'd taken another of Dr. Weller's pills and was welcoming the numbness she already recognized like an old friend.

"Well, from what I hear, it's just darling, Jess. An old guest-cottage. It's not on Maynard Hill. It's closer to the river. You ready? Why don't we get going then—I'm dying to see it myself." They dressed the children warmly, since there was a blustery wind, despite the sunshine.

The cottage was situated on a private drive off Oneida Street—a short street on the river side of Main Street, north of Wimbledon's business section. All of the large old houses had distinct personalities but reflected the pandemic of porches, pillars, and pediments that hit the homes of America's prosperous middle classes in the late nineteenth century. A circular gravel drive led them past a dark-brown shingled house, surrounded by nearly two acres of lawn and tall old trees. The cottage itself came as a complete surprise to Jessica. It was small, and its lines were unencumbered. There was a fine slate-covered mansard roof, a small porch, a graceful red brick chimney. The front door was polished yellow oak, and an oval cut-glass window, curtained in lace, sat primly in the middle of it.

"Do you have the key, Mary?" Jessica found she could hardly wait to step inside.

"No, but here comes Mrs. Murphy now. She'll show us through." Mary's face was set.

"Mrs. *Murphy?* Mary! You don't mean that this was . . ."

"*Sh!* Here she comes. Save your remarks for later, okay?"

Jessica, furious with Mary for not telling her the whole story beforehand, stood on the little porch and watched Mrs. Murphy, who was hurrying down the gravel path, with a bulky sweater thrown hastily over her shoulders. The Murphys must live in that big brown house. And this, this delightful little dollhouse, must be where poor old Nora Kelly lived. God! What did Mary take her for? They could never move in here—no matter how charming a place it was. Still, there was no way out, now. She'd have to go through the motions and let herself be shown around.

"I heard your car, Mary. I knew it'd be you and dear Mrs. Porter. How are you this morning? *Brr!* No point in standing out here in the cold. Let's go inside."

If it seemed like a dollhouse on the outside, the inside was nothing short of a jewel box. A graceful entry led to the front parlor on one side and a generous dining room on the other. Straight ahead a steep flight of steps, carpeted in bright red broadloom, led to the multi-eaved bedrooms upstairs.

"We haven't been able to show it to anybody until now, because of the investigation . . ." Mrs. Murphy hesitated, pausing to wipe her eyes with a tissue. "But, my son feels, and I think he's right, that we shouldn't let this lovely place stand empty. We thought—frankly— when Mrs. Smith told us how that crazy old Falconer woman was giving you a hard time—why not let Mrs. Porter see this place first? Wouldn't it be nice to have a cute little family living here? And we all agreed to let you have what you might call first refusal, Mrs. Porter. I don't have to tell you—I'm sure you can imagine all too well—the kind of horde of applicants just one tiny little ad in the New York *Times* would bring to our door. We'd just as soon avoid that. As well as the . . . you know, curiosity seekers"—more dabbing about the eyes— "that any type of local advertising might produce." Both Mrs. Murphy and Mary Smith were smiling now, looking at Jessica for an answering look of affirmation or gratitude or something. Jessica felt herself tighten up into a negative ball. They were not doing her any favors, thank you. Silently, hoping that at least the expression on her face would be neutral, and that she wasn't actually hurting anybody's feelings, Jessica followed as Mrs. Murphy ushered them systematically through the little house.

Though she pointed out each of the rooms' advantages in turn, her speech was perfunctory, at best. The rooms simply spoke for themselves. They were enchanting.

"We left some of the furniture . . . but we can store it all, if you'd like. We didn't know whether it'd be better to offer it furnished, so we sort of compromised and left just a few of the best pieces. . . ."

"It's charming, Mrs. Murphy," Jessica said.

"I don't expect you to decide right away, of course," Mrs. Murphy said. They were back in the parlor, which offered an excellent Adams-style fireplace flanked by tall French windows. Through the windows, the sun dappled a colonnade of majestic hemlock trees.

"The rent is two hundred seventy-five dollars a month," Mrs. Murphy announced. "Gas and electric are separate."

"That's very reasonable, Mrs. Murphy," Jessica told her. Mary was looking at her steadily; she seemed to be willing Jessica to take it right there on the spot. But Jessica couldn't. The place was exquisite. She loved it. But it was like a poisoned apple, She'd had enough of poisoned charm! The Falconer place was breathtakingly beautiful, too; yet they'd known nothing but fear and harassment there. Now here she was being offered the fragile nest of a cruelly murdered dove. When, in fact, a sterile two-bedroom apartment in an anonymous high-rise somewhere would probably be much more suited to her present needs.

"Now, Mrs. Porter, don't go rushing your decision. I'm going back to the house with Mary and your little ones, and we'll all have some cocoa. Why don't you just wander around one more time, on your own? Here's the key. Just be sure to lock up when you leave."

"That's a great idea, Mrs. Murphy!" Mary said enthusiastically. "Jess, just take your time—walk around, and see if you can't picture all your nice Porter things in this darling place!"

"There are plenty of closets, too, Mrs. Porter. You'll see. I forgot to point them out."

"Thank you." Jessie watched as the four round faces —two big and two small—beamed at her in cheerful farewell. The house was very quiet. She sat down at the window seat (hadn't she always wanted a window seat?) in the dining room and watched as the little group clambered up the Murphys' back steps. Was she being contrary? Was this in fact the lucky find of the century? Not for her. She could picture plenty of people who would light on this place, go into ecstasies over its precious charm, and cheerfully pay twice the price Mrs. Murphy was asking.

She'd better walk through the house one more time. She duly passed through the efficient kitchen, with its built-in booth for breakfast; the dining room, with its fine built-in cabinetry. Very nice, indeed. She walked up the stairs, knowing she would never, ever live here. Nora Kelly had lived here. How long? Thirty, forty years? Nora Kelly had been murdered. Jessica was through with the eccentric. She'd had enough of the macabre to last her the rest of her life. She didn't want Patience starting school in Wimbledon and having her playmates tell her she lived in a murdered lady's house. Was she being irrational? Well, feelings often were irrational. So what.

The bedrooms, not as small as she thought they'd be from the outside, were perfect. She stood by one of the three twelve-paned windows in the master bedroom and caught her breath when she saw the river. She watched a huge, flat barge pass practically under her nose. Then she heard the elegiac whistle of a Hudson Division train. Boy, it was really too much. No. Not for her. Not for the Porter family. Still. Sam would really dig it, wouldn't he? She walked over to the closet in the corner and opened it. A walk-in closet. Built-in drawers, a light fixture in the ceiling. All through the house were marvelous custom touches it took years of living in a place to provide. She turned on the little light and stood there in the closet for a minute, thinking, trying to be fair. She could feel herself wavering. There was something so alluring about this top floor. The main floor was almost too pretty. But up here she could sense real comfort, ease, coziness. She sniffed. Cedar. Sure enough, three of the drawers were built of cedar. She opened them: one, two, three. When she opened the third drawer, the one at the very bottom, something rolled about in it. Because all the shelves and drawers seemed to have been thoroughly cleaned out, Jessica stooped down to see what Mrs. Murphy's eagle-eyed cleaning might have overlooked.

When she grasped it, pulled it out and looked it over, her face went pale.

"Oh, my God—*no!*" She spoke aloud, kneeling alone on the floor of Nora Kelly's private closet. Still kneeling, holding the object, she closed her eyes for a brief moment, trying to decide what she must do next.

The little man was grinning lasciviously at her, baring a leering yellow row of celluloid teeth. His lips were much too red. She examined him more closely. There could be no doubt as to his identity. He was the mate to the doll they'd found in Patience's crib. She turned him around; sure enough, on the back, under his striped shirt, was stamped "Whoopee Novelties. Made in U.S.A." Vintage? Probably 1929 to 1934, somewhere in there. The man had slicked-down hair, parted almost in the middle, and features reminiscent of a John Held Jr. cartoon. He wore a snap-on bow tie and very wide, cuffed and pleated trousers, on which the fly buttoned with real buttons. Jessica undid the buttons, fairly certain what she'd find. Originally, no doubt, there had been some kind of spring mechanism, but this no longer functioned. Instead, a grotesquely exaggerated erection merely oozed through the opening, like an aging birthday balloon. The sponge-rubber-like material was badly corroded. Jessica covered it again and did up the buttons.

She slipped the doll in her purse and prepared to leave. Her heart had begun to beat violently, so she took another pill. She'd have to put Mrs. Murphy off with something vague and rush right to the police with this. When she rejoined the group at Mrs. Murphy's house, Jessica found she couldn't confide her discovery to Mary. The fact that Mary hadn't given her the full story about the house for rent made her feel shy toward her, as well as resentful. Jessica had always hated the sense of being manipulated, had hated hearing her parents talk about how best to handle her when she'd been standing right there with them in the room. She'd been a perfectly ordinary little girl, never much of a problem, perhaps just a bit shy. Yet once her parents had actually gotten her up to a summer camp on the pretext of visiting another child. Only after she arrived did her own suitcase—packed behind the scenes and without her knowledge—appear out of the blue. She'd stayed for two weeks and had enjoyed the camp very much. But she never forgave her parents the deception.

Now Mary had shown herself guilty of a similar crime, and Jess realized she'd have to keep her discovery to herself and go to the police on her own.

First, Jessica had to thank Mrs. Murphy for giving her "first refusal" on the house.

"Unfortunately, my husband is in California right now, and I really must wait until he returns before I can tell you one way or the other. Let's see, today's Friday . . . I'll call you by Tuesday morning at the latest. Is that all right with you?"

"Of course, Mrs. Porter, I understand." Mrs. Murphy did not understand, but her smile was kindly, all the same.

"You're really pissed off at me, aren't you, Jessica?" Mary said when they were all back in the car again.

"I'd rather not discuss it now, Mary. But something's just dawned on me that's important. I think I should go to the police about it. Besides, Dr. Weller said he thought I should go to the police about our prowler. . . ." Poor Jessie was not a good liar; in another minute, if she weren't very careful, she'd be telling Mary everything.

"You want me to take Patience for the afternoon?"

"You don't mind?"

"Of course not, Jess. I'm not the one that's angry, remember?" Mary smiled at her ingenuously.

"I may be awhile, Mary. But I'll pick Patience up before dinner, certainly." Jessie got out of the car at the foot of their steps. Patience and Violet remained in the cargo area of the big wagon. They waved. Jessica looked up at the house. Had it ever seemed this menacing before? Mary saw the look on Jessie's face.

"Jess, don't spend the night up there. Spend the night with us. What's the point of scaring yourself to death?"

"Yes, but Sam said he'd call me. . . ."

"Well, think about it. Wait until he calls, and then come over. Good luck with the police. Do you know where the station house is?"

"It's across the tracks, isn't it? Right next to Copper-Cable, on the river?" Jessie thought she remembered seeing it from the train station.

"Yes. That's it. I'll hear from you later, okay?"

"Right."

If only she had that other doll! Jessie looked up at the house once more and decided she wouldn't need even to go up. She got into the yellow VW instead and headed back down the hill.

As she turned left on Main Street, heading for the overpass that led to the other side of the railroad tracks, her car was observed by Dr. Wright. He was between appointments and standing in the big bay window on the second story of the old clapboard house, in which his father had first made his office so many years ago. As his father had before him, he enjoyed watching the passing scene from this private vantage. When he recognized Jessica driving by, he remembered her inquiry concerning Mrs. Falconer. Now would be a good time to check his files. There was something about that disconcerting young woman that made him feel responsible for her. "Ah, why kid yourself, Max, old boy," he said to himself, "you're attracted to her." If he had some useful information about her crazy landlady, it would give him an excuse to call her.

The police station, a dusty brownstone building with a steep flight of steps and a shiny brass handrail, had been erected in 1908, according to the legend engraved on the grimy cornerstone. Jessica hurried up the steps. It was even windier here next to the river. Little cinders were whipping through the air, and one landed in her eye, briefly. With one eye red and weepy, and her hair thoroughly disheveled, she walked into the police station as bravely as she knew how.

She asked the man at the desk for Detective Sergeant Orsini.

"It's about the Kelly murder," she heard herself say.

"I don't know if he's here right now, miss. Would you like to wait over there? I'll see if I can find him for you." The officer was polite. Jessica sat down on the hard oak bench he'd indicated. She thought about Nora Kelly's pretty little house. It was probably no more than three or four short blocks away from here. Yet all she could see out of the barred station-house windows were the same gigantic reels of cable in the CopperCable yard that had intrigued Sam as his train passed by.

Officer Orsini appeared. He ushered her into a small office.

"Now, you say you have information to give me on the Kelly case, Mrs. Porter?" He hadn't remembered her, at first. But now he recalled his visit to the Falconer house and the nervous, pretty little tenant, with the howling, bare-assed baby. She seemed calmer, today. But there could be no mistaking the fear in her eyes. What did she have to tell him? None of their hoped-for leads from the CopperCable computer had panned out. If Nora Kelly had been covering up some kind of illegal flim-flam from out of her past, she'd taken the secret with her to the grave. The payroll, pension, and profit-sharing accounts for which Nora Kelly had been responsible had revealed nothing out of order. Orsini was not convinced, though. Now old archives at Copper-Cable headquarters in Pittsburgh were being examined —by hand. It was pitifully slow going. He still had not interviewed the Falconer woman.

It was difficult for Jessica to get her story out. After all, she'd never even mentioned the first Kewpie doll to Orsini. She hadn't remembered it until after he'd gone that day. And though she had told him about Tweetie —that doll wasn't with her today. Dr. Weller had it, was running some tests on it. She could tell Orsini was listening to her with attention, waiting to isolate the useful kernel when she got to it. She hadn't managed to get it out, yet. His seriousness made her nervous. All of a sudden she had this wild impulse to just get up and leave. What did she, Jessica Porter, have to do with murders, perverts, pornographic Kewpie dolls? How had she ever gotten mixed up in this mess? And what made her think the police would know what to do with any of the tawdry information she was bringing to them? Was she, in fact, giving this quiet, serious police officer a valuable clue? Or was she merely muddying the waters for him? She stopped, pausing for breath.

"Go on, Mrs. Porter. I know how you feel; you think some of the stuff you're telling me may not be important. Just tell me the whole series of events, and let me decide what's important. I'm not sure what Mrs. Falconer's connection to Miss Kelly might have been. But I do know that Mr. Falconer knew Miss Kelly very well. They were friendly for many years."

"Yes, but he's been dead for many years."

"I know that, too."

Jessica took out the doll then.

"I found this in Nora Kelly's house this morning, Officer Orsini. It's the mate to a doll that was placed in my baby's crib the night after Nora Kelly's murder."

"Do you still have the first doll?"

"No. That's just it. It disappeared." She told how the doll had seemed to jump at Dorcas during their party, how they'd never seen it again after that. "It had a magnet on it, you see. The magnet jumped at the magnet on Dorcas's potholder. This doll had one, too, I'll bet—you know like those little kissing dolls you see in novelty shops. You know, put 'em together and they lock into a passionate embrace."

"Well, without that other doll, Mrs. Porter, this is all just hearsay. Where do you think it is now? Up in Mrs. Falconer's flat? We could get a search warrant, but we don't really have enough to go on to do that. Almost, but not quite." He shook his head. Jessica told him about the prowler, the cigar, the old Tweetie's sudden reappearance in Patience's crib.

"Mrs. Porter, perhaps you could bring some of that other stuff down—the cigar stub, that other doll. I'll put a man on your prowler complaint. That's the place to start. We'll have to get that old woman to let us in. We'll get right on it. Thank you for coming. I don't know where these facts are leading us yet; but I appreciate your coming. The very fact that there's some kind of connection between old lady Falconer and Nora Kelly gives us something to go on. I'll be in touch with you." He stood up, still looking thoughtfully at his notes. There was something here, he knew it.

"If I find that other Kewpie doll—the female one—would that give you enough to tie it to Mrs. Falconer?"

"It should certainly help," he replied, still reading over his notes.

"Okay then." Jessica realized she'd have to get that doll. She prepared to leave.

"Oh, and Mrs. Porter . . ."

"Yes?"

"I wouldn't stay up in that apartment of yours anymore, if I were you. Do you have some place you can go to for the next few days?"

"Yes. Yes, I'll stay at George Smith's house up on Riverview. Thanks for the advice." She looked over her shoulder at him and saw that he was already on the phone. "Yes, operator, get me Pittsburgh, please." That made no sense at all to Jessica. She walked down the steps and headed for the parking lot. As she got behind the wheel of her car, she took a moment to slip another of Dr. Weller's pills in her mouth. She knew she would need it.

Chapter 22

INSTEAD of pulling into the driveway at 33 Granite Terrace, Jessica drove all the way up Maynard, to Mrs. Falconer's entrance. She parked about half a block down the street, then calmly walked back to Mrs. Falconer's garage door. By standing on tiptoe she could just peer in. She didn't dare believe her luck. The big old 1949 Pontiac was not there. Jessica knew very little about Mrs. Falconer's daily routines. She knew the woman arose early—at dawn; Mrs. Falconer herself had mentioned that she did her marketing on Thursdays. Where would she be now, a Friday afternoon? It was just after two. She'd have to hurry.

Though it was still early in the afternoon, the sun had disappeared. Heavy clouds were building for a blustery rainstorm. She lifted the latch, undid the hook and eye, and turned the knob on their side door. She peered up the steps. No tobacco smoke today. No sounds of any kind. Dimly, she made out the little velvet curtain where the steps turned a corner midway. She was scared but, thanks to Dr. Weller's pills, calm. She walked up. She got to the curtain—a greasy, dusty, filthy thing, with tarnished gold braid and grimy tassels. She pushed it aside. The steps went up for another half flight. She came out in Mrs. Falconer's kitchen. It was not clean, but it didn't look used, either. Though the floor felt gritty underfoot, and the windowsill was laden with a sooty accumulation that bespoke long neglect, the sink—an old, cracked, marble edifice standing precariously on uneven legs—was wiped clean. No dirty dishes or pots were about. Mrs. Falconer's world was shrinking daily. Pretty soon all she would know or care about would be the path from her bedroom to her bath to this kitchen sink. *The doll might be right here,* she thought. No—the bedroom was more likely.

Jessica walked quickly through the kitchen, which was at the front of the house, but for one room in front of it—a gracious foyer. Jessica looked in and saw it had been painted a sunny yellow not long ago, perhaps when Mrs. F had their flat downstairs done. This room looked fresh and inviting. The parquet floor was polished, a small divan was covered with a crisp Indian throw, and to Jessica's further surprise a still life by Matisse decorated the wall. The room was not at all what she would have expected. But—she thought to herself —if Mrs. Falconer ever opened the door to strangers, which she evidently had to do from time to time, wouldn't this innocuous, pleasant room put them at their ease? The room was about as sinister as a pat of butter. It made a good cover. As there were no shelves or chests of drawers to hide anything in, Jessica wasted no further time in it.

Her next surprise came when she walked through four connected rooms—large, well-proportioned, formal rooms—that were completely empty. Not a stick of furniture, no rugs, no curtains or blinds at the windows. One room had shelves on all four walls—the library, it had been, no doubt. But no books. Mrs. Falconer must have sold everything of value she'd ever had to make ends meet. Jessica, who'd never really tried to come to grips with Mrs. Falconer as a real person, simply because the threat of her actual presence obviated any kind of rational character analysis, suddenly caught a glimpse of the loneliness, fear, and pathetic pride that had shaped the eccentric woman in her old age.

All of the succeeding rooms were either completely empty or were littered with old packing boxes and an assortment of debris—she saw one carton, containing God knew what, marked WE DO OUR PART—SPAM. FEEDING OUR SOLDIERS, SAILORS AND MARINES! DO YOUR PART —BUY WAR BONDS TODAY! The carton was further decorated with the silhouette of a revolutionary soldier in profile, carrying a musket. Jessica was quite sure she knew where the bedroom would be. That was where she always heard that early dawn activity. It would be way in the back, facing the river. Above their own porch and living room. She was following a molelike furrow through the rooms. The house was square and well designed. In the middle of the square a generous central hall connected four large rooms on either side. At the front were the entrance way, kitchen, and a bathroom. And then, in the rear, another bath that was apparently directly above their own, downstairs, and two small rooms, perhaps originally meant to be children's rooms, and Mrs. Falconer's real home—the many-windowed back room. Jessica could see it as she came nearer, edging by the old cardboard boxes that filled the last of the small rooms. The dust was making her nose itch. She bumped into a table—the first actual piece of furniture she'd passed since she left the entrance.

She looked at the table, and its purpose dawned on her. It was a doctor's examining table, covered in ancient, peeling, black leather. At the base a pair of stirrups, looking more like manacles intended for some unspeakable sinner in the dark ages. But the dark ages this table served were not that long ago. Silent, long disused, it seemed to warn Jessica of the seriousness of the evil she'd come to disturb. The conclusion she reached, almost without pausing to think, was fairly obvious. Mrs. Falconer had evidently been more than just a nurse, back in her heyday. She'd apparently done her share of illegal abortions, too. Jessica's heart was starting its uneven, noisy pounding again. Her hands were slippery with perspiration. What the hell, she'd come this far. What could this sordid old table do to her anyway? On legs she could barely feel, with a sensation of swimming underwater through a sulfurous grotto, she entered the final room.

Downstairs the phone rang. She jumped. The phone rang and rang. She stood perfectly still. Who was trying to reach her? She looked at her watch. Two thirty! And she hadn't even gotten what she came for yet!

After twelve rings Dr. Wright hung up. He'd asked his father about Mrs. Falconer at lunch.

"Vile woman!" Max, Sr., had said. "Nasty disposition. Lah-dee-dah airs. Most perfect set of teeth in all of Wimbledon. Never did more than clean 'em." Max, Jr., was puzzled. "You mean you didn't make a set of false teeth for her?"

"False teeth? Loretta Cavendish Falconer? Never! Now, that poor sod she married, young Frederick the meek, I finally had to put a pretty good set into him. Poor fellow, he took years to pay. She never let him have any of her money. Tighter than—" But Max, Jr., interrupted.

"So Mrs. Falconer's teeth were perfect, eh?"

"Yep. There's no justice, you know, son. The wicked have the last laugh, every time—even here in Wimbledon." Max, Sr., chuckled.

So that was all he'd had to tell Jessica. He also wanted to find out—as tactfully as possible—about her marital status. He didn't know why, but he'd been assuming she was divorced or separated. But for all he knew, a Mr. Porter might be around. He'd call again later.

Jessica didn't notice when the telephone downstairs finally stopped ringing. Because the room Mrs. Falconer spent all her time in was a nightmare. Jessica wished she had a cane like Mrs. Falconer's, just to help her carve a trail through the jungle of worthless junk and debris that was piled almost to the ceiling. Six-foot stacks of newspapers and magazines—some still in the brown wrappers they were mailed in—coffee cans, hundreds of them; Christmas cards, twenty years' worth, at the very least; picture postcards tacked randomly to the walls, to the backs of derelict chairs, nestled in the corners of most of the windowpanes. She stopped to examine one of the picture postcards—two kittens playing with colored yarn—and read the message on the back. There was no date, but the card had grown yellow around the edges and was brittle to the touch. "Wednesday is out," it read. "Friday two dolls." It was unsigned. Two dolls. A tantalizing clue, that made no sense to her . . . yet. She hurried on through the mounds of litter. Empty food boxes—Ritz Crackers, Premium Saltines, and hundreds, perhaps thousands, of empty tins: sardines, cans of Campbell's beans, Dinty Moore beef stew, Franco-American spaghetti—the room was so littered with moldy remains of lonely meals it was impossible to take it all in. Finally, over in the corner, she saw the bed. It was a lovely old bedstead—dark cherry wood, with massive posts carved in an elegant pineapple motif at the tips. On it was just a bare mattress . . . filthy . . . and an ancient pillow covered in blackened ticking. A luxurious red silk comforter—luxurious still, despite its age and dirt—was the only covering. Next to the bed stood a delicately bow-fronted nightstand, drawers opened and bulging with further detritus, on which rested a little electric hotplate and a venerable Atwater Kent table radio, shaped like a cathedral window. There was one more item on the nightstand. The item she'd come for.

She felt neither surprise nor satisfaction in finding it just where she thought it would be. The doll leaned against the radio, in a sitting position. The nonchalance of its position reminded Jessica of pictures she'd seen of prostitutes sitting at lit second-story windows advertising their trade to pedestrians below. How could she get to it, across this murderous, debris-strewn room? With the kind of convulsive revulsion reserved for cockroaches, slimy snakes, and white grubs under rocks, Jessica found herself traversing the filthy bed—there simply was no other way to get to the night table. She grabbed the doll and she rushed out of the room, knocking down one of the mountainous piles of newsprint by the door. The sound echoed eerily throughout the large apartment. At the far end came a sound like the slamming of a door. Was it an echo—or had Mrs. Falconer just returned? She edged through the next two rooms on tiptoe, holding her breath. All she had to do was get to the side stairs. She was nearly there. She didn't hear another sound. Then the telephone downstairs began to ring again. Jessica felt an absurd regret —surely it would be ringing its last ring just as she got downstairs to answer it. She'd never know who it was.

Dr. Weller let the phone ring eight times. He was a busy man. He was calling to tell what he'd found out about Tweetie. The sticky coating on the doll was, as he'd suspected, semen. He told his secretary to remind him to try Jessica's number again in thirty minutes. Perhaps she'd gone to the police to report that prowler. He sincerely hoped that she had.

By the time the phone stopped ringing, Jessica had reached the kitchen. She was just twelve feet from the little side door. She took just one second to turn to her purse and place the doll in it. In a mad moment she delayed her departure to take the male doll out of her purse and hold the two together. It was an aberrant, stupid thing for her to do. Later on, she would blame it on the excessive amounts of tranquilizer in her system. Fascinated for one split second, she watched as the male doll and the female doll met and collided—locked into a magnetic embrace.

Clump. Clump. Clump.

Jessica froze.

Mrs. Falconer, her face flushed from the cold, her mad blue eyes tearing profusely from the sharp wind, her gnarled old hand still holding the keys to the Pontiac, had entered the kitchen. Jessica simply stood, staring. She didn't even try to hide the coupled dolls in her hands. She could have tried to slip them in her bag—but she stopped thinking. If there was any coherent thought in her brain at all, it was simply, "Please, God, don't let me die!"

Mrs. Falconer stared at Jessica in disbelief.

"What?" she said. "You here? Come back, have you?" She laughed. "Wanting a bit of fun, eh?" Her attention was focused on the dolls—she barely saw Jessica. She came closer, close enough for Jessica to smell her. Mrs. Falconer leaned over and fondled the dolls—making them move in a sinuous, rhythmic way.

"Hee hee. A little fun, eh? It isn't safe up here. You know that. Downstairs. That way, she'll never know. Deaf as a post, she is. Hee hee." She took off her coat. Jessica, paralyzed by fear, did not dare let go of the dolls. She had but one goal: to get herself and the dolls down the side stairs to safety. But just then the old woman grabbed the dolls and, turning from Jessica, began a shuffling sort of dance. The old face became set, square, distant . . . the eyes shut. The old voice began a gravelly sort of humming. A clicking, sucking sound, some words Jessica couldn't make out, and all the time the circular, shuffling steps. Then, a wicked cackle—followed by wild, phlegmy laughter.

"Oh, baby!" the voice said. The coital charade between the two dolls gathered momentum.

"Oh, baby, mum, mum, hee-hee, heh-heh!" The old hands shook convulsively and placed the dolls on the kitchen table. Freed of their salacious burden, Mrs. Falconer's hands reached for the hem of her tattered skirt. Jessica suddenly knew what was happening.

"No!" she gasped. "No!"

The old person in front of her continued the shuffling dance, though the humming was muffled now by the gaudily flowered dress being pulled over the head. The dress dropped to the floor. The dance continued. And Jessica saw Frederick Falconer, in a dirty undershirt, a vest, and old pleated trousers, rolled up nearly to the knees, emerge from his daytime disguise. His blue eyes opened. He reached into the pocket of his vest, and withdrew a cheap cigar. He lit the cigar with a wooden kitchen match and exhaled expansively. And now the old arms reached out toward her . . . and the old face laughed and laughed.

"Hee hee. Heh heh. Puff puff. Here I am, baby! C'mon, now, Nora—do me! Hee hee hee." The graying white nurse's shoes were trampling on the flowered dress. Frederick Falconer reached for the female doll. He tweaked it in the obvious places and gestured meaningfully with it. More laughter.

"She won't hear a thing. Deaf as a post! Hah hah!"

"Not here, Frederick!" Jessica heard herself say. "Let's go downstairs." Jessica had edged herself forward so that there were just three feet between her and the side door.

"No! Not down there. Our love nest's become a trap! She'll come crawling out at us. You'll see! You did it, too, Nora! You helped!" His eyes bulged accusingly. "Loretta's dead, Nora—dead. You're dead, too. You came back; she can come back, too, any time. First the baby. We let her kill the baby, Nora. And then we killed her. Killed her and buried her—right in our little love nest."

"And then you killed me, Frederick, didn't you?" Jessica said.

"Yes. And now you've come back. I'll get you yet. Retiring to Florida, computer's taking over. Leaving me without a pension check! You didn't think I'd let you get away with that, did you?"

Jessica was within reach of the door. She wanted to keep him talking, but she didn't understand enough about what he was hallucinating to know what to say next. Best just to agree.

"Yes, Frederick, I understand."

"No you don't! You don't know anything about it. That woman is all over the house. Twelve years dead and she's everywhere. She's down there now, Nora! Buried in that wall. And you, you with that little sugar and spice house with your ladies in for tea and your library committee and butter wouldn't melt in your mouth! You killed her same as me! You think I'd let you run away to Florida?"

"Frederick. Why do you think I'm here now?" A desperate ploy.

"Huh?"

"I've come to fix everything up, Frederick! . . . Make everything all right." Jessica's voice was shaking. Jessica was shaking. Falconer seemed in a dream. "Meet me downstairs in five minutes. I'll have a surprise for you." Jessica fought to maintain control. The door was just two feet away. She no longer trusted herself to fool the mad person in front of her. He might snap any second. She made a dash for it. In one swift movement she lurched through the side door. The momentum caused her to trip halfway down the stairs. She ran through their apartment and out the rear door. It was raining hard, and there was a cold, gusty wind. She ran down the street toward her car. She didn't hear their phone begin to ring.

Detective Sergeant Orsini let the phone ring only five times. Hadn't Mrs. Porter told him she'd be staying with friends? No need to warn her.

"C'mon, let's just go get Falconer. We've got enough information now."

The call to Pittsburgh had done the trick. Eyeballing forty years of record books was slow going. Especially if you didn't know what you were looking for. But looking up forty years of records for just one name—Falconer—was much easier. An hour after Orsini had placed his request the return call came.

"Yeah. We've got a Falconer, Frederick, R., on the full-pension list: born, November 18, 1902/ employed at the Wimbledon plant on July 1, 1926/ retired at full pension as of July 1, 1956. And then, we've got 'im on the deceased list as of August, 1962."

"Still on the full-pension list after 1962?" An anticipatory smile was on Orsini's intent face.

"Last check went out just a week ago."

Orsini nodded. That was all he needed.

Jessica couldn't believe that she was still alive. She hadn't gotten the dolls back from him—but, God! what difference did that make now? Mr. Falconer. Mr. Frederick Falconer had killed Nora Kelly, his mistress. Thirteen years before, he'd (they'd?) killed his wife. He'd been impersonating her ever since. Why, she hadn't a clue—but the police would be able to put the rest of it together.

She was driving downhill on Firehouse Lane, heading

for the police station and safety. The dark, stormy weather had caused streetlamps to be turned on. Hers was the only car on Firehouse Lane. But just as she neared the busy Main Street crossing, where she could see there was plenty of traffic, she looked into the rearview mirror of the Volkswagen and saw the high, grinning hood of a black, 1949 Pontiac looming erratically into view and gaining speed. God only knew when he realized she'd gone. God only knew what kind of retribution he was planning. The traffic light on Main Street was red. She had to stop. Again she looked in her rearview mirror. He was so close now that she could see his face behind the wheel. Hoping that the rain would provide cover to prevent Falconer from noticing her, she turned off the ignition, opened the car door on the passenger side, and ran out. It seemed to her that leaving the car behind would give her a time advantage, and make her less conspicuous. If she could just make it to the police station, everything would be all right. And, sure enough, the big black Pontiac hesitated when the light changed to green, and the Volkswagen failed to move forward. It cost Falconer precious seconds. But then he saw Jessica a block away, as she ran across the railroad bridge. He stepped on the gas.

Staying close to the nondescript buildings on the other side of the bridge, Jessica neared the street that led to CopperCable and the police station. She was soaked through, and her shoes were filled with water. She heard a siren in the distance. Two police cars were now speeding up Maynard. She stopped to catch her breath. She saw the horizontal teeth of the Pontiac's radiator grill reflected in the streetlight on the corner she'd just passed. No time. She had to run again.

Now the car was actually chasing her. Though she tried to head right—toward the police station, the car was forcing her to the left—into an obscure corner of the

CopperCable yard, at the very edge of the Hudson River. Jessica was close to collapse. He could simply have run her down, there and then. But somehow she managed to keep moving, until she realized that she could go no farther; she was cornered. The car stopped. The headlights remained on. Frederick Falconer came out. He was wearing a black oilskin slicker. His cane led the way. Jessica looked desperately around. There was no cover. There was a chain-link fence all around the area and nothing but stacks of spools and reels for cable between her and Falconer. The only way she could go was . . . up. The cable spools were all different sizes. She clambered up a small one and from it onto a bigger one. From the big one she climbed farther up, to the top of several that had been stacked.

Falconer was right behind her. She hesitated for a minute. There was another spool at the top of a pile just six feet away from her, at the same height she was at now. Could she jump to that one, in this rain, without falling? There was no choice. Falconer was right there. She jumped—and made it. As she stood up on the enormous spool, Jessica saw the old man pause— Could he jump it, too? He picked up his cane.

"I've got you now. You can't get away."

Jessica looked around. He was right! This was as far as she could go. There were no more spools to jump to. No more steps up or across she could take. Falconer's cane clicked and opened. A long steel blade shot out.

"This is for you, Mrs. Porter! You had me fooled, but not for long. You're next. You think I'd let you get away? After all I've been through?" He gestured with the blade, flailing the air.

Jessica was so high above the ground on her crazy pedestal of spools she did not think she could survive the drop down. She would jump only if there were no other way to escape from him. First she would have to

238

try to talk to this unbelievable, mad person standing just six feet away from her on his own column of piled-up spools and reels, hell-bent to kill her. She would have to try to talk him out of it. The rain made everything so difficult. Difficult to see. Difficult to make herself heard.

"But why, Mr. Falconer?" she shouted into the dark, wet air between them. "Why kill me? You can't possibly get away with it. It's all over now, can't you see that? The police are on to you . . . they're after you. Look down, Mr. Falconer . . . that's a long drop. How do you plan to get back to the ground?" She could see him appear to hesitate. *Oh, please, God! Just a little more time!* "After all, Mr. Falconer," she went on, still shouting to make herself heard above the noise of the downpour, "even if you jump over here and succeed in killing me with that blade—how do you plan to get down from here, afterward? Personally, Mr. Falconer, I don't think you can make it. What possible good will it do to kill me?" That was when she lost him. He shook his head, a mad, possessed old man, pursuing some wild dream of retribution that no longer made any sense.

"Nobody knew. Nobody would ever have known. You and that ugly long nose of yours. Poking into things you had no business to. Now it's your turn." He was going to jump over to her. Jessica did not wait. She jumped. What would happen to Falconer no longer mattered to her. She was so sure, as she fell through the air and saw the ground loom darkly up—it seemed to take a very long time—that this terrible fall would kill her.

Yet Falconer's dying scream, as he, too, came crashing down, was the last thing Jessica was to hear . . . until much, much later.

Chapter 23

THE pain in her leg told her she was still alive. Cautiously she opened her eyes. She saw an insistent, circling red light—was that the pain? No, an ambulance, of course. There was a blue light, too. A police car. It was still raining hard, but something was protecting her. A large umbrella was being held above her by . . .

"Sam?" Her voice was a croak.

"Mrs. Porter, how are you feeling now? It's Dr. Wright." She recognized the face beneath the umbrella. "I saw part of what happened from my window. . . . We're moving you to the hospital now. I put a temporary splint on your leg . . . I'm afraid you've got a pretty bad break there. But you're lucky to be alive."

"Falconer?"

Dr. Wright shook his head.

"Oh."

They moved her stretcher then, and the pain was so bad she fainted.

Chapter 24

FIVE days later Jessica was doing her best at sitting up, with a leg encased in plaster, in a bed that was festooned with the best pulleys, wires, and sand bags the little hospital in Dobbs Ferry could provide. Sam, three days back from his visit to the coast, had just sat down in the visitor's chair. Jessica's eyes had been closed when he entered the room. Now they opened.

"Hello, Sam, is it four o'clock already? I must have dozed off."

"Good, good. Get all the rest you can, honey. Patience and I are counting on you to heal up real fast. . . ." He paused to look at all the flowers in the room, some already starting to wilt. "And so are all your friends." Jessica followed his glance. The Roths had sent an exquisite terrarium from a very expensive Park Avenue florist. . . . There were crimson roses from the Smiths, and a big pot of purple mums from the Tarpinians. Jessica'd been especially touched to receive a large bunch of daisies from Dorcas Dillingham—no mention of Pierre on her card; nor had Pierre sent anything on his own. As for the two dozen carnations with extravagantly long stems from the two Max Wrights—Jr. and Sr.—Sam had yet to ask (though Jessica could see the question on his face) who the hell they might be. Jessica smiled at Sam.

"Not bad for a colorless little muddlehead, huh?"

"I never said you were colorless."

"Do you and Orsini have anything new to report to me today?" Since his return Sam had coped with caring for Patience, moving out of the Falconer house—the Smiths were putting them up—and giving Orsini and his men a hand with the gargantuan task of sifting through the debris upstairs. There were still some unanswered questions to be cleared up.

"Ask me anything," he said. "I'll see what I can come up with for you."

"Well, I can't understand why, if Nora and Frederick were so involved with one another, how come he went and married, er, Loretta Cavendish?"

. Sam explained.

"This goes way, way back, Jess. See, in 1931 Nora and Frederick were planning to get married; but they had no money. Nobody did in those days, that was the depths of the Depression. So, when she became pregnant, they were really in big trouble. But Frederick got wind of Nurse Cavendish's back-room operation up on Maynard Hill. Poor Mrs. Murphy never knew any of this, by the way; she was just a little kid at the time. Anyway, though this is mostly a reconstruction, we—or rather the police—haven't found much proof . . . but they're turning up more every day in that mess upstairs! Evidently after the abortion Nora had a kind of breakdown. She left Wimbledon. Took a six-month leave of absence from CopperCable and stayed with relatives out of state. Mrs. Murphy does dimly remember that; and some of the older residents do, too. But by the time she returned to Wimbledon and began working again Frederick had already married the Cavendish woman."

"Wow! How'd they ever get back together after that?"

"They didn't for quite some time. But Nora never dated anybody else, though she was damned attractive and very well thought of. Of course, he'd see her every day—they both worked in the same place. Soon it became common knowledge that Mrs. Falconer treated Frederick terribly. So he and Nora began to meet in our apartment. It was vacant for years and years. Mrs. Falconer didn't start renting it out until some time in the fifties. And even after that it was often vacant—tenants were always moving out, breaking their leases, because of her overbearing, nasty ways. So, whenever the flat was empty, old Fred and Nora would reunite. These dolls —ugly and lurid as they are now—began as a private joke between them. Apparently they became part of a ritualized system of signals to arrange meeting in their "love nest." First they'd send a picture postcard; then they'd set up their dolls. Just today we found a postcard, dated in July, 1938, that refers to 'our two love dolls in the back window.' Evidently the window in Patience's room was where they placed their signals. It's close enough to the ground there so that Nora could reach it. Believe it or not, they kept their secret so well that nobody ever knew about the affair . . . and it went on for thirty years. Poor Mrs. Murphy is just horrified; she can't get over it."

"Why didn't Frederick just divorce Mrs. Falconer?"

"She had quite a hold on him. You've got to realize what disclosure of the abortion would have meant to somebody like Nora Kelly, living in a village like Wimbledon. It was simply unthinkable."

"So finally they killed her."

"The police—that Orsini fellow—thinks they were caught in the act one day, and that she may actually have been killed in self-defense. Falconer's cane may have been the weapon then, too. Mrs. Falconer had had that cane specially made—it was hers to begin with, Frederick just took it over."

"But why did Frederick assume Mrs. Falconer's identity, anyway? What did he hope to gain by that?"

"That was the beginning of his madness, you see. It was a simple act of transference, by which he denied the fact that he'd killed her. Obviously she wasn't dead if she was still living up there on Maynard and driving through town in that big old car. He felt safer within her identity—after all, she was the dominant one—than he did in his own. 'Frederick the meek' people used to call him. Not exactly your run-of-the-mill mad-dog killer."

"Oh, Sam. Doesn't it sound almost logical? That's the thing with madness, isn't it . . . that weird logic. I can almost feel for him." Jessica leaned back and closed her eyes for a minute. Sam was so tired—this obligatory visit to the hospital was but one brief stop in a series of nonstop days. He wished he could just lie down next to her for a snooze. An ordinary, everyday thing that now seemed very precious. How long had it been since there'd been any coziness, any everydayness, between them? How long would she lie here, waiting for the broken pieces to mend? He stood up and looked down at her. He bent over and kissed her closed lids, Then he kissed the purple circles below them. To his dismay she flinched.

"What is it?"

"It's nothing, Sam. I'm just all tied up in knots."

"I can certainly see that." He smiled, indicating her harnesses.

"I don't mean that." No answering smile. "I'm all tied up in knots inside. Did I tell you Dr. Weller came to see me this morning?" She hadn't told him. Nor did Sam tell Jessica that it had been at his suggestion that Dr. Weller dropped by.

"Oh?"

"Dr. Weller and I both think Falconer's madness dated back to the abortion. Killing his baby inside Nora did something to him. That helps explain his morbid

244

interest in babies . . . his sexual problem or perversion or whatever . . . masturbating with a doll in front of a baby. Well, that had to be related to his guilt over killing their love child. The horror of it!" She shuddered. She looked ready to break down. Sam tried to comfort her. He gave her a glass of water and one of the pills on her bedside table. It was hard to tell whether this fragile, changeable state she was in was due to the horror of her experience or to her weakened physical condition. According to the doctor, she'd suffered severe and continuous pain for the first thirty-six hours and was still subject to intermittent attacks of pain that took a lot out of her. It was almost time for him to leave. Jessica, sensing his departure, gestured for him to stay. She wanted more information. Information seemed to bring a kind of solace.

"And his pension," she persisted, "Nora was the only person who knew Frederick Falconer was still alive, right? It was because of Nora that Falconer continued to receive his pension checks, even though he was supposed to be dead."

"Right. It turned out, you see, that in spite of all her fancy airs, Loretta Falconer had no money of her own at all. Orsini tells me that though they've done a lot of digging, here, upstate, all over, they can't locate any Cavendishes related to Mrs. Falconer. Her branch of the family pretty much died out with her generation. As did the money. And she'd be over eighty years old if she were alive today. So Frederick would not have survived without that pension. Nora's manipulated books kept poor old Fred alive."

"Poor old Fred! Sam! He practically *killed* me. I don't think I'll ever get over it . . . the horror . . . that awful, awful man! And when I think of what might have happened to Patience! . . ."

"Please, Jessica. Don't think about it. Just concentrate

on those bones knitting. We're all waiting for you. According to the doctors, you're doing real well. Everything's going to be all right."

"You'll be here again tomorrow?"

"Of course."

"What's happening at the house tomorrow?" Sam wondered whether he should tell her. He decided he would.

"The police are going to—what do you call it?—exhume Mrs. Falconer's body. It's been buried there in the wall between the kitchen and the bathroom all these years."

"That's why the kitchen was so small. That's why she—I mean, he—threw such a fit when I hung up Patience's paintings. . . . Oh, God." She looked up at Sam. "Sam, you didn't throw those paintings out, I hope? I especially wanted to keep those."

"That's what Mary said. We kept them. They're quite safe. Get some rest now. I'll be back tomorrow. You'll be feeling better by then."

Chapter 25

AND the next day Jessica did seem better. Her color had improved, and the ghastly purple shadows beneath her eyes had faded. She seemed alert, almost efficient, in her pursuit of the whole story. She wasn't talking to Sam so much as interrogating him. But there was a reserve, a kind of unreachable quality, that hadn't been there before. It made Sam nervous.

"How come nobody ever got wise to the impersonation? In a village the size of Wimbledon, with all the gossip and everything?"

"Well, as you might expect, there are now several old-timers who claim they always knew *something* funny was going on. Sounds more like twenty-twenty hindsight to me, though. You've got to realize how thoroughly unpopular Mrs. Falconer was. She had no friends at all. The few people she dealt with during the forty-odd years she lived in Wimbledon were on business—either shopkeepers or repairmen or, in the early days, clients. When you don't like somebody, you tend not to look at his face too carefully. Also, according to people who remember them together, even though Frederick was years younger than she was, they were of a similar build and coloring. Most important of all, Frederick was a damn good mimic. That was about the only way he could deal with the misery of living with the old bitch—he was known to do a wicked imitation of her behind her back."

"I guess, after a while, as the years passed, he got so he didn't know *who* he was, for much of the time. All that time we were there, we were dealing with a man . . . and never knew it! What about Nora Kelly—did she go on seeing him, after the murder?"

"Orsini thinks not. But she arranged for him to receive his checks right up until the end. We think he killed her when she told him she was moving to Florida. He didn't realize that she'd covered up his secret perfectly. She saw to it that the computer was programmed to continue sending the checks, month after month. It was a very neat job. She probably never had a chance to explain." They were both quiet for a moment.

"Sam, Dr. Weller stopped by again this morning. Why?"

"Well, he only lives up in Tarrytown, so it's probably just a friendly gesture on his part, to stop by on his way to the office."

"You think so? I don't know. I almost have the feeling his visits are, well, professional."

"Well, if they are, he'd better not send us any bills . . . because this is the first I heard about it!" Sam was lying. Dr. Weller had mentioned to Sam that it would be easy to look in on Jessie on his way to work and had offered to keep an eye on her emotional state. Sam had been grateful for the help.

"I tried to tell him, this morning, how this thing has made me come to terms with the idea of evil . . . the *reality* of evil. We all seem to go through life denying the presence of evil, by giving it clinical, psychological names. But it doesn't work. I remember, at school, when we'd write papers and stuff in philosophy, I'd deal with evil by referring to it as 'the other side of the coin.' So neat! Give it a name, define it, and then look the other way for the rest of your life. But it doesn't go away, you know. Evil is more than just a way to define good as its opposite. Evil is real, Sam . . . and it's in all of us, all of the time." Sam felt himself getting nervous. He hated philosophical discussions. "I guess what I'm trying to tell you concerns something fundamental that's happened to me. It has to do with this discovery that I've made about myself. Do you remember, at the party, when Sarah said that awful Kewpie doll looked as though it knew her?"

Sam nodded. *Now what?*

"We all sensed it, remember? A familiarity? Well, the doll was so lurid, so ugly, it reminded us of all the things inside us that we keep hidden. I've been so good all my life, Sam. But I just *assumed* my goodness . . . I was never tempted to do anything bad—at least, I don't recall ever having been. Well brought up. No temptations, no derelictions. Well. Evil was there all the time! An old friend. I don't quite know how to explain this to you, but you must let me try. . . ." She looked to see whether she'd caught his interest, and was disheartened by his polite, bland expression.

Sam wished she'd stop. On the one hand, he was afraid she might get all riled up again, and it would be bad for her. On the other, he simply hated to hear her talk this way. Always had. He'd always hated the look on Jessica's face when she tried to engage him in half-assed, high-brow discussions. It didn't seem feminine, somehow. It turned him off. He shuddered inwardly. Pretty soon, now, she'd be using terms like *a priori* and *agape*. "Really, Jessica? In what way have you changed? I'd like to hear about it."

"The only way I can explain it is that I've looked back and recognized things about myself that I've kept hidden up till now. For instance, when we were living up there in the Falconer place . . . didn't we *know* that

249

there was something . . . well, evil there? Didn't we feel its presence? Be honest! Look back. I mean, we had to be crazy to put up with that mess as long as we did. But we were afraid to call our fear by its true name. It seemed too messy . . . too frightening. So we pretended not to notice things. Forgot about things after they happened. Why, I forgot about the existence of that damn doll. I should have jumped right out of my skin when I saw it. It was such a clear warning. But I wasn't going to admit it. So I put it out of my mind.

"When I was finally face-to-face with Falconer . . . I wasn't surprised. Terrified, yes. But surprised? Not really. Something inside me had known. Known and understood. We are all of us on familiar terms with the most horrendous, murderous behavior! It doesn't surprise us because it's occurred to us to behave that way—subconsciously—many times. So, when we see somebody that actually goes and does it . . . acts the way we've imagined acting . . . we're not surprised. We see ourselves in the act. As I did. I wasn't shocked . . . I almost had a sense of *déjà vu* . . ." Sam winced. There was one he hadn't anticipated. Jessica registered his lack of attention. She interrupted herself.

"Oh, hell, Sam, I can see you don't really want to hear all this. What it means is that I want a chance to get to know myself better before we live together again. I've discussed it with Dr. Weller, and he seems to feel it would be the sensible thing to do. I found out about myself when old Falconer was chasing me across those rainy streets. I discovered my cunning. I would have killed him without remorse, Sam. He simply beat me to it. There's just a lot more to life than I was willing to recognize. And now that I've been forced to recognize it, I want to find out more. And more, and more! Until I see where this leads me, I wouldn't be much good as your wife. Can you understand?"

Sam's heart sank. He'd known.

"I catch your drift, Jessica."

"Much as I love you, Sam—and I do!—I can't help but feel I'm not your type."

"Jessica, I love you. I love Patience. We'll all be together again, you'll see. Look. I have a plan. I didn't want to worry you about this, but now I think it may please you. Chris Banning called last night. There is another job for me out on the coast. . . ."

"Oh! Something other than the detective thing?"

"The detective thing is out. Somebody put out a survey saying detective series are out for next season, and the whole project folded. No, this thing isn't all that exciting, but the pay is good and the work is steady—twenty-six weeks of it. Why don't I accept? Move out there. Leave you here, to think things through the way you claim you need to. For a minute I was afraid you were going religious on me. Frankly, all that stuff about evil doesn't cut any ice with me. But you seem to need time to work things out for yourself. And we could use the bread . . . it's a second lead. What do you say?"

"I say yes, Sam."

"That's it, then."

"When do you leave?"

"Oh, not for a little while yet. There'll be time for you to heal and get settled somewhere." There were tears in his eyes. He hoped she wouldn't see them.

Chapter 26

A month later Jessica, using one crutch and wearing a smaller cast on her left leg, was once again moving into a new apartment. This time it was a boxy two-and-a-half on the twelfth floor of Wimbledon's Hudson View Towers.

There'd been a heavy snow the night before. This morning everything was white and crystallized under a blinding blue sky. Jessica hobbled about the small flat. It had no charm, other than its view of the river. She could see from Manhattan, on the left, all the way up to the Tappan Zee Bridge on the right—a range of nearly twenty miles. Patience was in the kitchen, happily opening and closing all the cabinet doors. How much she understood about Mommy's and Daddy's separation Jessica could not tell.

Sam was leaving for California on Monday to start his new job. He'd be back for a visit at Christmas. He was spending his last few days in Wimbledon in a motel.

"Is Daddy coming now? How come you're not going with us?" Patience was waiting for Sam to take her to see the Christmas displays. They were going to buy some decorations.

"Well, dear, I still can't move about too well, you know. I'd spoil your fun."

"Poor, poor Mommy!" Patience walked to her and gave her a hug.

The doorbell rang, and Sam arrived to pick Patience up. No real talk between them. Just things like "Here, I'll help her with those boots" and "Do you have your money, Patience?" and "We'll be back by five."

"Good-bye, you two!"

Good-bye, Sam.

She looked out the window at the icy blue dazzle and willed herself to find some kind of promise in the view before her. She wanted a sign. A glimpse into a future that had, by some miracle, been divested of the recent past. Everything she'd been most afraid of had actually happened to her, and now it was over. She'd survived.

Tomorrow was her twenty-fifth birthday.

She was on her own.

MARY RENAULT

"MARY RENAULT WRITES LIKE A STREAK OF WHITE LIGHTNING"

—*Chicago Sun*

☐ **FIRE FROM HEAVEN**   #00091 – $1.25

☐ **MIDDLE MIST**   #03077 – $1.50

☐ **NORTH FACE**   #00206 – $1.25

Queen-Size Gothics

are a new idea. They offer the very best in novels of romantic suspense, by the top writers, greater in length and drama, richer in reading pleasure. Each book is guaranteed to be:

"READING FIT FOR A QUEEN"